I0761809

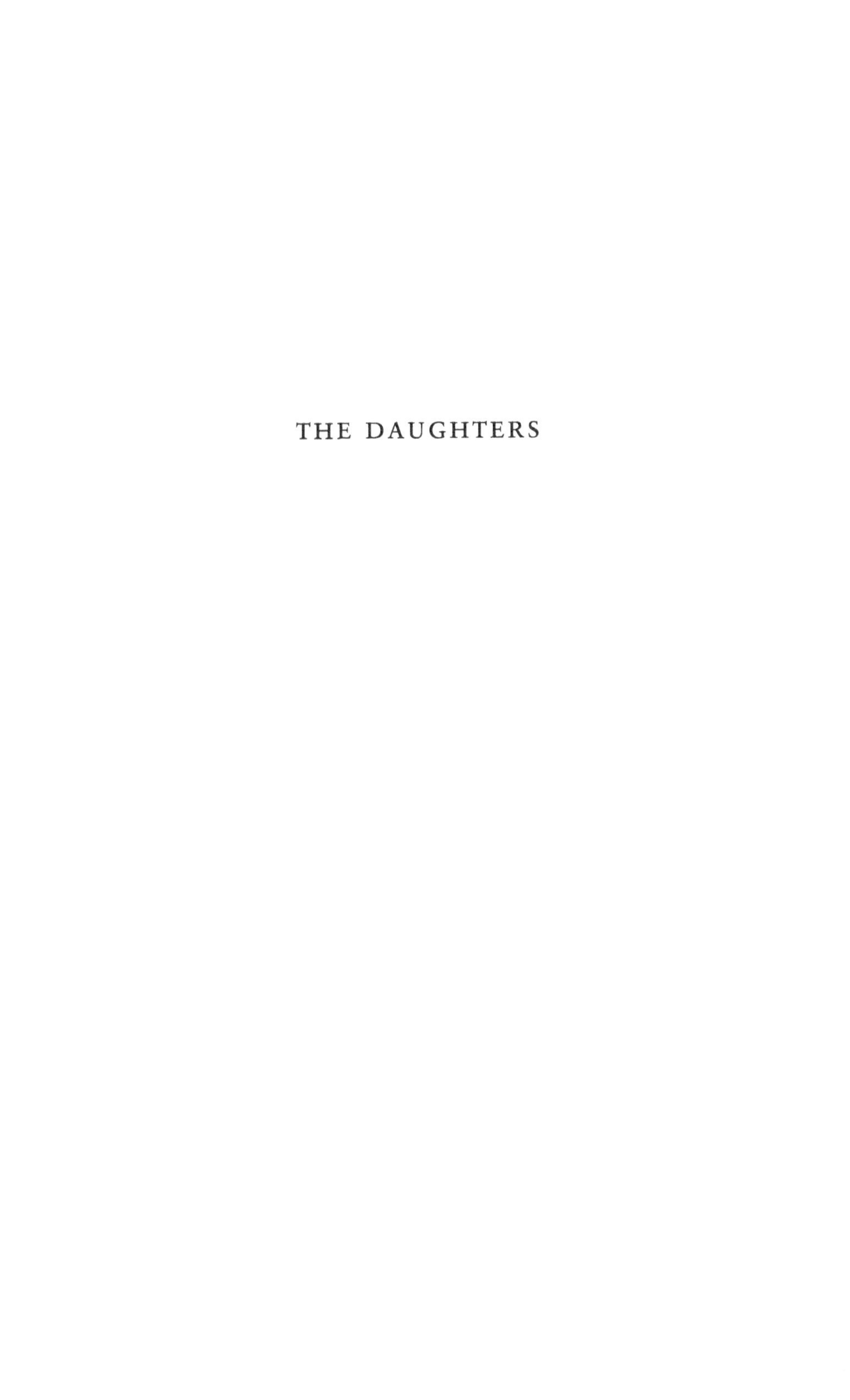

THE DAUGHTERS

The Daughters

A Novel

BEN ROGERS

UNIVERSITY OF NEVADA PRESS | *Reno & Las Vegas*

University of Nevada Press | Reno, Nevada 89557 USA
www.unpress.nevada.edu

A prior version of the chapter "Zhiyu/Jerry (1986)" was published as a short story, "Zhiyu/Jerry," in *The Rumpus* in 2017.

Manufactured in the United States of America

FIRST PRINTING

Cover design by TG Design
Cover illustration by Flamma, Shutterstock

Library of Congress Cataloging-in-Publication Data is on file.

ISBN 978-1-64779-201-5 (cloth)
ISBN 978-1-64779-202-2 (ebook)
LCCN: 2025005662

The paper used in this book meets the requirements of American National Standard for Information Sciences—Permanence of Paper for Printed Library Materials, ANSI/NISO Z39.48–1992 (R2002).

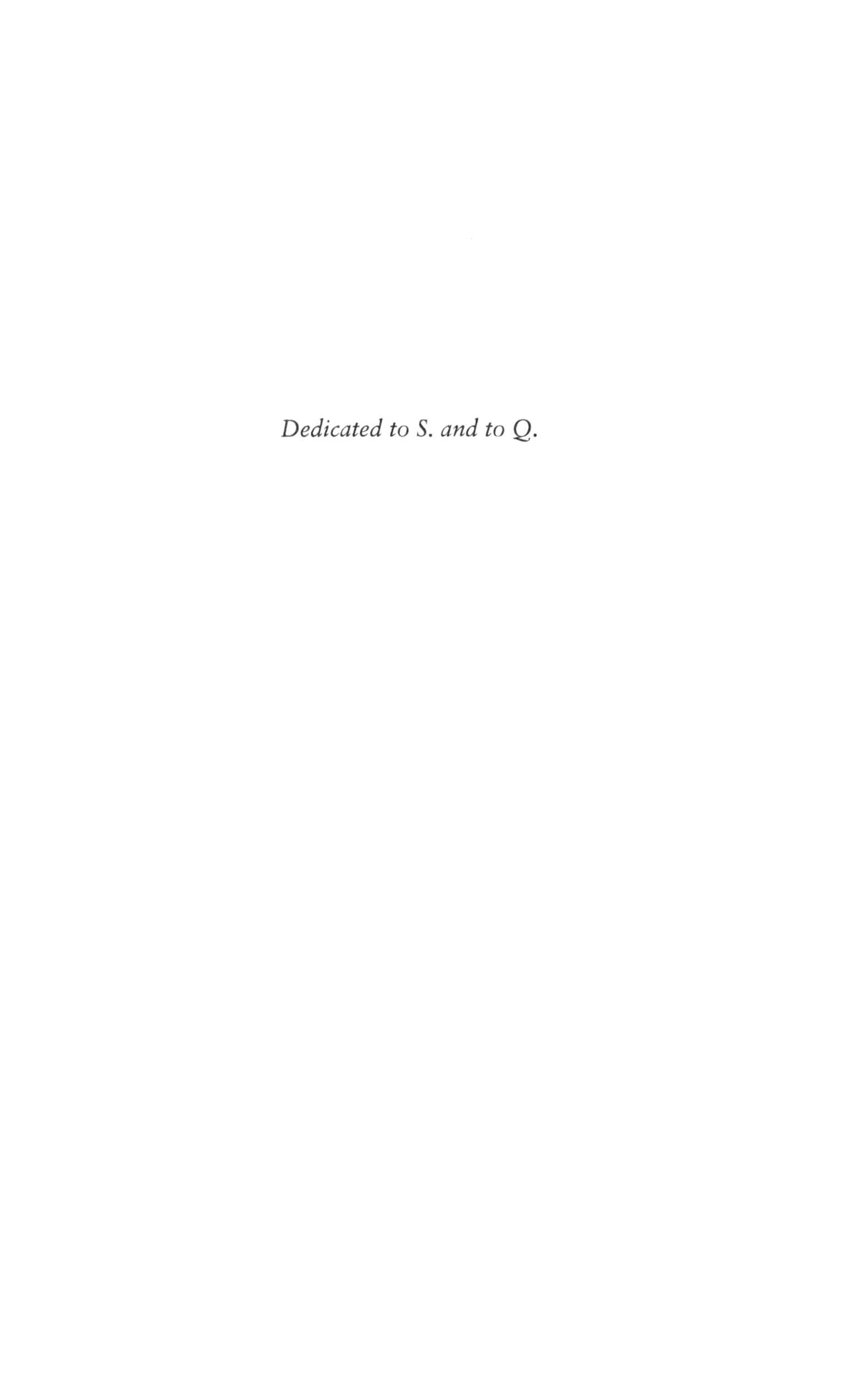

Dedicated to S. and to Q.

Like a wave in the physical world, in the infinite ocean of the medium which pervades all, so in the world of organisms, in life, an impulse started proceeds onward, at times, may be, with the speed of light, at times, again, so slowly that for ages and ages it seems to stay, passing through processes of a complexity inconceivable to men, but in all its forms, in all its stages, its energy ever and ever integrally present. A single ray of light from a distant star falling upon the eye of a tyrant in bygone times may have altered the course of his life, may have changed the destiny of nations, may have transformed the surface of the globe, so intricate, so inconceivably complex are the processes in Nature. In no way can we get such an overwhelming idea of the grandeur of Nature than when we consider, in that accordance with the law of the conservation of energy, throughout the Infinite, the forces are in a perfect balance, and hence the energy of a single thought may determine the motion of a universe.

—NIKOLA TESLA, "On Light and Other High Frequency Phenomena," lecture delivered before the Franklin Institute, Philadelphia, February 1893, and before the National Electric Light Association, St. Louis, March 1893

Contents

THE DAUGHTERS

Prologue

I, Z (2012)

I TOWELED DUST FROM THE BOTTLE. Tugged the knife from the wooden knife block. Gripped the bottle by its throat. Circumnavigated the foil with the blade. A lovely woman watched me closely. But suddenly I could see all the ladies who'd watched before. Their legs crossed as they leaned in—nibbling necklaces, fingering earrings—the way polite children watch ice cream being scooped. A gaze of controlled ravenousness.

I always used the winged variety of corkscrew, the type with geared arms. An elegant tool, but that's not why I used it. It was the loaded question this particular tool allowed me to ask: *Do you know what they call these in France?* How many times had I asked it? How many bottles had it opened?

They call it a *de Gaulle*, I'd say. Like the French president.

And I'd push and pull the screw to make the wine opener's chrome head bob, its chrome arms flap. I'd explain that that's how de Gaulle used to look when he gave speeches. A tidbit I'd picked up years before and had worn ragged with retelling. (I wonder if it's even true. I know it's not *funny*.) Still, I told it. Every time. If I'd learned anything over the years, it was not to go off-script. The script worked. Half an hour before I opened this particular bottle of wine for this particular woman—*Sue*—I'd stood at a vessel sink in the men's room of a Pan-Asian bistro in downtown La Jolla, California, and swallowed a light-blue diamond with a handful of tap water. I'd guessed then (correctly) that I'd be back in my bungalow with Sue now.

Call me Cocksure. Moby Dickhead.

For the love of god: look at me. I'd actually walked to the restaurant, having arranged to meet Sue in the bar. Over dinner, I'd explained that my Jeep was already hitched to my trailer, that I was headed to Joshua Tree first thing in the morning. This was my move. It preempted the possibility of sleepovers and awkward breakfasts. From what I could tell, my dates appreciated it. They, too, seemed to prefer slipping away to sleep in *their* own beds, to wake up to *their* own perfect, single lives.

Two bulls stand on a hill, looking out over a scattered herd. The young bull overzealous: Let's run down there and fuck one of them cows! The elder bull advising otherwise: No, let's *walk* down there and fuck 'em all . . .

My monogamous, churchgoing father told me that joke.

(While we're on the topic . . . A few paragraphs ago I used the word "god" and did not capitalize it. I will do so throughout this story, for both myself and others, except when the word is used to start a sentence because, well, that would be a sin. Don't worry: I will not bore us here with the vagaries of my spirituality. I hope (pray?) this minor style choice suffices.

There will be one exception: Doreen. Doreen's an uppercase God kind of gal.)

I'd been single at this point for sixty-four years. In college, the girls wanted to be girlfriends, to rent with option to buy. Then the girls became *women*. I could hear their clocks ticking. I had nothing against children. I viewed kids the way I viewed swimming pools and boats—great fun, so long as someone else handled all the upkeep.

Somehow, I stayed slippery. Over the years I'd been partial to a few women. Two, I think I loved. Just not enough. Apparently. Because I had not changed. I had my routines. My hyacinth. My Frisbee golf. I did whatever the fuck I pleased, whenever the fuck I pleased, with whomever the fuck cared to join me. Translation: I was usually alone.

I just didn't know I was also lonely.

Since I'd "retired" to La Jolla two years earlier—though one could argue, and plenty of critics and publishers and pundits did, that Peter Zemeckis retired the day *A Wake* won the National Book Award in 1997, and that everything the bastard has put to paper since is shit, or, more specifically, "pathetic," "self-indulgent," "victory-lappy," "out of touch," "cranky," or "pompous" (or, incompatibly: "absent the clout and audacity of his masterwork," et cetera)—I'd opened wine for all walks of women of a certain age. Divorcées, widows, grandmothers (!), and pantsuit professionals. Women who, like me, married a career. Sure, their bodies sagged a bit. Some had some liver spots on their hands. A little gray at the roots of the blonde. But I was on equal footing, and no sexier. What with my hairy shoulders. My worsening jowls. My limp dick.

We get stuck in our ways, our skins.

These ladies had gotten wise to me, though. I'd seen how they rolled their eyes, shook their heads—all too familiar with my modus operandi. I'd reconciled myself to that. To my predictability. For they, too, were predictable. They still drank my wine. They laughed. They flirted. Women of a certain age are not bashful, I've learned. I miss bashful.

Anyway. There we were, Sue and I. I pierced the cork with the screw and twisted the key. The geared arms rose. I set the bottle on the counter and pried them back down.

Cork squeaked against glass. The wine drew its first breath in sixteen years.

I got the decanter from the shelf. It has a broad belly and a neck tapering to a slanted lip. In contrast to the deftness with which I'd *opened* the bottle, I emptied it into the decanter like I was dumping it down the disposal. The wine glugged and bubbled. I wiped my hands off on a towel. While the bubbles migrated around on the surface and burst, I walked right out of the kitchen, leaving Sue to toy with the empty stemware.

I'd found over the years that the best way to get wine to open up is to treat it like you don't even plan to drink it. Just pour it out. Walk away. Wait.

The crimson sediment was streaked along the curvaceous inner surface of the decanter, marking the path of my last pour. Nearby, two glasses. One empty, with burgundy lipstick on the rim. The other had a few sips left. Little blue diamonds can't do their trick if you're drunk. A lesson I learned the soft way.

It had been *Sue*, actually, who'd taken my hand and—putting an end to the pretext of a tango lesson in my front room—led us here, to the bedroom. We had not come stumbling and giggling, as our younger selves might have.

My eyes had not yet adjusted to the darkness of the bedroom. I palmed Sue's expensive bra. Her darting tongue was tinged with merlot. She slid her hands up my chest and pinched apart the topmost button of my shirt, then worked her way down the rest. We stopped kissing. I sucked in my feeble paunch. Starlight—pinpricks of radiance en route for millennia—poured in through the window and struck Sue's skin, if for no other reason than to make her glow imperceptibly more. Right there, in the moment.

This moment, when everything is about to change.

Sue has rendered my shirtfront an open v, exposing my over-sunned skin, my tuft of wiry gray chest hair. The corner of her mouth curls into a smirk. Her hands slip to my belt. I reach out to untie the ribbon cinching her cocktail dress at her bust. But I hesitate. I feel strange. Numb. I feel . . . bored. I have seen this movie too many times.

What if I make no effort whatsoever? I wonder. *Just stand here like a child as she strips off my clothes, while I in turn remove nothing of hers? How far will she go, unreciprocated?*

I am not long in contemplating this before it is out of the question. Sue starts undressing herself. She kicks away her heels. Unties her bow, teasing out the loose end. Her arms go to work within it. The dress seems to lift itself off. She drapes it over the lacquered chest at the foot of my bed so as not to wrinkle it.

Here she stands. Jade silk push-up bra. Skin-tone Spanx from navel to thigh. The impressions of her bra straps in the supple skin of her shoulders.

Here it comes. Three knocks at my front door. Sue turns toward the sound like a startled doe. She picks her dress up and clutches it to her breast. She looks to me for an explanation. I frown. I have no idea. We hold our breath together in the back of my darkened bungalow.

Five more knocks. Louder than the last. I refasten my belt. I leave Sue in the bedroom and make my way down the hallway. My unbuttoned shirt billows behind me like a cape.

It strikes me, then and there. I'm grateful for this interruption.

A twist!

I brush aside the curtain on the tall window beside the front door. I peer out at the porch. Simultaneously, Dr. Nancy Chu—my neighbor, my unrequited love—puts her face to the other side of the glass, the angle of her head complementary to mine, as if it is *we* who are about to kiss. She cups her hands to her face like she's holding up binoculars. You can see it, the instant her focus penetrates the mirrored pane and she sees beyond her own reflection. What she sees, of course, is *me*, mere inches away.

She jolts backward. Lets out a precious little shriek. I fumble with the deadbolt and step outside. I try to embrace her. She retreats to the top of my steps. A breeze stirs my shirt-cape. I rebutton it. I try to calm her.

The last time I saw Nancy—two weeks ago—she dumped

my half-drunk glass of Mario Perelli-Minetti cabernet sauvignon onto my all-white Tommy Hilfiger shorts. We have not spoken since.

She is wearing a green, sand-encrusted hoodie, rolled-up canvas pants, and the ridiculous khaki cargo vest she favors. She provides no preamble. I need to borrow your Jeep, she says.

I reach back and, ever so casually, tug the front door shut. Right now? I say.

Yes, right now, she says. It's Charlotte. She needs me.

Charlotte is Nancy's daughter. I ask what's wrong.

She's an alcoholic is Nancy's reply.

Where is she? I ask.

A bar. The Gaslight . . .

Gas*lamp*? I clarify.

Right.

The Gaslamp *Quarter*, you mean. That's a lot of bars.

She hands me a slip of paper with the name of the bar scratched on it.

I called for a taxi, she says. They said it'd be half an hour! I can't wait that long. Charlotte'll leave, or change her mind. I told her I was on my way. *Please, Z.* I'm begging you. Just give me the keys and I'll leave you alone. Looks like you were going to bed.

Sure, I say. Sounds good. Just unhook the trailer before you go, okay?

I nod at the Airstream parked on my curb. Its bulbous aluminum chassis gleams in the streetlight. I watch Nancy deflate. She must have been too flustered to notice the trailer before, or probably just too determined. In the six months I've known her, I've taken what consolation I can in writing her book backwards. I imagine the woman she must have been, before. I've crossed paths with her type a few times—whip smart and decisive; accustomed to breaking wills; never giving or expecting quarter. A bird of prey: a fierce, independent thing, a predator at heart, and yet so frail; just feathers and hollow bones that would crumple if you were to snatch her into your hands and squeeze. And tonight, she is completely out of her element. A kestrel in a bounce house.

How long does it take to unhook? she asks.

Ten, fifteen minutes, I say—overestimating. (The key to the tow-hitch is on the dresser. In my bedroom.)

Nancy closes her eyes.

I slip back inside. Wriggle my feet into my Crocs. Nab the keys to the Jeep and my wallet. I sense movement in the room. I turn to see Sue standing half-naked in the hallway. I grimace and turn up my palms. I do feel sorry for her. I say it, even: *Sorry, Sue.*

Who's out there? she asks.

My friend, I say. I have to go.

I apologize again. Before Sue can say more, I slip back out the front door. I find Nancy kneeling at the trailer hitch. She grips the handle of the lift jack and starts to crank in frenzied, herky-jerky motions. The little wheel descends toward the pavement. I start across the lawn.

Stop, I say.

Nancy straightens up. Her dirtied palm curls into a fist. She sets it against her hip. She looks near tears, and I hug her with one arm. She seems to need this, but I dare not linger. Any moment now, a woman scorned could, and should, reemerge—high heels dangling from painted fingertips—and storm across my yard to an Audi two-seater. The Walk of Blame.

Am I doing it wrong or something? Nancy asks. Just help me finish and I'll—

Get in the Jeep, I say. I'm driving you.

What about the trailer?

Leave it. There's no time.

You don't have to do this, Z. Just go to bed . . .

Nancy, I tell her. I love you. You're a very capable woman. But you don't know where the Gaslamp Quarter is, and you don't know how to tow a trailer. So, please. Just shut up and let me help.

She frowns. I step past her and crank the jack in the opposite direction. Nancy watches her efforts negated. She walks around to the front of the Jeep and climbs in the passenger seat. I keep an eye on her through the rear window. She stares out into the night that has made a hostage of her daughter, and I am put in mind of a boy in grade school who asked our teacher why the words *daughter* and *laughter* don't rhyme.

I unplug the extension cord and leave it lying across the yard. I climb into the Jeep.

Nancy touches my hand.

A thrill runs through me.

We get underway without another word.

I crack a window and join Interstate 5, heading south, wondering if I'd pass a breathalyzer. Nancy turns talkative.

I listen and drive, changing lanes and subjects as needed.

How'd we get here? she asks.

Here? I ask.

This, she says. How'd it come to this?

Mm, I say.

Isn't this all my fault? I mean, aren't I her mother?

Nancy's tone doesn't ring rhetorical, so I field the question. Yes, I say. You are her mother.

Mothers are supposed to watch over their babies, Nancy says. Not just *hatch* them.

She wants me to agree with her, and in so doing, impugn her. She wants me to help her punish herself. But I will not be further party to that. I do not take the bait.

As someone who's made a career of people watching, I shall attest: death and trouble find us all. Misfortune is therefore generic and undeserving of ink. But, as someone who's lived next door to the various incarnations of Nancy's family, I shall add: the misfortun*ate* themselves can be endlessly fascinating.

Individual is a word I hate, the parlance of police reports. So let us say *granular*, *particular*. Particu*late*. Each of us, in minute and troubled little ways, is singular. And in my book—this one, here, in your hand— the mere attempt, successful or not, to memorialize specificity will always be worth the ink.

Isn't this what I'm supposed to do? Nancy is asking. Swoop in and save her from herself?

I think we protect our children when they can't protect themselves, I suggest. When they're young.

Our?

You know what I mean. Just, children. In general.

Is twenty-three young?

Is sixty-four old?

Nancy nods, and I am disheartened. Then I catch the distant look in her eye. She's not answering *my* question.

She says, She's got a drinking problem, Z. An *addiction*.

I smile. Nancy's hair is matted, her eyes sunken, her unjacked headphones dangling from the pocket of her cargo vest—a junkie in her own right.

She just needs to get out of the rut she's in, Nancy says. Get away from all this *history*.

Move away, you mean, I say.

Well, Nancy says. No.

I exit the freeway into downtown San Diego. Nancy fidgets. We're getting close, I assure her.

We pass an Irish pub, a sushi bar, a Thai joint, a frozen yogurt shop. The warmly lit streets teem. Short skirts, backward hats. *Kids*. Their motives gloriously transparent. Here are bodies hunting bodies. The sight of them gets me feeling nostalgic. Then impotent.

Gonna be tricky trying to park, I mutter.

Hey! Nancy says. That's Carter's truck! See . . . that big red one?

I nod. I find a yellow-curbed loading zone. I park. I leave my hazards blinking. Before I've locked up the Jeep, Nancy has already found a pair of partiers to point her toward the right bar. She sets out. I have to jog to catch up. I feel eyes on us. We're as conspicuous as two parents crossing a schoolyard at recess.

The bar is a shitty, popular one. Its doorway exhales muggy, boozy air and thumping music. We elbow through young people holding plastic cups, thumbing at their phones in the dimness. There's a TV on the wall showing a man riding a toilet off a jump. Nancy grips my arm and knifes through the crowd. We come to a hallway where people are queued outside four unisex bathrooms. Nancy pounds on the door of the first one.

There's a line, bitch, someone says.

Charlotte! Nancy shouts. Charlotte!

She moves to the next door and repeats the pounding, the yelling. The fourth door opens. Charlotte peeks out.

Her hair is pulled up in a chaotic bun. Mascara is blurred across her temples and cheekbones. A cigarette is tucked behind her ear. She shoulders a knit bag and shuffles out of the bathroom with her head bowed.

Nancy gathers her into her arms. She turns to me and points back toward the street. *Go!* she says.

I cut us a path. The kids make faces at me. We spill back onto the sidewalk. Nancy pants as though she's just dragged Charlotte up from deep water.

I tail Charlotte and Nancy like a secret service detail in my green Crocs. My phone buzzes in my pocket. I've missed two calls from Sue, with accompanying messages.

You're barefoot, Charlotte says to Nancy. Nancy looks down at her feet as if seeing them for the first time. Her toes are painted. She has well-taken-care-of feet. There was a time not long ago when she'd let me rub them after one of her marathon sessions at the beach.

We saw Carter's truck, Nancy says.

But not him? Charlotte asks.

Let's keep moving, I say.

Nancy and Charlotte choose to ride together in the back seat of the Jeep. They hold hands. I happily accept my change in assignment from bodyguard to chauffeur. I've never seen them like this with each other. Quiet descends on the car. I ease my little train away from the curb and head toward the freeway.

At a red light, Nancy breaks the silence. Are you drunk? she asks.

No/No, Charlotte and I say over each other. Thankfully, Charlotte is the more defensive, and louder.

Do I seem drunk? Charlotte adds.

I can never tell, Nancy says.

We ride in silence.

Nancy says, Earlier. When I called you . . . I . . . I found something. At the beach.

I turn an ear, but I am distracted by the approach of some unnaturally high headlights in my driver-side mirror.

Down by Scripps Pier, Nancy says.

The truck to which the lights belong materializes outside my window. Burgundy red. Matte black metal rims. Nancy starts in with her story. In my rearview, I see recognition creep across Charlotte's face, followed by fear. She stares up from her window at the truck's impenetrably tinted windows.

It's okay, I whisper. He might not even know we're here. He could just be driving.

He's fucking wasted, Charlotte says.

Who? Nancy asks, and then she turns and sees the truck, too.

I keep an eye on the traffic light. It's still red. A car pulls up behind the truck. The light turns green, but I keep my foot on the brake. We stay put behind the crosswalk. The red truck doesn't budge, either. The car behind the truck starts honking. I peer up into the truck's muscular undercarriage. Even at idle it shudders with gratuitous horsepower.

The tinted passenger-side window scrolls down to reveal an angry, tattooed young man. He levels a pistol across the cabin at us.

I do not own a gun. But if I did—if I had one at this moment, I swear I would use it. Looking up at him, I want to shoot him. I want to shoot him for being so goddamn frightening and so fucking stupid. For being so childish as to make the situation no longer safe for children. I want to shoot his truck at least.

I cannot remember the last time life caught me so off guard, or had me feeling vulnerable, let alone violent. And I realize: I've gotten more than my share of fucks, but it's been way too long since I gave one.

I am ready and willing to take a bullet for these daughters from next door.

Is this how fathers and husbands feel? Is this how Eric felt? And Zhiyu?

Earlier, Nancy had asked me how we got here. It's an excellent question. *Once upon a time, a father found a pebble in his rice and thought nothing of it . . .*

I'll get to that. First, I think we ought to go to the rodeo.

Amy

1977

IF IT HADN'T BEEN FOR A SPAN OF DAYS in Texas some thirty-five years ago, Nancy wouldn't have shown up frazzled on my porch in La Jolla tonight. It is therefore with Amy that we must start our story. See her there atop Patton. (The horse, not the general.) Calm as ever beneath Amy's saddle. Amy not so much. Amy was giddy. The beef brisket she'd had for lunch refused to settle. She didn't tend to get like this. You see, this was not her first rodeo.

Nor did she know it would be her last.

She thought, *Focus on your progressions, Amy.*

She pictured the perfect run, as Doreen had trained her. *One right, two lefts, go like hell.* Amy couldn't see Doreen at that moment, but The Daughter knew The Mother was out there, in the bleachers. See Doreen there, fiddling with the ruby crucifix in her cleavage. Doreen didn't believe Jesus had much to say about barrel racing though. *Decide what you want and go get it*, Doreen told Amy all the time. *Hard work, good decisions.*

Amy took a deep breath. The arena smelled like cotton candy and alfalfa and chew spit and dust and sweaty horseflesh and barbeque and beer and horseshit and cowshit and perfume and fear. Playing on the PA was the same Steve Miller Band song that was everywhere that summer. (I was twenty-nine and working on my second novel. The manuscript for the first was hostage in a dresser drawer in Santa Cruz in the house of a thirty-four-year-old English lit professor I'd been shacking up with. She had summarily rejected me, just as every major and minor U.S. publisher had rejected the manuscript. On the grounds that I/it was objectively rotten.)

Here's what Amy loved about rodeos: being on her own a little. Free to walk the grounds and mingle with the other girls in the morning, before they became her enemies in the afternoon. Home for Amy was like a blanket. Warm and cozy, sure, but now that it was summer and she'd graduated from high school, it was a little too snug.

Here's what Amy hated about rodeos: everything else. The humidity and the heat, and on account of these, she hated the dress code—long-sleeved button-downs and jeans and felt hats. She hated being hurt all the time. She'd broken her left ankle twice and her right foot once. All from bad ground. Dirt too thin or too muddy to hold a horse that turned as hard as Patton. Amy hated the feeling of her mother's eyes on her, like God's eyes.

Outside of rodeos, Amy hated taking care of horses. She considered them pampered and stubborn animals. *Founder soon as look at you*, Doreen liked to say.

But: Amy did love goin' like hell.

She draped her reins over Patton's pommel. She loosened her belt by one hole and renotched the buckle. Her boyfriend Tommy had given her this particular buckle to mark their one-year anniversary. It was huge and silver with a turquoise number 1. Doreen didn't care for the buckle because she didn't care for Tommy. But since Amy insisted on wearing it, Doreen told her the 1 could at least remind Amy of The Goal.

Sweat and Aqua Net leaked down from Amy's Stetson. The hairspray wasn't for Amy's hair. It was to keep her hat stuck against her forehead. It also gave Amy zits. But there were fines for those who lost hats in the arena. Lost hats slowed down the show. But Amy refused to use a stampede string. (Because Doreen called them doofus straps.)

Amy didn't throw up, and this felt to her like victory already. She took off her hat and wiped at her eyes with the non-sequin side of her sleeve.

There was one team left to go before Amy and Patton—a girl on a palomino mare. The girl wore a shimmering red button-down with piping on her saddle to match. She cantered away from Amy down the chute, hardly holding her mare back until—at that very last second—she spurred her. The horse dipped her hindquarters. The big muscles rippled beneath her hide. Girl and horse together ate up ground.

For Amy, watching their run from the chute was like seeing it through a keyhole. The crowd went through its own "progressions." There was clapping when the team flew out into the sunlight, veering left to where Amy lost sight of them. Bigger applause when they made the first turn clean. Shooting back across Amy's view, they disappeared again to the right. Then some whistling and whooping. A clean run so far, then.

The team came back into Amy's sights, making the last turn of the cloverleaf, clods of dirt rooster-tailing, the girl whipping at the mare's flank. The horse threw out her feet and all but ran in place, so tight was the turn she made around a huge can of Coors: the barrel. Which teetered, which tottered, but stayed standing, and so the crowd roared. The girl stood out of her saddle. The mare's mane flapping. Together they bore down on the chute that had birthed them.

They came flying right at Amy, who put Patton against the fence rail to make room. The girl tugged on her red reins to make the mare skid. Her front legs straightened to fight her momentum. The time soon displayed on the big board was the quickest so far that day. The crowd roared again.

But the day was young. Celebrating at this point was

premature, and the girl hardly reacted. She turned and guided her mare back up the two-way road of the chute, avoiding Amy's eyes as well as those of every other girl down the line. All of whom were now raring to beat her.

The Steve Miller Band faded. The announcer came over the PA: *Folks, she's only nineteen, but she must have a big ol' piggy bank, because this sweet young lady walked home with $3,000 from the Nacogdoches Rodeo two weeks ago . . .*

Said sweet young lady—who'd won that money while riding with a cast on her ankle and who did in fact have a piggy bank, porcelain and pink, although it had no prize money in it (those checks got deposited in a college account only Doreen could touch)—looked down the chute. There was dust in the sunbeams that came through the bleachers.

Amy knew she was expected to go to college eventually, but Doreen had been letting her put it off while she was still barrel racing. Amy's grades from high school were good enough for Texas State. Doreen had never gone to college. She'd gotten pregnant and quit the pre-vet program at A&M. *Best mistake of my life*, Doreen always told Amy. A mistake she'd chosen to make twice more, after Amy—both boys. Doreen also told Amy that to follow in her footsteps would mean stepping over Doreen's dead body. *Good cowgirls keep their calves together.* That was Doreen's joke. Ha ha. Yeehaw.

Patton was antsy. He'd come a long way from the horse Doreen paid just $900 for at an auction three years before. Amy had been there that morning. She'd seen the horse led out onto the bidding platform and had written him off. *Too fat.* But Doreen had insisted he was merely *stout*, that he had great bones and a long back for weaseling around barrels.

When Amy's friends were all getting trucks for their sweet sixteens, she'd gotten a horse. She'd named him Patton after the American general. Not the actual general. The one from the movie. Amy's father, Hank, loved that movie. They quoted it to each other: "*We're not just going to shoot the bastards, we're going to cut out their living guts and use them to grease the treads on our tanks . . .*"

The first time Amy ever mounted Patton, she'd put the spur to him right away and he'd come unglued. But she'd held on. She'd ridden the buck clean out to let him know she wasn't scared of him and didn't ever plan to be. Doreen and Amy had spent months teaching Patton to run barrels. He'd taken to it. Doreen told anyone who'd listen that Patton was grittier than any horse she'd ever trained. A horse with a hell of a lot of try, and you can't teach try. The gospel according to Doreen. Who told anyone who made an offer on Patten that she turned down such offers all the time and always would.

Amy started to slide off the saddle. She lay a gloved hand on the rail of the chute. It was one hundred degrees in the shade, and plenty humid to boot. Amy prayed: *Lord, hold me together. Just one more minute.*

She did not hold herself together.

Patton turned to stare back at her with one eye. She slumped over his neck and found herself staring down at the brisket and lemonade she'd had for lunch, now splattered in the hoof-cupped dirt. The back of her throat burned. The rider in line behind Amy sidled her horse up alongside. Patton headbutted him.

We okay here? asked an official, also on horseback. Amy stared at him over her right shoulder, then over her left, as Patton pivoted. A string of spit connected her mouth to her shirt. A rectangle of light awaited her at the end of the chute.

The official asked Amy if she wished to withdraw. Amy spit. Shook her head no. Leather creaked as she tightened her grip on the reins. She pointed Patton. Spurred him into the light.

Mom. Pull over.

Here?

Yes, *here!*

Doreen checked her mirrors, then merged the F-250 and accompanying trailer across two lanes of I-27. Amy unbuckled and opened the door as the truck tipped onto the shoulder, gravel pinging in the wheel wells. Hot air gushed in.

Can you wait just a damn second? Doreen asked.

Amy could not. She got one hand on the oh-shit handle, one boot on the running board, and hopped out. She made it only a few steps before vomiting into a patch of foxtails. Doreen came around the front of the truck to find Amy with her hands on her knees, dry heaving.

Good Lord, Doreen said.

Waves of heat rose from the truck hood, from the asphalt. Amy pulled her hair into a ponytail. A semi roared by, pushing a hot wind. Patton nickered and kicked inside the metal trailer. They'd come about an hour from Lubbock, heading up the Panhandle. They were still two hours from home in Amarillo. Patton had done all the work in Lubbock. Amy had finished only a second off the winning time: top 20, but out of the prize money. Doreen had met them in the cool-down corral. When Amy saw her, she shook her head so Doreen would know the run hadn't been to Amy's liking either. Doreen had patted her daughter's boot, then reached under Patton to loosen his girth. That had been that. There was work to do. With horses there always is.

When the traffic on the highway calmed, the cicadas' buzzing was omnipresent.

This just come on then? Doreen asked. She rubbed Amy's back. What'd you eat for lunch?

Brisket.

Doreen huffed. That coulda done it, she said.

They loaded back up and got rolling and Amy started to feel like she was out of the woods but Doreen never turned the radio back on and it was spooky quiet.

Amy woke to see the truck's headlights swing off the two-lane road and light up the family mailbox, shaped like a barn.

Home.

Amy's father, Hank, had built the place. Well, Hank's *company* had. He was the first to admit he hadn't lifted a hammer since he started his concrete and construction company in 1966. The homestead was seven acres alongside Timbercreek Canyon on the outskirts of Amarillo. The house faced south, toward the bulk of Texas (the house's ass to the rest of the country, Hank liked to say). The property had a detached three-car garage and a massive six-stall barn. Behind the barn was a split-rail corral. Doreen taught riding to local girls who gaped at Amy's accumulated trophies and pictures. The corral got tilled every Tuesday by one of Hank's men on a company tractor.

Doreen pulled the truck under the yard light and killed the engine. I'll put up the horses, she said. You head in.

You sure?

There's plenty that needs doing. But most of it'll wait till tomorrow.

Inside, Amy found Hank and her brothers watching TV. Pizza on the coffee table.

Doreen had called Hank from a payphone outside Lubbock, so he knew that Amy lost. But Amy knew that he didn't give a shit. He'd never taken much interest in horses, other than to pay for them. Doreen sometimes suggested that the money she brought in teaching lessons made it all about a wash. But Amy knew how much a single vet visit cost. A wash it certainly was not.

Amy leaned against Hank's recliner. She hugged him where he sat. He asked how she was doing. She nodded to her brothers and excused herself. She went straight to her room and picked up the phone.

Her boyfriend Tommy was ashamed of *his* house, of how messy and cramped it was. His mother was always in her pajamas and his father in his booze. So whenever Tommy and Amy hung out, they were nearly always at Amy's house. Amy was not allowed to have Tommy in her room for "extended periods." Meaning they were rarely alone together.

Phone calls were the exception. Amy would spend hours with her door shut and Tommy all to herself. She'd work a pinky into the cord as she probed his deepest thoughts, his feelings, what he wanted from life, and what he wanted from her. He could be funny— no one else realized that about Tommy—and Amy would start laughing, which would get Tommy even more excited. Amy's laugh had always had that effect on boys. Sometimes late at night on the phone she felt the need to muffle it with a pillow, as if it were a moan.

Hey, Tommy answered.

Come over, Amy said.

Amy undressed in the bathroom. She looked at herself in the mirror as if with Tommy's eyes. She'd packed on ten extra pounds in the year since graduation, despite Doreen's nitpicking. Tommy said he *liked* Amy curvy. He was no bean pole himself.

Doreen told Amy that she could do better than Tommy. That she hadn't *chosen* him. That he was just the leftovers after all the other boys left Amarillo. If dumb was dirt, Doreen said, Tommy'd cover 'bout an acre. She called Tommy "Slim," which Tommy thought was a joke about his weight. He didn't know the version Doreen used when he wasn't around: *Slim Pickens*. (And even if he did know, he would have had no idea who Slim Pickens was.)

Amy didn't give a shit. Tommy was her man. She knew that he hadn't lingered in Amarillo because he was dumb. He'd stayed because his father had offered to let Tommy start to buy him out of his car repair shop. Tommy knew a good thing when he saw one.

Simple as this: Tommy was a car guy; Amy was a horse girl. Don't it just sound like the opening of a great country song?

Having showered, Amy lay down on her four-poster bed in such a way that her freshly feathered hair could dangle off the side of the mattress. She almost fell asleep before the doorbell sounded.

When Amy got to the door she found Doreen stuffing cash into the back pocket of Tommy's cutoff jeans. Tommy had recently replaced a squealing belt in Doreen's truck. He'd insisted it would be no charge, but Doreen didn't like owing anyone—especially Slim—a favor.

Well, look who's all gussied up, Doreen said. And to think I was getting to feel sorry for you . . .

Amy took Tommy's hand. I ain't sick, she said. Just a little tired is all.

She led Tommy back to her bedroom. She shut the door and kissed him and he reached up under her shirt. She tapped once on his button fly. Down, boy, she said.

Let's drive somewhere, he said.

Amy wanted to. She'd been traveling and training so much. But she was also able to wait. She kind of *preferred* the waiting. It kept Tommy in a chivalrous mood. What's more, she'd already played up her stomach sickness for maximum pity from Doreen. To head out into the night with Tommy would be unwise. So she proposed they bake some cookies. Amy loved baking. Tommy was usually a sport and helped, but Amy knew: a nineteen-year-old boy could only be kept satisfied for so long by licking batter off a finger.

They wound up in the family room watching NASCAR with Amy's brothers. She snuggled up to Tommy and teased them all for following such a silly sport.

At least NASCAR's got parity, Tommy said.

Amy's brothers nodded from the other end of the couch.

Y'all don't know what that word even means, Amy told them.

Neither do you, one of them said.

They all looked at Tommy. He reached a hand toward the TV.

What're you trying to say? Amy asked.

It's *stock car* racing, he said. That's the whole point. Means it's about the *drivers*. Richard Petty could swap cars with any driver on that track and still smoke 'em all.

So could Farah McGovern, Amy said. (You may not know: Farah was the 1976 National Finals Rodeo champion.)

Yeah? Tommy said. And who'd Farah thank right after she won?

God, Amy said.

That stallion of hers, Tommy said.

Rico, Amy said. That was just her being modest.

Or *honest*, Tommy said.

Amy looked him over, knowing that Farah made more money studding Rico out than she did barrel racing.

You think I just hold onto Patton and he does all the work? Amy said.

C'mon now, Tommy said. You know we're all just talking. That's all.

Doreen's voice rang out from the kitchen: Well, I'd say you're doing most of it, Slim!

Usually Doreen's eavesdropping pissed Amy off. But when Tommy looked now to her for some backup, she stood up from the couch and announced, I'm gonna make cookies.

Leaving Tommy no choice, really, but to leave.

The next morning there were five horses in the barn that were not going to feed, water, or exercise themselves. Nor was Amy. She couldn't summon the energy to get out of bed.

Chores, Amy! Doreen shouted from the hallway. It's past 9!

A lazy Amy might have groaned at this, or begged for a few more minutes. A rebellious Amy might have argued. So when Amy did nothing but stare off the side of her bed at the orange shag carpet, Doreen didn't stride in and tear the covers off the bed.

That's it, Doreen said. I'm calling Dr. Ferris.

Amy dozed off. The next time she looked up, Doreen was in her doorway. Got us an appointment, she said. Get dressed.

Amy groaned.

Now, Doreen said.

Bare feet to carpet. To the bathroom, to the closet. Wranglers.

White blouse. Boots. Something in Doreen's tone had Amy worried.

They drove the eight miles to Amarillo. The land in the midday sun looked washed out. The hills were dried brown and yellow, the sky was a diluted blue. Hot as hell. The air-conditioner worked as hard as it could. Amy pretended to sleep. Doreen seemed willing to keep up her half of that silence until, out of nowhere, she broke it.

Are you and Slim having sex? she asked.

Amy stared out the windshield. Paralyzed.

What? she said.

She was a smart girl, but she wasn't playing dumb. Wasn't pretending shock.

Because it simply hadn't yet crossed Amy's mind. It hit her like a hot wind.

She and Tommy were very careful. But there had been times . . . Once, he'd fingered her right after he took a condom off, and she'd told him he should have washed his hands. Another time a condom came off inside her.

Holy fucking shit.

Amy had hardly ever thought of herself in that way. As a *mother*. (What? Like *Doreen*?) It had never seemed like something that could or would happen to her, not unless she tried for it. Unless she wanted it. Unless she went after it.

You heard me, Doreen said.

No! Amy said. Then she said it again, with all the conviction she could muster: *No.*

Doreen looked over. Amy kept her eyes on the twisting road.

Thank God, Doreen said.

Despite her age, Amy still saw her longtime pediatrician, Dr. Ferris. In the waiting room, kids were climbing all over a carpeted play structure. A TV on a shelf played *The Price Is Right*. While Doreen checked in, Amy found a seat next to a little rollercoaster track of wooden beads. One by one, she nudged them into freefall.

A nurse called Amy's name. Mother and daughter followed her down a maze of corridors. Amy could sense herself being led deeper and deeper into trouble. Doreen walked just behind and to the side of Amy. As if she were Amy's attorney. They were shown to an exam room. Doreen took a chair. Amy was instructed to sit on the exam table. She kicked at the air. The paper she sat on crackled.

Sit still, Doreen muttered.

Dr. Ferris knocked on the door as he came through it. He smiled at Doreen, then frowned like a clown at Amy. Not feeling good? he said.

Mostly just tired, Amy said. A little dizzy.

Going around all those barrels'll do that, he said, winking at Doreen. He took a popsicle stick from a jar and pointed it at Amy. We haven't seen this one in some time, he told Doreen.

He edged closer to Amy. He shined a light in her eyes, her ears, her mouth. He took the liberty of lifting Amy's blouse to use his stethoscope. The only sound in the room was Amy's forced breathing.

Good, Dr. Ferris said, sliding the stethoscope around Amy's heaving chest. Again . . .

When he was done, he pulled a stool on wheels out from under the desk and sat. His face was at Amy's waist level. One of his big knees stuck out of his white coat. Well, he said. We can do this next part with your mom in here or out in the hall. It's all the same to me.

I think the hall, Amy said. She turned to Doreen and added, If that's okay.

Doreen picked up her purse. Dr. Ferris rose from the stool to give her a wide berth as she stormed out.

Amy stared at a framed photo of a hot air balloon. Do I . . . um, lay back? she asked.

Amy, Dr. Ferris said, I'm very busy this morning. I'd like to cut right to it, if you don't mind.

Amy tried to smile—as if being pleasant would influence his verdict, her sentence.

Are you sexually active, honey? he asked—the second time she'd fielded this question in an hour. The second time in her lifetime. She recalled the smell of Tommy's neck, the animal look in his eye when he was driving away at her.

Amy nodded.

And when was your last period? Dr. Ferris asked.

Amy straightened, bracing herself. The paper rustled. She feared she might cry. This month's hasn't come quite yet, she said.

Dr. Ferris gave a sad little smile. Have you ever taken a pregnancy test? he asked. An EPT?

Amy's bangs swung back and forth as she shook her head. Dr. Ferris looked out the window and rubbed his palm on his bald head.

We don't tend to see girls your age in here, he said. We might not even stock . . . Well—tell you what. Let me step out, talk to Gayle, see if we can't find us what we need. Give me just a minute, honey . . .

At first Amy felt thankful for this stay of execution. Then she thought: *What's another minute, at this point? What's another hour?*

When Dr. Ferris returned Doreen was with him. She didn't look at Amy. Just sat down with her purse in her lap. Politely fuming. Amy kept her eyes down while Dr. Ferris explained the test Amy was going to take.

Answer the doctor's question, honey, Doreen said.

Amy realized she'd stopped listening, stopped breathing.

It's fine, darling, Dr. Ferris said. I was just asking if you had any questions at this point.

Amy had a hundred questions. But to ask even one of them would show her for the stupid teenager she surely must be to have gotten herself into this. To ask a single question would make all of this real. Questions were therefore out of the question.

Not right now, she said.

Dr. Ferris handed her a little cup wrapped in plastic. Amy took it to a bathroom across the hall. Unwrapped it. Pissed her life away.

We'll have an answer in two hours, Dr. Ferris said.

That long? Amy thought.

That fast? Doreen said.

Dr. Ferris excused himself, leaving the door ajar. Doreen got up and walked out. Amy followed her back to the waiting room. The only place to sit was an undersized bench painted to look like a circus train. They sat.

I *trusted* you, Doreen muttered.

On the TV a woman in heels used her whole body to spin a wheel of glitzy numbers. The audience shouting. The wheel bleeping. The woman held her hands to her face like she was sucking on a blankie. The wheel spun slower. Slower. *Bleep, bleep . . . bleep . . .*

Doreen got off the train. I'm leaving, she said.

Most everyone at Amy's high school knew the story of the Clark sisters, who'd faked a robbery of their own house, pawned all the stuff they took, and gone shopping with the proceeds. When Mr. Clark figured it out, he'd driven the girls straight to the police station. He had them booked. *Sure I coulda grounded 'em*, he'd told KAMR news. *But ain't no match for a night in a cell.*

Doreen couldn't have done much better than leaving Amy in that waiting room, in limbo, among Amarillo's sickest, snot-sodden kids and their exasperated mothers.

Time forked. Amy lived each passing minute in the past, the present, and the future. Her legs wrapped around Tommy's hips in the bed of his pickup; these same legs lost circulation on the circus-train bench; and they wobbled as she stepped into her father's den with something to tell him.

An hour went by. Doreen did not return.

From her bench, Amy had a bird's-eye view of the street. There were so many new things to be afraid of down there. Speeding cars. Electricity. Amy had always been flighty. Hermit crabs and hamsters had died, hot and thirsty, on her watch. Patton might have too, without Doreen. How, then, could Amy not fail at this?

Amy's answer: *This isn't anything. Not yet. Because maybe I'm not pregnant.*

But probably I am.

And if so, Amy's answer was simple. It was drawn from a well she'd never gone to before. It was so simple it had to be true.

You just don't fail, Amy. Because you can't.

It played over and over in her head like a mantra. A negative about which she was positive: *You just don't, you just don't . . .*

You're a mother. You came here as one person, but you're going home as two.

Barrel horses weren't the only things that could turn on a dime.

No more rodeos . . .

No more rodeos!

Amy thought about finding a pay phone to call Tommy, but she didn't have any coins. Plus it could wait. She didn't know for sure yet.

Children and mothers (no fathers) kept coming through the waiting room. The nurses' desk went unmanned for a long time. Amy glanced around, trying to catch the eyes of other mothers to see if they were as concerned as she was.

Yesterday afternoon, Amy had been in Lubbock riding in front of thousands of people who were rooting for her. Today she was completely alone.

Finally, a nurse. Who grabbed some paperwork, disappeared. Amy got up. Started across the room, only to turn back. Because what was she going to do? Knock on the glass like some lunatic? Put her lips through the little hole and start screaming?

It already felt to Amy like she'd been in that waiting room for nine months.

Doreen walked back into Dr. Ferris's office as if she'd only gone to ladies' room. She'd changed into shorts, boots, and a red blouse. Her hair was up in bun.

You went home? Amy said.

Someone has to deal with the horses, Doreen said.

(We've got to hand it to Doreen: guilt shoveled on guilt.)

Still no word? she said.

Amy shook her head.

Doreen crossed to the nurses' desk. Had a brief chat with them. Then she turned to Amy and flipped her hand the way Hank did to call the dogs.

Back to the corridors! Amy saw skylights she hadn't noticed before. Sunlight on the carpets. They were shown into the exam room right next to the one they'd been in before. It was a mirror image. Amy plunked down on a fresh sheet of paper. She was steel. She had never felt so sure of herself.

You seem awful calm, Doreen complained.

Dr. Ferris came in right away. Shut the door. He set a clipboard down on the Formica and stared at Amy. You're not pregnant, he said.

What? Amy said.

So what is it, then? Doreen said. What's the matter with her?

My guess? Dr. Ferris said. Food poisoning . . .

But she *missed her period*, Doreen said.

Dr. Ferris frowned. Fair point, he said. But it can happen. Or she's just late. Overexercise'll do it, too. Stress. Travel. Any of that sound familiar?

He winked at Amy. But she was already gone, already somewhere else. She was not ready to be "one" again, when just a minute ago she'd been "two." Her brand-new world popped and shriveled back to a little exam room, almost but not exactly the room from this morning, with its picture of a hot air balloon, its ten cubbies full of little pamphlets, its four drawers. Its two adults, one teenager, one fetus.

Now, three adults. Period.

Doreen usually drove fast on the highway, but now she was lingering in the slow lane. She had one hand on the wheel while the other fiddled with her crucifix. Her window was down, the country station volume up. Amy left her own window shut. This created an uncomfortable pressurization in the cabin. Amy watched the density and verticality of Amarillo's downtown smear into the space and horizontality of its outskirts. She was heading back to her flat, yellow, unchanged life.

You know when I went home, Doreen shouted, I exercised your horse. I got him bridled and all, and I was leading him outta the barn, but he halted by the wagon wheel. I tugged on him, but he didn't budge. Just kinda stood there. Staring at me with that big ol' black eye of his. I could see my reflection in it, and I thought—well, that's it, Doreen. You done *failed* . . .

It struck Amy then for the first time all day that her push-up-bra-wearing mother had nearly became a grandmother in her thirties. No wonder Doreen was so shell-shocked. No wonder she was so relieved.

Doreen was saying, All your plans, all your hard work. All the things we've got lined up. It would have been: *Poof.* Gone.

Fine by me, Amy said.

Their exit came. Doreen took the off ramp. Rolled to a halt at a stoplight. And then, finally, asked: What's that supposed to mean?

Amy thought about it. Being pregnant for a few hours had changed things. A baby fell out of thin air and she had let go of everything to make sure she could catch it. Maybe she didn't want to pick all that stuff back up.

Now she knew why she hardly ever got nervous at rodeos. She hardly cared.

I don't want to do any more rodeos this summer, Amy said.

Doreen laughed this off. It's been a long morning, she said. How about we just survive the rest of the day.

Amy looked out her window, past the four-strand fences that paralleled the road, to the flatness further out. The telephone lines headed out into infinity. Drifting clouds. Grazing cattle.

I'm near twenty now, Mom, Amy said. And I still live at home. I don't have any good girlfriends left. All I do is ride that damn horse and ride in this damn truck.

And Slim, Doreen said. Don't forget him.

The look Amy gave Doreen was truly one for the ages.

I was scared as shit today, Amy said. Does *that* make you happy?

No comment from Doreen.

But then, Amy continued, I don't know. I felt . . . strong. Maybe that's how you felt— with me? It felt *right*—like something I was supposed to do.

What's gotten into you? Doreen asked, both hands back on the wheel.

Don't worry, Amy said. I ain't fixing to run out and get pregnant. But there's things I want to do, I think. On my own. I can see 'em clearly now.

Name one, Doreen challenged.

Cooking school, Amy replied immediately.

This is crazy, honey, Doreen said. You *love* riding. You're one to the saddle born . . .

I don't know, Amy said. I think maybe I've just been holding on.

Amy called Tommy as soon as they got home. Having carried the weight of the world by herself all morning, she eagerly tossed it right into his lap. I was at the doctor all day, she said.

So you were sick? he asked.

Pregnant, Amy said.

Tommy laughed, then laughed a little more. I know that laugh. I have laughed it. (The aforementioned English professor—the one with whom I had been sleeping for the six months leading up to that same summer of '77? She'd once noticed an engagement ring in a shop window as we strolled by after an otherwise lovely dinner of linguine and clams and white wine, and she'd veered us over to peer in at it. Isn't it gorgeous? she'd said, and I'd shrugged and agreed and tried to start walking again. Well. You can tell where this is going. I thought we'd been walking down a sidewalk but I walked right off a cliff. And when I laughed about the prospect of purchasing such a ring in my near future, she didn't, and I laughed a little more, and that was the beginning of the end for us.)

Amy told Tommy she wasn't joking. This took a lot of convincing. She explained what happened, how she'd thought she was pregnant but wasn't.

Holy shit, he said. Holy *shit.*

I know.

So you told Doreen, he said. About . . . *us.*

Everybody thought I was pregnant, Amy said. Including me.

But you aren't. Thank god!

Yeah.

Tommy paused. Amy? he said.

Mm.

How come you sound like you're not relieved?

It's just, for a little while there, I was ready.

Jesus, Amy! This is crazy. How come you didn't call me right away? I should be the first one to hear things. Even bad news . . .

Our baby is bad news?

Our baby? Tommy said. Amy, what the fuck!

I thought you'd be supportive, she said.

Of what? Having a goddamn baby?

Of *us*, Amy said. Of whatever happens.

Amy was looking at a picture of her and Tommy pinned to her dresser mirror. It had been professionally taken at the Rodeo Gala. With Tommy in his rental tux, graciously escorting Amy—the "Rising Texas Talent." They looked happy—or at least Amy did. Tommy always looked . . . well, like maybe Doreen had it backwards: maybe Slim Pickens was the one settling.

By the way, Amy said. I thought about what you said last night. About how my horse does all the work.

Seriously? Amy, I think that's not really—

You were right.

Tommy sighed. He said, That was just me arguing.

I know. And you were right.

I gotta get back to work, Tommy said.

The next morning Amy was in the shower when she felt a menstrual cramp. All of a sudden she was crying. She cried for a long time standing there in the hot water.

Her phone rang. Leaving the water running, she wrapped herself in a towel and went to answer it. Passing the mirror, she saw that her chest and face and eyes were all bright red. She left wet footprints across the carpet.

Hey, she answered.

Tommy started talking. More than usual. He said he'd been up most of the night thinking. That he'd started to understand things better. *Good*, Amy thought. She knew Tommy was a thoughtful guy, deep down: it just took him time to realize what she'd been through. She realized it was partially her own fault for dumping the news on him the way she had. Whereas she'd had a whole day to sit with it.

Just come over, she said—watching steam billow from the bathroom. We'll talk.

I don't think so, Tommy said.

And Amy realized that Tommy was surely not interested in facing her parents any time soon. Right, she said. I'll come to your house.

Actually . . . , Tommy said.

(Eric—whom we haven't met yet—told me once that a significant, and annoying, milestone in his daughter Charlotte's development was the proper deployment of that word *actually* to start a sentence. It does so much heavy lifting, that word. It says: I understand what you're saying, but the truth of the matter is different, and how about I tell you what that truth is. Tommy hit this selfsame milestone in his relationship with Amy at that moment.)

Amy could hear him breathing through the phone. But before she realized what was happening—before the ground she stood on cracked—she felt big waves moving through her, like the low notes from concert speakers that can shake your guts. Or how horses can tell when there's an earthquake coming and they get skittish and feel an urge to run, and they do run, to try to get ahead of whatever's coming, whether or not that's even possible.

I think we should break up, Tommy said. You're different than I thought.

What? Amy said. No, I'm not! I'm the same. Nothing's changed.

Actually . . .

Oh honey, Doreen said. You look positively wrung out.

She'd found Amy sitting on her bedroom floor in her towel, the shower still running, hair still wet.

Doreen clucked and went to shut off the water. She came back and puttered around Amy's room, picking up clothes from the floor. C'mon now, Doreen said, get dressed. I can't let you out of chores two days in a row.

Tommy broke up with me, Amy muttered. She peeked out through her knees to catch her mother's reaction.

Doreen stopped puttering. *No*, she gasped.

He's just scared is all. He's not acting like himself.

I'll bet. Boy's probably scared shitless. (Bingo, Doreen.)

Amy was shivering. Doreen knelt beside her. She squeezed her daughter's shoulder. Trust me, Doreen said. Best thing to do is just get movin' again.

I have to talk to him, Amy said. He's just overreacting.

Doreen stood up and made fists on her hips. I don't know, she said. I think ol' Slim's reaction is about right. I wish *you* were more shook by all this. My God! You complain about taking care of *horses*! Your life would have completely changed . . .

Exactly, Amy said.

This hit mother right where daughter had been aiming.

You ungrateful little . . . , Doreen said, then paused, collecting herself. Do your girlfriends talk to their mothers this way? she asked.

What girlfriends, Amy muttered.

Daughters, Doreen mused. So damn melodramatic. Your brothers never brood like this. They just go punch a wall.

You're a fuckin' daughter too, Amy said.

The *mouth* on you. Get up!

Doreen's boots were almost standing on Amy's bare toes.

I ain't going in that barn, Amy said.

Doreen pulled Amy's hands off her knees and yanked her up from the floor. Amy grabbed hold of the towel in time to keep it from falling off. Doreen breathed though her nose like Patton. She looked like she wanted to do violence, and Amy worried she'd finally pushed her too far.

You're making some very poor choices, young lady, Doreen said. And it's time you start facing up to 'em. Starting with that horse of yours, who I'll not see you neglect another day.

He's *your* horse, Amy said. I just ride him. They're all your horses, in that barn.

Patton is *yours*, Doreen said. You know that.

Hank arrived then in the bedroom doorway, asking about the commotion.

Doreen explained: Our daughter here is no longer interested in doing chores.

That so? Hank said, crossing his big arms and leaning against the doorjamb.

Amy stood. She was all cried out. She'd lost a baby and a boyfriend. She had nothing on but a towel. She felt like a wet varmint in a trap. And she got the urge to do something rash. To finish whatever it was she seemed to have started here.

Doreen was lecturing about how living under her roof meant *blah blah blah . . .*

Yes, ma'am, Amy interrupted. Understood.

Doreen straightened up, not expecting this. She looked to Hank. But he was watching Amy. He was often the first to see what his daughter was getting at.

Okay, then, Doreen said. Sounds like we're in agreement.

I'm moving out, Amy said.

She didn't wait for a reaction. Just went straight back to the bathroom and locked the door. She expected Doreen to come pound on the door, but there was only an eerie quiet. Amy turned on the shower again. She held her hand into the spray for a minute but it only got lukewarm. All the hot water in the house had been used up.

Amy got in and finished what she'd started.

Days went by. Tommy didn't call. Not that Amy really expected him to. She tried to guess his mind. *Does he feel like he's made a mistake? Is he just too proud to say so?* Maybe all it would take to get him back would be the smallest thing—the pushing of a single speed-dial button. A giggle. She was the most desperate at night, in the dark. Twice she picked up the phone. Once she even dialed, but hung up before it rang. She unplugged her phone, then plugged it back in.

She hadn't forgotten what she wanted, what she'd threatened to do. She *was* moving out, she just didn't know *how*. She looked through the classifieds in the *Amarillo Globe-News*. There was a one-bedroom/one-bath studio available downtown for $165 a month. Amy could cover the first month plus the $100 deposit with what was in her piggy bank. It boiled her blood to think of the 15 grand she'd taken home in winnings over the past two summers. All of it was out of her reach, in a stupid college account. Amy didn't want to go to college. She wanted a one-bedroom/one-bath studio in downtown Amarillo.

In those days, some of you may recall, the real estate section and the personals were one column apart. They read about the same. All business. Short and sweet. Kitchenette, brunette. Square feet, height. "Pets okay," "Loves kids." There was one key difference, though. A word, used over and over: *seeks.* Places aren't so picky about what they're looking for, other than someone who can pay the rent. Not so with people. People can be very specific in their wanting.

Amy scanned the personals and wondered: was Tommy in there somewhere? Was he the five foot ten, 180-pound, brown-haired car lover seeking a girl to ride shotgun? If so, he'd lied about his weight.

Were we to craft a personal ad for Amy, what would it say? *Bottom-heavy brunette, barrel racer/dropout seeks cheap apartment where she can sleep and cook dinners for friends (also seeking those) . . . ?* Was that all she wanted, then? Just . . . freedom? Not really. More the opposite. *Cute, young, sassy (but not too sassy!), and independent (but not too independent!) former semi-pro athlete seeks dependable, supportive man to make babies with (not right away, but sooner rather than later!). Are you out there? Is this really that hard, are the pickings really this slim?*

Amy avoided Doreen. She got the feeling her mother was returning the favor.

Early one morning Amy slipped out the front door. The clouds had pink bellies. She walked barefoot on the cool asphalt to grab the *Globe-News*. There was yet another section of the classifieds, one she was ready to stop avoiding: the want ads.

Back inside the still-dark house, Amy stopped dead. Doreen was on the couch in her red robe, drinking coffee.

You're up early, Doreen said. Can't say I've known you to read the paper. She rose from the couch and came to stand in front of Amy. You've been missed in the corral, she said. I've been exercising Patton, but he needs to run barrels. Be a shame to let him get out of practice, don't you think?

Shelly can ride him, Amy said.

Shelly was a girl Amy's age who lived a few miles down the road. Amy had never really liked Shelly. Maybe because Doreen liked Shelly so much. Or because Shelly loved riding, even though she'd never be great at it. Shelly's father bought her the best horses, and endless lessons with Doreen.

Shelly can't boss him through a turn like he needs, Doreen said.

I need the money from my bank account, Amy replied.

Okay, well. When you need it, it's yours.

Not for college.

Yes, for college.

But it's *my* money. I won it. I need it.

Oh? And what is it you *need*, Amy?

Rent, Amy said.

Oh, for God's sake! Are you doing all this to spite your poor mother? Are you tryin' to make some kind of stand? Well, point taken. You're not the first little bird to want to fly the nest.

I know.

You know *shit*, Amy. But that ain't your fault. You're nineteen.

I know more than you think.

You're damn well *capable* of more'n I thought. You and that boyfriend of yours.

Ex-boyfriend, Amy said.

Indeed, Doreen said. The silver lining in all this.

Amy turned to go, but Doreen stepped in her way. I'm sorry, Doreen said. You're a strong young lady. Strongest I ever saw on a horse. It's just, I've been thinking back to *myself* when I was nineteen, and frankly, it scares the hell out of me. What I thought I knew . . . And that was the '*50s*. Things are so different now.

So.

So, people ain't horses, Amy. They don't just fall out of their mammas and lick themselves clean and take off runnin'.

Remember the first time I got up on Patton? Amy asked. How he came loose on me? I wasn't scared until I looked over and saw how scared you were.

That horse's been a stubborn bastard since day one.

Mom, are you even listening? I'm trying to make an analogy.

An *analogy*?

Yeah. Like how you compare two—

I know what it is, honey.

You just didn't think *I* did. I reckon there's other things too.

Maybe so, Doreen allowed.

Can I have that money in the account?

No.

No?

No, Doreen said. And please don't ask again.

The want ads were "seeking" too. At least the ones for good-paying jobs. They sought experience. Degrees. Certifications.

Amy sought out Hank. She met him one evening in the garage as he got home from work. Gave him a hug and made some chitchat and then put the question to him. I was wondering, she said. Can I have the money in the savings account?

What'd your mother say?

Amy looked down. Hank squinted at her for a moment.

I heard they lost a dispatcher over at W&C, he said. They're missing concrete drops. They could probably use someone . . .

What's the pay?

Hot damn! Hank laughed. That's my girl . . .

Amy stared at him, waiting.

A dispatcher? Hank said. Maybe 4 an hour. Or thereabouts. You'd pick it up quick. There's a big board for tracking deliveries, and a radio for wrangling the drivers.

I've never used a radio, Amy said.

You've sure as hell used a phone, he said. You push a button, you talk.

Amy had been thinking a lot about wages. Four dollars an hour wasn't far from the wage she'd more or less been earning already, over thousands of hours, racing barrels. Well, so long as she didn't factor in expenses—the money Hank spent on alfalfa and gas, trucks and trailers, hairspray and sequins. *Actually*, Amy was deep in the hole. She owed Hank many thousands.

You just let me know if you're interested, he said. I'm happy to make a call.

Amy thanked him. He nodded, but Amy could sense he was patronizing her. Words didn't mean shit to Hank.

Amy had been force-fed *The Scarlett Letter* in senior English. She'd found it boring and had purged Hester Prynne from her memory as soon as she took the final. To the point that, one night soon after her breakup, as she stood in front of her mirror and gazed at her belt buckle, the damned A did not cross her mind.

It does of course come to my mind, though. For she wore The Turquoise Number. Like the A, the 1 started out symbolizing one thing (an anniversary), became another (victory), and finally settled into something else. It represented . . . *her. Amy*. Amy was all Amy had.

She took walks on the dusty dirt roads near the house. These roads led nowhere. Still, it helped, putting one boot in front of the other. She liked getting baked in the Texas sun, sweating out whatever was in her, watching dust devils rise up and spin themselves out. One day she was out walking when she heard motors, then a couple dirt bikers came over a rise. She stepped into the brush to let them pass. But the first rider stopped. He lifted off his helmet and yelled to ask if Amy was okay. The armpits of her blouse were sweated through.

I'm fine, she said.

What? he yelled.

I'm *fine*!

The second rider rolled up. They sat their bikes, their gloved hands resting on their gas tanks the way Amy used to lay hers on a pommel. Their engines thrummed and popped.

Helluva buckle, the first rider yelled. He pointed at Amy's waist.

Thanks, Amy yelled back, but he wasn't looking at her. He was talking to the other rider. Amy got the sense they were deciding something. Something bad.

Lemme see it, he yelled.

Amy felt the big waves in her gut again. She felt outmanned, out here where she lived, in the middle of nowhere. The first rider threw his boot over his seat and rocked his bike up on its stand.

Amy unbuckled the belt, yanked it out through the loops in her cutoffs. It dangled from her hand like a whip. The buckle end plopped in the dirt. The second rider raised his palms the way one does to calm a spooked horse. But Amy was already swinging the belt like a helicopter blade. She wanted them to look at her and see a dangerous desert creature. To know: this one stings. She wanted them to see she had nothing left to lose.

This proved easy.

Moments later their tires were spitting dirt and they were out of sight again over a rise and Amy couldn't hear their bikes for the wind.

She caught her breath. There was sweat trickling down her ribs. The way one of the riders had waved when he remounted his bike—it had been . . . *cute*. Amy realized that maybe he'd really only wanted to admire her buckle. Maybe he'd liked the curve of her shorts. Maybe he'd have asked her out if she hadn't gone crazy.

She put the belt to her teeth and bit in, leaving tooth marks in the leather. She thought, *Goddamn if I ain't misjudging men lately*.

Ten days after losing a rodeo and a baby and a boyfriend in one fell swoop, Amy stole Doreen's little notebook. She closed the door to her bedroom and dialed one of the numbers in it.

Hello?

Shelly? Hi, it's Amy!

Oh, hi, Amy. I was so sorry to hear about you and Tommy.

I'm calling to—wait, who told you about that?

Doreen.

Maddening as this was, Amy refused to be sidetracked. Anyway, she said, I called to ask if y'all want to buy my horse.

You mean . . . *Patton?*

The one and only.

I didn't know he was for sale.

He is now.

Did you get another horse?

No. It ain't like that.

Amy felt the power of her position. (I know the other side of that position. I went out for wrestling my freshman year of high school. And in each of my matches, right before I got slammed to the mat, there was that same horrible moment when I could feel my feet or my hands lose touch with the ground, when I lost all leverage. It might be said I am not a writer so much as a failed wrestler. It might be said that all writers are failed *somethings*.)

I'm calling you first, Amy said.

Wow! That's awful kind of you.

Fifteen grand, Amy said. I'll even hand-deliver him. But you gotta let me know real quick. I got a list of folks who've made offers.

I bet! Can you hold just on a minute? I need to go get my dad.

Attagirl, Amy thought. *Go ask Daddy*.

Amy left the house through the garage and crossed the driveway. It was close to noon and scorching outside. The winds were picking up. She could see Doreen in the round pen working a horse on a lunge line. Doreen's back was turned. Amy slipped into the barn.

It was dark and a little cooler inside. Amy walked past the trophies and pictures and came to the second stall. Patton came over and hung his head on the rail. Amy lay her hands on his muzzle, the velvet on his nose. He blew his sweet alfalfa breath in her face. It made her sad. Doreen had been right about his big, black eye. It saw right through you.

Amy knew to keep her own eye on the prize. Doreen had been right about that, too.

There was dust in the beams of sunlight coming into the barn. Amy could hear her mother outside, could hear her tongue clicking. Amy was surrounded by feeding bins and water troughs and hayforks and brushes and rolls of tape and saddle pads and bits and latigos and hackamores—all the things one needs to keep a girl so busy she can't tell she's the one who's bridled.

Amy wanted a studio apartment with a big queen bed. She wanted a three-ring binder with a syllabus in the front pocket and copies of homework recipes in tabbed sections she'd carefully labeled in pink pen. She wanted a checkbook for an account only she could draw from. She wanted friends. Friends from cooking school or wherever—just not high school—who talked about things other than cars and horses and high school. And Amy wanted a boyfriend with strong arms and a big heart to taste the things she made and take her out and fall in love with her. And make a baby with her. That's it. That's all she wanted.

A big rectangle of light waited in the door at the end of the barn.

Amy bridled Patton but skipped the saddle. She led him down the alleyway. Before they got to the big door, Amy put a boot up on a rail of the last stall and boosted herself up onto Patton's long back. He trotted sideways, not used to being mounted like this. The door at the back of the barn creaked as it opened. A breeze stole through. The dust in the sunlight swirled in it.

Amy heard her mother's voice. Amy? That you, honey?

Amy tapped Patton with her heel. Trotted them out into the light.

When they reached the two-lane road, Amy set Patton into a canter. Staying in the weeds between the asphalt and the barbed-wire fence, they picked their way toward Shelly's. Half a mile down, Amy heard a truck pull onto the shoulder behind her.

Doreen shouted out the passenger window of her F-250: Damn it, Amy! What the hell are you doing!

Sold my horse, Amy said, riding through a crosswind. To Sally. Mr. Cooper said he'd pay me today.

You sold Patton to *Shelly*? Jesus on the cross. Please, Amy. You gotta call this off. This is plain crazy.

Never before had Amy heard her mother talk like this. Doreen was *begging*.

Amy slowed Patton to a trot and said, Will you let me have that money in my account?

Is that all this is about?

Amy kept riding, staring out toward the Coopers' property line. It's 15 grand either way, Mom, she said. So you pick. I don't care.

I can't decide if I should come over there and slap you silly or shake your hand.

Amy rode along.

I give up, Doreen said. Just take that damn money. You've earned it, I suppose.

Amy gave the reins a gentle tug. Patton halted.

Doreen stopped the truck. Now, will you *please* take that poor horse back to the barn before y'all melt?

Yes, ma'am, Amy said.

She turned her horse and set him galloping home. Her hair blowing out behind her.

Doreen had been right. Amy *had* earned the money. And on the back of a horse, to boot.

Just not in a rodeo.

Zhiyu/Jerry

1986

EARLIER, I HUMBLE-BRAGGED about my National Book Award. I wish to add here that I am actually prouder of my Hugo for Best Science Fiction Novel of 1986. Thank you. Please hold your applause.

Not the award itself. The book: *Dividing Light*. It wasn't very widely read. Or at least not widely *purchased*, judging by the royalties. But that's one of the few titles of mine I can pull off the shelf and read from and not feel ashamed or annoyed, nor compelled to call my editor and beg to pull it from circulation, or at least be allowed to make changes.

Dividing Light was based in part on the Arecibo message, an FM radio message encoded with basic details about humans and the Earth that we, humanity, broadcast from the Arecibo Telescope in Puerto Rico on November 16, 1974. We chose to aim the transmission at a cluster of stars twenty-five thousand light years away.

That transmission got a young Z thinking, which tended to get him writing. Anyway, the novel ended up being in three parts: (beginning) the composition of the message, (middle) the reception by the alien culture, and (end) their response. In my story, both of the messages, despite attempts at generality and objectivity on the part of the cultures that sent them, were imbued ever so subtly with the personal histories and predilections of their particular composers. The composers on both sides struggled with writers' block (what does one say to the universe!). Early in the book, the human tasked with drafting ours cranked out a shitty first draft as a joke, just to get something down. It was rife with petty struggles, infernal longing, indecision, inappropriate musings. My hope being that readers would find the silly, hyper-personal draft the more compelling. That its specificity would convey things actually far more universal than did the final message. Same thing on the alien side. The final versions of both cultures being recomposed by committees and saying, predictably, what *should* be said. Of course—inevitably—both messages were made irrelevant by the light years before either arrived. A conversation cannot be held at such a remove. Hence the title.

You'll be surprised (or maybe unconvinced) to know I bring all this up not in furtherance of my own ego. You'll *not* be surprised that I am a sucker for metaphor. I bring it up because I cannot help but see parallels in the message sent in 1974 across outer space and the one sent in 1986 across a front stoop.

Zhiyu wanted the very fattest duck. He pointed it out to the lady. She nodded and leaned into the cage to nab the bird by its neck and carry it, flapping against her clutch, into the back room. Zhiyu waited. The lady returned with a drooping plastic sack. The sack was warm. Zhiyu took it with him on the bus home from work. By the time he got to his stop the sack was cool.

Work was a corner store Zhiyu and his wife Fei Yen had managed for nearly twenty years and had owned for the last eight. Home was a two-bedroom apartment on a busy street in South San Francisco. All three of their children had been raised in this apartment, paid for by the money earned at the store.

In the coat closet by the front door was a bike pump. The pump had a screw-on needle valve. Back when Zhiyu rode still rode a bike most everywhere, he'd kept this valve in a drawer in the kitchen. He had only attached it to the pump a few times a year, on occasions like this. Zhiyu had not pumped up a flat tire in a long time. The needle stayed on the pump now. *Maybe the* pump *should be kept in the kitchen!* he thought.

Fei Yen came into the front room. At home, they spoke in Mandarin.

You shouldn't go to all this trouble, she said. The boy might not even like duck.

Everyone likes duck, Zhiyu replied.

I'll make extra dumplings, Fei Yen said. Just in case.

Zhiyu took the duck from the sack. Arranged it on a metal tray. He punctured the defeathered breast skin with the needle. Fei Yen bent over to grip the pump's T-shaped handle. She started to pump, up and down, up and down. The pump wheezed. Neither of them spoke.

Zhiyu moved the needle around the carcass as she pumped, and soon the inflating skin started to separate from the underlayer of fat. When it was separated to Zhiyu's satisfaction he nodded, and Fei Yen smiled and shook her head and left him in the kitchen. As he always did, Zhiyu boiled the duck for the time it took to smoke one cigarette. Then he toweled the bird dry and rubbed it with his father's secret six-spice mix. He hung it on a wire hanger bent just for this purpose, then glazed the skin with honey, vinegar, and soy sauce. He got out an electric fan and left the duck dangling in the breeze it made. Zhiyu and Fei Yen could hear the fan whirring from their bedroom as they fell asleep. A reassuring sound, like an ocean.

In the morning the skin was as dry as parchment. Zhiyu glazed it again.

It was Sunday. He and Fei Yen mopped and dusted and

swept the apartment with more purpose than usual. By noon the day was warm and sunny and they opened the windows to air out the rooms. They put a tablecloth and linen napkins on the table. Fei Yen made her dumplings.

At 4:30, Zhiyu put the duck in the oven. Then he sat down at the kitchen table and balanced the checkbook while half-listening to Chinese AM radio.

The shirt—a blue button-up with yellow pinstripes—had arrived in the mail that week. Inside was a note from Zhiyu's daughter, Nancy. The note said: *Please? Thanks!* The shirt was still in its package. Zhiyu tugged the pins out one by one and put it on. The tag itched. He preferred to button his shirts all the way to the top, but even so the collar of this one hung loose. It was huge: a "medium."

For his fifty-sixth birthday, Nancy had given him a big blue sweatshirt with golden letters—BERKELEY—and a pair of "pre-faded" jeans. Both had also been far too big for his body. The father Nancy remembered, and still saw, was bigger.

By 6:00 p.m., there was nothing left to do. Zhiyu sat in the bedroom in his new shirt and savored what he knew would be his last cigarette for hours. Autumn light came through the drapes. Zhiyu smiled to think of how afraid his daughter was of the clothes he might have worn. He used to feel the same toward his own parents, except for the opposite reason. *They* wore the jeans. *They* watched the subtitled Roy Rogers shows. *They* were amateur Americans, and their ugly yearning for a life they would never actually lead was so embarrassing to a young Zhiyu that he'd crossed the Pacific just to spite it. To show them what it *actually* looked like. He believed there was nothing so pathetic as hoping without seeking, as wearing a cowboy hat as you stand ankle deep in the mud of your rice paddies. The doorbell. Zhiyu stabbed and stabbed and stabbed his cigarette out in the ashtray and fanned at the dying tendril of smoke. He hoped its stink would be masked, or at least forgiven, by the smells coming from the kitchen.

Fei Yen was at the front door, waiting for Zhiyu. He scratched at his neck where the shirt irritated him. He and Fei Yen had two grown sons, both of them strong and hardworking and independent. But it was their daughter—now waiting on the other side of the door—who, no matter how she'd turned out, would always have been Zhiyu's favorite. And she'd turned out stronger and harder working and more independent than anyone Zhiyu had ever known. However, Nancy was not a hugger. This made it hard for Zhiyu and Fei Yen to believe there was actually someone else out there with her on the porch.

Yet there was. Wearing jeans and a sport coat. A gift in one arm and Zhiyu's favorite person (besides Fei Yen) in the other.

Zhiyu had expected someone shorter. Skinnier. More steel-eyed. More Asian. This kid was tall with light hair and blue eyes. And grinning.

Fools grin.

Fei Yen spoke first, in English. Her English had never been great—nor was Zhiyu's. However, both spoke infinitely better English than their guests' Mandarin, Nancy included.

Eric, Fei Yen said, bowing a little. It's so wonderful to finally meet you!

Eric tried to bow back. Thank you so much for having us, he said.

Zhiyu looked over at Nancy. Their eyes met and spoke the full truth, without the clunky translation of speech. Nancy's eyes thanked her father for wearing the shirt, and begged him not to be embarrassing, to give this brave boy a chance. Zhiyu's eyes in turn told his daughter that he would withhold judgment.

The smell of roasting duck floated out of the apartment. Eric leaned into Nancy, but her eyes stayed with Zhiyu and said something else—something they had never said before: *I need your help.*

Fei Yen and Eric were chatting. Then they looked at Nancy and Zhiyu. Neither of whom had spoken yet.

Eric, Nancy finally said. This is my father, Zhiyu.

Zhiyu bowed. Extended his hand. They shook.

Call me Jerry, Zhiyu said—looking again at Nancy. He wondered whether his daughter appreciated that he'd insisted on his Western name for Eric's sake. Or whether she saw it for what it was: a denial of intimacy, a buffer.

When Nancy first started preschool, Zhiyu had met many parents and teachers. None of whom could pronounce his name. One of Nancy's favorite cartoons was *Tom and Jerry*. Zhiyu watched it with her (there wasn't much dialogue). He laughed just as loud as she did to see the mouse outwit and outwork the cat. He felt like he'd moved to a country of cats—domesticated ones, accustomed to easy meals. And he'd realized, sitting there on the rug watching TV with his American daughter, that he might always be feral. He started asking people to call him Jerry.

Smells amazing in there, Eric said, peeking over Zhiyu's shoulder.

Mm, Zhiyu said in something like agreement. The boy was right: it was time they all went inside. Please, Zhiyu said. Come in, come in!

He stepped aside to let the young couple through. Nancy stopped to hug Fei Yen.

Then Zhiyu.

The older couple shared a look. *Hugs?*

Zhiyu found Eric to be smarter than he looked. The boy knew when to hold his tongue. He passed the plates of dumplings and duck before serving himself. From the way he described his position at IBM, he came off as capable and hardworking, but not obsessed. He kept complimenting Nancy, saying IBM owed her a promotion. Zhiyu noticed that the skin in the low v of Eric's collar was quite tanned. Eric had the kind of muscles that come from exercise for exercise's sake—weight rooms, not store rooms.

Eric liked the duck. Loved it, actually. He asked question after question about how it was prepared.

Zhiyu answered them all.

You mean, like, a regular bike pump? Eric asked.

Zhiyu nodded. He couldn't tell if Eric was put off. *Does he taste the pump somehow?* Zhiyu wondered. *Some trace of machine oil?* Zhiyu snuck a look at Nancy, wondering whether this boy of hers was being condescending or curious. She kept her eyes on her plate.

Amazing! Eric said. Can I see it?

The pump? Zhiyu asked.

Yeah!

Of course, Zhiyu said. It's no problem.

Zhiyu decided he'd get it out when they were done eating, but Eric set his chopsticks on the side of his plate and wiped his hands on his napkin and stood up. Zhiyu couldn't help but marvel. Here was the genuine article: a young American man who expected the things he wanted to come quickly, with just a word, a smile.

Zhiyu got up. He carried his napkin with him across the room to the coat closet, Eric in tow. Zhiyu hauled out the pump and handed it over. Its chrome smudged with grease, its hose frayed. *And yet I have cooked dinner with it*, Zhiyu thought. *No wonder the boy is shocked.*

Eric cradled it like a trophy. I used to *hunt* ducks, he said.

You never told me that, Nancy said from across the room.

In Colorado, Eric said. Northern Front Range. We belonged to a club.

A club? Fei Yen asked.

A duck club, Eric explained as the two men return to the table. I was never much of a hunter, though. I mean, I was okay with a shotgun, but I didn't like getting up at 4 in the morning, plus the ponds are all covered in ice that time of year. It's just so much *work!* Eric laughed.

Fei Yen smiled and nodded, pretending to commiserate.

Eric went on: Eventually, it got to be that I'd go out to the club with my brothers and my dad, but I'd sleep in. And when they came home in the middle of the day, they'd all take naps and watch football while I cleaned their ducks and got 'em roasting. I'd fry up some of the meat on toothpicks with some bacon. Some water chestnuts. Some jalapeños . . . So good.

Mmm, Fei Yen said.

She like food spicy, Zhiyu explained.

Eric smiled. Me too, he said.

Eric's a *fantastic* cook, Nancy said.

Eric rested his big hand on Nancy's thin thigh. She patted it, then nudged it off.

I got pretty good at cooking ducks, Eric said. But I never cooked one that even comes close to this, Jerry. I mean that. This is the best duck I've ever tasted. I could go back to Colorado with this recipe and blow people's minds!

I don't know, Zhiyu said. This method maybe not so good for that kind of duck.

Oh, right, Eric said. You probably want 'em domesticated, huh?

Yes, Zhiyu said. Nice and fat.

At this, the two men began to laugh. Zhiyu laughed because he was anxious: he had just inadvertently insulted his domesticated guest. But Eric's feathers seemed unruffled. He puffed out his cheeks and patted a big, pretend belly with his hands—enjoying this image of a fat, flightless duck. It *was* funny, so Zhiyu kept laughing. The women stared as if worried for their two men's sanity.

Zhiyu sent the plate of duck around again. Eric helped himself to seconds.

Further to his credit, Eric insisted on doing dishes. He stood at the kitchen sink with a wide stance like a cowboy, relegating Fei Yen and Nancy to the kitchen table, where they sat sipping tea. Zhiyu took the opportunity to slip out the front door with a teacup of Hennessy. He sat on the steps of the stoop. His stoop. Except, if it were truly his, wouldn't he smoke a cigarette? But he couldn't. Not with his daughter around to catch him, chide him. Nancy was a drug far stronger than nicotine.

The evening was warm. No wind. Zhiyu's shirt still itched. He untucked it and lifted it off without unbuttoning it and hung it on the railing, and he sat there in just his undershirt. A woman walking a golden retriever waved up at him. He waved back. To her, this was just another evening. A walk with the dog at the western edge of America.

Zhiyu was not having just another evening, though. He was on the verge of tears. He couldn't remember the last time he'd felt so worked up. He didn't know what had brought it on—not specifically. There was nothing anyone had said or did. It was just—a *lifetime*. A long march. Something sought, a purpose, that tonight seemed . . .

Nancy knocked on the front door from the *inside*.

Who is it? Zhiyu said.

Father looked daughter over, there on the stoop. He wished he could tell her that he knew the spell she was under, that he was willing to accept that she leaned on another man now. But Zhiyu's eyes couldn't lie. They saw that it was not Nancy doing the leaning. Zhiyu was the one who stood to topple.

Nor could Nancy's eyes hide the look Zhiyu had seen in them when she first arrived.

She was not silly with young love. She was in need.

What happened to your shirt? she asked, in English. The only language she really knew, if you didn't count math.

It *your* shirt, Zhiyu said.

This made Nancy smile. You and Mom made a great dinner, she said. Thank you.

Thank you for coming, Zhiyu said. I know how you busy. It good you busy.

Nancy nodded toward the house, and therefore toward Eric. So, she said, what do you think?

The boy?

Yes. The *boy*.

Nice, Zhiyu said.

Definitely, Nancy said. A far-off look on her face, like it was not *definite* at all, like she'd come out here not for approval but for convincing.

You both have good job, Zhiyu said. You both hard workers. So . . . these are important.

Eric's very smart, she said. And very sweet.

Zhiyu laced his two hands into a fist. He held it up to her. Together, he said. Strong team. Make grandsons!

Dad! she said.

Or granddaughters, he added.

Nancy laughed, but her features rehardened. For Zhiyu, it was frightening to see just how tippy was the scale upon which she seemed to be weighing such heavy things. It seemed that a single pearl of advice could tip it either way.

You love him, Zhiyu said bluntly, almost like a command.

I think so, Nancy said. I don't know what that's supposed to feel like.

Zhiyu watched the street. He sensed that he needed to pick his words carefully. He wished Nancy spoke Mandarin so he could be more subtle.

I think you not a little girl now, he said. And he not a little boy. That is a *man*.

Maybe something in between, Nancy laughed. He's not so serious all the time. Not like us . . .

Zhiyu put an arm around her. Well, he said, he *is* doing dishes.

What am I doing? Zhiyu thought. He knew that Eric was not man enough for his daughter. But who would be? Maybe strong wasn't even what Nancy needed. Maybe this suitor, with his tanned chest and his Colorado club and, more than anything, his genuine affection for Nancy (and therefore his fine taste!), was the reason Zhiyu had abandoned everything he knew and crossed an ocean, the reason he'd gone by another name and hustled like a mouse and disappeared even to himself most days. Zhiyu didn't do all that so his daughter could end up with a Jerry.

Eric was the fattest duck.

I should go back in, Nancy said, rising from the step.

Before she could go though, Zhiyu told her, You pick a good one.

Nancy bowed her head a little in thanks, or deference. It both heartened and saddened Zhiyu to know his daughter could still be humbled by his tiniest assessment. And he knew without question, as the door closed again between them, that he'd just told her the one thing she'd come outside to hear. He knew it was the message he was supposed to have sent across the light years between them, and he also knew that he should not have sent it, in any language.

Eric

2001

WE NOW COME TO the father with whom I feel an odd kinship. I say odd. For it could be assumed I begrudge the man whose shortcomings later led his wife and daughter to crash-land on my doorstep and need my help. This is not the case. Eric and I have too much in common, probably. Love for the aforementioned wife and daughter, yes. But I started college as a physics major before language stole my heart. Poets and physicists are more alike than not. We end up wrestling with similar stuff. An atom and a person are both difficult to see into, and as such, alluring. So we make our attempts. To see what we're made of.

Of course, I'm not a poet per se. Nor was Eric exactly a physicist. Nonetheless! I feel I know him the best, if also the least. We talked across our fence. I'd be out in my yard, puttering, and he'd be out in his, tinkering. We'd start to chat. Half an hour later we'd still be there at the fence, tools in our hands, shooting the shit.

He, like me, enjoyed trip planning. On the Thanksgiving that a different kind of shit first hit the fan, he'd booked a cottage in Carmel for his family. But on the Tuesday afternoon before that little family was to depart, his wife Nancy emerged from her home office to microwave a French bread pizza. Eric looked up from a magazine and reminded her that she'd resolved to eat healthier. The microwave beeped. Nancy took her pizza, left. When next their paths crossed that evening, Eric watched in the bathroom mirror as Nancy took her electric toothbrush through its paces, her lips tugged back, showing her teeth. She spat and turned to go.

C'mon, he said. I was trying to be supportive.

It's a few pounds, Eric, she said. We can't all go to the *pool* every day.

She grabbed a jar from her medicine cabinet. Smeared a muddy concoction on her forehead. Back and forth they trumped each other with stale grievances. Nancy moved to slathering her cheekbones.

Do you have to do that right now? Eric asked. I'm trying to talk to you.

This is when I have time, she said.

The day is twenty-four hours long, Eric said. For everybody. You just . . .

Just what, Eric? Nancy asked, but Eric was looking past her. Their only child, a daughter—Charlotte—had just shuffled into the bathroom, eyes bleary, hair mussed.

Are you guys fighting? she asked.

Nancy and Eric hugged Charlotte in turn. They allayed her concerns with lies. Bid her goodnight. They did not speak to each other again until the next morning, when Eric was loading the car for Carmel and discovered that Nancy had not packed. When he questioned her, she waved her hands. She cited fires to be fought at work.

Are you serious? Eric said. It's *Thanksgiving*.

It's a holiday, Nancy said. There'll be another one next year.

Don't do this because you're mad at me, he said.

Okay.

What's *that* mean?

It means, okay. I won't.

What the hell's going on, Nancy?

I'm behind. That's all.

You're *ahead*, Eric said.

Nancy shook her head.

Don't you think this sends a horrible message? Eric asked.

How so? They'll see I'm working on a holiday.

To *Charlotte*, he said.

Who do you think I'm doing this for, Eric? she said.

That's such bullshit.

In fact, Nancy doubled down. I'd say I'm sending exactly the message I want. That hard work is hard, but it gets rewarded. Charlotte needs to see that her mother isn't just that.

What, Eric said, just a mother?

Exactly, Nancy said.

But, that's all she needs you to be.

Look at my parents, Nancy said. The most important lesson they taught me was their *not* being around. Because they were at work.

You're seriously not coming to Carmel.

Are you even listening, Eric? Do you hear what I'm saying?

Loud and clear, he said.

Dazed, Eric did his best. He drove with Charlotte to Carmel. The cottage was as cozy as he'd envisioned. They dropped their stuff off and headed straight to the shopping district. He tried taking succor in retail. He caved to his daughter's half-hearted pleadings. They ate frozen yogurt for lunch. He bought her an overpriced, fashionably distressed canvas jacket.

On Thanksgiving Day, given the option of helping her old man cook a turkey with all the trimmings in the cottage's well-apportioned kitchenette, Charlotte opted instead to go out. She wanted Thai food. So they walked three quiet blocks to a restaurant as the afternoon faded, the sunset just a gradual darkening of a fogbank. They were ushered through an empty main room to a window table overlooking the streetscape.

Eric draped his napkin over his lap like a warm blanket. He opened the menu like a storybook. How about some shrimp Rangoon to share? he said. He peeked over his menu to find that his daughter's eyes were wet. There came a flipping in his guts. What's the matter, sweetie? he asked.

Charlotte said: You and Mom are gonna *divorce*, aren't you?

It was as if the word had never before been uttered by anyone, and now that it had . . . Well. Eric tried, but he could not look across the table. He could only stare out the window. Still Charlotte pressed him. She had another question, in fact, that was just as difficult to stomach. A question Eric didn't expect. Hearing it, he realized that Charlotte had stood by, watching him pack up the boxes. She'd asked him then what he was doing. And it had been so simple to say he was just getting his radio equipment together so he could sell it.

The streetlights on the boulevard were not lit yet. No one passed on the sidewalk.

No cars went up or down the street. From where Eric sat—across from his daughter in a Thai restaurant in Carmel on Thanksgiving Day—it truly looked like the world had just ended.

The world did not end. But Charlotte had been dead on. By the time she turned twelve, her parents were divorced.

In June of the following year, she and Eric left San Jose riding on opposite ends of a vinyl bench seat in a seventeen-foot U-Haul. They towed Eric's Saab. The little train rattled all day down I-5 through the heart of California's central valley, picking up and losing radio stations. Charlotte kept to herself. Eric didn't pry. He'd decided she was just waiting to see how this all played out. As was he.

In La Jolla, the unloading of all their possessions into a two-bed/two-bath bungalow took less than an hour with help from a spry Guatemalan man hired outside the Del Mar Home

Depot. Eric located the light switch. Evening had crept up on them. Somehow it had gotten dark.

The ceiling lamp flickered. One of its bulbs gave off a tiny supernova and died. Eric stepped onto the coffee table and unscrewed the frosted dome. Dust and insect bits spilled onto his face. He sneezed. Charlotte giggled—Eric's favorite sound. He stepped down and zombie-walked toward her. She shrieked and retreated. Eric didn't give chase. To do so would have meant crossing a line, treating her too much like a child for her taste. He was always trying to stay on her good side. This was absolutely exhausting.

Radioactive atoms also have "daughters." Parent atoms expend their energy in waves until eventually decaying into different elements altogether. Uranium, over time, gives so much of itself it turns to lead. Why? *Because*. Just the way of the universe. But ask any father, and he'll probably tell you: that's just fine with him.

Eric didn't have anything to sleep on. Knowing Nancy had neither the time nor the inclination to refurnish, he'd left her with the king-size bed and all the bedroom pieces. He had, however, helped himself to most of the kitchen items. He took his books, left the bookshelves. He took the barbeque, and the TV/VCR and, of course, *The Boxes*. Containing the stuff Eric was supposed to have sold, but instead had tucked away behind blankets in the basement storage closet. On the afternoon he'd moved his things out of this closet to pack them up for La Jolla, Nancy had come home from work early to "help." (She'd always had a world-class bullshit detector. It's what made her so good at her job.) She even lugged some of *The Boxes* to the U-Haul herself. Even after Eric told her they were too heavy. This was the type of remark he'd once kept to himself around Nancy. (The Nancy who'd been his girlfriend, and later, the Nancy who'd been his wife.) She'd carried one box right up to Eric and, before he could take it, let it fall to the sidewalk with an expensive-sounding clang.

Eric had held his tongue. Whatever couldn't be fixed could be replaced. Electronics are so much easier that way.

Long day, Eric said. I bet you're hungry.

Is that bathroom in the hallway yours? Charlotte asked.

Would you like it? he asked. He was eager to spin this as a father's land grant, not a daughter's eminent domain.

Charlotte nodded, kissed him on the cheek, and took her toiletries off to unpack.

Later, he looked in on her sleeping. Her furniture—a double bed, a dresser with matching nightstand, and a white secretary desk—was clustered in the way she used to half-heartedly arrange her dollhouse. She'd never taken much to dolls. This had pleased Nancy and Eric, both.

Eric headed out to the yard and stared at it for a while. Deciding.

Eric stepped onto the shoulder of the shovel blade and leveraged out a slab of rotted turf. A severed worm floundered at the hole's lip. When Eric was a boy he'd once torn a worm in half. He'd been told it would become two worms. But when he'd peered into his bucket the next day, only the head part was still moving.

He ran water into the hole. It made the digging easier. He took a sip from the hose. La Jolla's water tasted different than San Jose's. It was softer. It would take getting used to.

When the hole was deep enough he took an eight-foot, copper-coated steel rod and jabbed it in and pounded it with a sledgehammer until it drew flush with the grass. He threaded copper wire through an eyelet on the tip of the rod and ran the wire to the house.

There was no going back. La Jolla was ground now.

The sun was well up by the time Eric woke. He found himself on a couch. In La Jolla. A breeze through the open front window carried the scent of an ocean. The Pacific. He went to find Charlotte. She squinted at him from her bed. She held a pillow up to shield herself from the daylight he was letting in.

We'll get you some curtains, he promised.

Charlotte extended a thumbs-up from the eiderdown.

He went down the hallway to his room and sat at his two-tiered desk, upon which the contents of the boxes were now set up. Anticipation flickered within his shame like lightning within a cloudbank.

The boxes. Some still taped up and boxy. Some flayed open and brimming with bubble wrap. Some reduced to two-dimensionality, their flaps amputated. Coiled strips of discarded packing tape bore velvety brown skins. Seeing it all in the light of day shamed Eric in the way a countertop of empty bottles does a relapsing alcoholic. He had failed to contain himself.

For here it was, all of it. Chassis stacked on chassis. Knobs of varying diameter. Rows of buttons. Toggle switches. Input jacks. Gray-on-gray numbers in the utilitarian font of calculators and clock radios. Fickle little needles that swayed inside circular windows. As a toddler standing on the very chair in which Eric now sat, Charlotte had loved to fiddle with it all.

And how could Eric blame her? It was all engineered for human touch.

Behind the desk was a circulatory system of cables. Eric had kept some of the lines well isolated. Some had required co-ax. Some had been arranged to be as short as possible.

Out front, upon the desktop, was the most familiar component, the one Charlotte seemed to understand the first time she saw it—a golf-ball-sized mesh sphere atop a bendy arm, affixed to a sturdy base. A microphone. With a big rectangular button. Simple.

As Hank had told Amy: You push a button, you talk.

The desk was below the window. This location had been chosen not last night but in early February, when Eric first toured the house. The realtor had steered toward the kitchen, but Eric had slipped down the hallway. She'd found him in this bedroom. He had a hip propped on the window sill, his face against the glass. He was peering up.

The realtor came over to take a look herself. All she saw was a blank swath of sky.

Eric was already headed back down the hallway, shouting a question about the yard. Minutes later, standing together on the half-dead back lawn, Eric and the realtor shook hands in commemoration of a nearly full-price offer, the unkempt palm in whose paltry shade they shook having sealed the deal. The realtor didn't understand or care why.

Eric was on the roof when he heard Charlotte calling, *Dad!* She sounded frightened. They had now lived in La Jolla for exactly one day. He retracted a tape measure and crawled across the sinusoidal Spanish tile. He heard the croak of a spring-loaded screen door.

I'm up here, honey, Eric said.

He peered over the eaves to find Charlotte in the backyard. She was holding sunlight at arm's length to peer back up at him. He gripped a nylon rope tied to the base of the chimney and rappelled himself off the roof, his running shoes stepping backward down brick. He hadn't yet bought a ladder. He'd gotten onto the roof by climbing a tree.

Was Charlotte chiding him for leading her to believe she'd been left alone? Even though he'd never once left her alone, and so the insinuation would suggest something fundamental had changed? Yes, it had and she was.

Eric consoled her. She softened, then stated the obvious like she was handing a knife over, blade first: You're building an antenna, she said.

Eric wiped his brow with the back of his hand. Of course she'd already seen the equipment in his room. But also she knew, because he'd taught her, that the equipment was just expensive junk without an antenna.

I know, he said.

She had a request. Eric almost said no by reflex. For years now, no had been his immediate reaction to most any request she made. Charlotte was old enough to know what was kosher. If she was thirsty, she could get herself a drink. If she was lonely, she could call a pal. And so, if she had to ask, she probably wanted something outside the boundaries. A PG-13 movie. Body glitter. So, *no*.

Have you called your mother yet like I asked? Eric said.

Tonight, Charlotte promised.

Okay.

So he said yes. And they walked to the beach, four blocks away. The crowds stretched half a mile down the sand. Eric unfolded a chair and flipped up the brim of his UCSD Gilligan hat—included in his new-faculty welcome basket.

This was a good idea, Eric said.

I know, Charlotte said.

Eric got out of his chair and started to dig. The deeper sand was charcoal gray. He soon had a basin. A wall. Around which he dredged canals that drained into the basin. He and Charlotte watched the surf come and go, come and go. Waves darkening higher and higher crescents of sand. None quite reaching his kingdom.

Until one did. Quicker and thicker than its predecessors, it rode up the face of the wall and surged simultaneously into both canals and filled up the basin.

The basin was big enough to sit in, so Eric did just that. Charlotte pushed sand onto his legs. When he didn't complain, she escalated the assault, plastering his lap and chest with handfuls, laughing in an unaffected way Eric hadn't heard before. It was equal parts abandon and menace. It wasn't a tentative, pre-teen laugh; nor was it a girl's giggle. It frightened him.

Okay, okay, he said. That's enough.

The sand atop his chest cracked and bulged as he breathed. He rose, sloughing sand as he ran out into the breakers.

Shuffle! Charlotte shouted after him.

(Shuffling is how we ward off the ever-present stingrays here in La Jolla.)

Eric did shuffle. (He'd seen the bloody ankles; he'd heard a grown man wail.)

As he dove headlong through a wave the water filled his ears. He heard the garbled underwater violence. Plus another, fainter sound—the crackling of particles, pebbles. He rolled over and backstroked. A v of pelicans was gliding overhead. He was wearing his waterproof Omega watch. He felt its weight on every other stroke.

Were this story a trick—and who's to say every story isn't?—this would be the moment I held out this watch for you to get a good look at it before I hid it under one of three cups and told you: keep track of it.

Eric was treading water as he unfastened the watch's clasp, ready to let it go in some therapeutic, symbolic, bullshit way, when Charlotte shouted at him from the beach. She waved. He waved back, glad to have been interrupted.

Coming back in from a swim, there must of course always be a moment when one's feet have to touch down upon stingray-infested sand without having first shuffled. The chance of landing right on one of the bastards is slim, but nonzero nonetheless. My old man was an amateur pilot, and like all pilots he liked to say that flying was easy, it's the takeoffs and landings that'll kill you. The transitions. I miss my father. He died when I was too young to realize I wanted his advice. I was forty-four.

Eric's feet settled onto soft, ribbed sand. He shuffled in and lumbered out of the surf and right up to his daughter and handed her the watch. I'd like you to have this, he said.

Charlotte cupped it in one hand as if to gage its weight.

It was Mom's, Eric said. She got it as an award.

For what? Charlotte said.

Doing a good job.

At what?

Her job.

A ghostly white band of flesh encircled his wrist. It would soon tan and disappear, Eric knew, just as the band on his ring finger had.

Eric needed twelve-gauge, copper-clad steel wire. He made some calls and located a spool at a farm supply store in La Mesa that sold it to local dairies for electric fencing. The twenty-five-minute drive inland was the Saab's first voyage under its own power in San Diego County. To Eric's surprise, Charlotte elected to come along without needing to be cajoled.

On their way home they stopped at a furniture store. Eric picked out a new single bed for himself and arranged to have it delivered. They also stopped at a supermarket to stock up on staples, plus the ingredients for baked ziti. But before Eric cooked Charlotte's favorite dish, he attached Teflon insulators and guide rope to his new wire, then headed back up to the roof to anchor one end to the chimney. Returning to the lawn, he donned a medieval-looking set of tree spurs. The spurs dated back to a summer spent repairing power lines and fishing for halibut in Seward, Alaska in the days before PhD, IBM, and Mr. and Mrs. He dug the spurs in and shimmied up the palm trunk.

What if something happens? Charlotte asked, staring up at him.

Nothing's gonna happen, he muttered. He was concentrating on his climb.

Who should I call, though? Mom?

Mom?

Well, we don't know anybody here . . .

Nothing's gonna happen, he said. He was now twenty feet up. He lashed a steel collar with a welded grommet to the palm's trunk. To this grommet he affixed the other guide rope. He pulled the assembly tight. It stretched like a tightrope from chimney to palm tree, so taut it sung a little in the breeze. Installing his San Jose antenna had entailed a year-long legal squabble with the building superintendent, plus permits, fees, and special scaffolding.

His La Jolla antenna had entailed a joyride to La Mesa and a little monkeying around.

Eric connected ladder line to the center of his antenna. He'd once used co-ax cable for this purpose. He'd once done a lot of things. He'd once been Nancy's husband. He'd once let thirty watts of a one-hundred-watt signal go to waste as heat, as friction.

On his way back down he lost his grip for an instant and hugged the tree by reflex, bloodying his forearms and thighs as he arrested his fall. Fucker! he growled.

He eased his way down, wincing as the striated bark grated his lacerations. Blood ran down his calf and soaked into his sock.

Do you need stitches? Charlotte asked when he was back on the ground.

I need hydrogen peroxide, he said.

Do we have that?

Let's keep this little incident to ourselves, okay?

Why?

Because.

Eric hated that answer and so did Charlotte, but sometimes it's the only one.

Because you fell, she pressed. Or because . . . the antenna . . .

Did you tell your Mom about the watch? he asked.

I hate being in the middle of this, Charlotte said.

Her eyes were steel, but Eric detected a shakiness in her voice, one so subtle only a father might detect it—a father who'd been there for her first leap off a dock, her first monkey-bar crossing. He nodded empathetically. Charlotte retreated to her room.

Eric left her to sulk. He made her favorite ziti. While it baked he fashioned a bandage from a dish towel and some electrical tape. He set the table. When the ziti was ready he called to Charlotte and they sat down across from each other.

Pass the bread, Charlotte said.

Eric was about to prompt her with *Please?* But before he could, Charlotte tacked it on herself—*please*—and that was that. They moved on. They had to.

The fall semester began. Eric was teaching two sections of Intermediate Physics and one of Numerical Methods for Engineers. His salary was less than half of what it had been at IBM. He worked twice as hard as he had at IBM.

I can say: it's nontrivial, developing two courses from scratch. I once taught a creative writing workshop. I figured the gig would entail occasionally spouting my opinion like gospel. Some men make a similar miscalculation before becoming fathers.

At first Eric relied on textbooks, but his mind was something of a fair booth that'd been collapsed down in storage. It reexpanded to display some impressive wares. He quickly ditched the textbooks and started improvising. One day he brought in a metal detector he'd built from cannibalized parts. The class watched as he hijacked the analog signals and displayed them on an oscilloscope. He handed the gadget over to the class. They probed each other's groins, giggling at the beeps it made on their zippers and pocket change.

His lecture notes comprised scribbled equations and diagrams only he could decipher—he, and maybe Nancy, who knew his handwriting and shared his belief that math was the only honest language. They'd both spoken it more fluently than

English. Both of them engineers at heart. He'd once made her a Valentine's card with a transfer function flow chart:

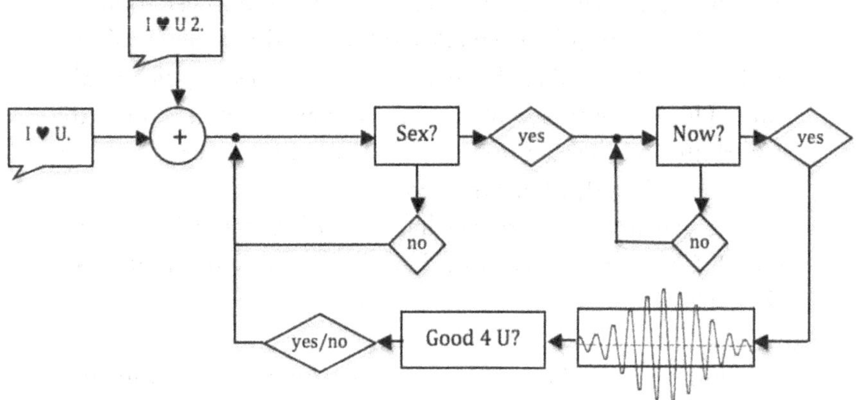

Nancy'd loved that card. Eric didn't know it, but she'd allowed herself to keep it.

So much had been wasted.

He taught in the afternoons. He'd given Charlotte the option of attending an afterschool program, but she'd made a face at that idea and elected to sit in on his lectures instead. She always sat in the same spot: the rightmost chair of the front row (his left, looking out). She'd doodle or read or pick polish off her fingernails.

He escaped into his lectures. All three chalkboards would crawl with hasty art. Chalk lines transcended the board onto adjacent walls. He often used his palm as an eraser. Chalk coated his shirtsleeves, dotted the tip of his nose. As he talked, he sipped tepid coffee from a mug Charlotte had painted for Father's Day. This had been back in the days when she'd accompany him to the YMCA pool. When she'd play in the shallow end while he swam laps. The mug had a smiley face with two raised arms bobbing among blue zigzags—a man either expertly treading water or happily drowning.

Eric signed off each class with, *Queries? Complaints? Epiphanies?* Prompting increasingly uproarious pronouncements as the semester wore on. (Four that made Eric smile, against his better judgment: *Photons are bogus. I'm either hungover or dead. Why can't there be more* ladies *in this major? I got poison oak on my undercarriage.*)

Eric walked Charlotte to school in the mornings. Watching her dissolve into the busy playground was a sight that sustained him. His daughter was adapting. He was, too. He'd grown a goatee, his first since grad school. There was some salt in the pepper now. He did push-ups and sit-ups. He was getting used to the taste of La Jolla's water.

He was as lonely as he'd ever been.

On a night years ago, Charlotte had been sitting on his lap, leaning her elbows on the radio desk as they stared together at a motionless indicator. As if hope alone would make its needle teeter to life. And so when it did quiver, she'd turned to Eric and smiled: *See?* But he'd shaken his head and spun a dial, seeking more promising channels. Sorry, bud, he'd told her. That's just interference on that frequency.

But can we wait and see? she'd asked.

The way Charlotte had looked at him in those days—the lift of the brow, the glint in the eye—it had been enough to make Eric scan back to the frequency. They'd sat there together for a long time, listening optimistically to static.

On a Monday in mid-November, Eric was pulled out of a staff meeting by the physics department secretary. Who had just gotten off the phone with Charlotte's school nurse. Apparently, she said, your daughter's been in a fight.

My daughter? Eric said.

He spent the afternoon on auto-parent. He rushed to Charlotte's school, expecting to be met at the campus gate by medical personnel who would brief him as he jogged toward the scene. Instead he searched empty corridors and loped up and down stairwells. It took him ten minutes to find the nurse's office.

Charlotte's right hand and forearm had been wrapped in a club of gauze. There were bandages around her head, too, holding in place an absorbent pad, stained blood-pink. He took her to the hospital. All told, Charlotte ended up with six stitches in her right hand and three in her eyebrow. Plus a ruined T-shirt and a citation for unruly conduct.

She refused to call it a fight. She told the ER nurse that she'd been pushed, hard . . . and next thing she knew she was flying into a display case outside the multipurpose room . . . glass and trophies falling out . . . This was the story she stuck to later, while she and Eric ate pizza in front of the TV. Eric asked her to please elaborate. She gaped at an ad for carpet cleaner. He switched off the television. She continued staring at it.

C'mon, he said. Let's deal with this. It's just you and me, bud. That's all we've got. I'm the guy you have to talk to.

She knotted her legs up underneath her in an extreme version of Indian style.

I called Olivia a bitch, she said.

She resituated herself on the couch, her upper lip peeling back slightly. Eric put a hand on her foot and rubbed it, buying time. For he was at a loss. Nancy had always been better at helping Charlotte navigate the gauntlet of girlhood.

I don't want a birthday party this year, Charlotte said.

I have a doctorate in physics, Eric thought, *and most everything I know is useless.*

What he ended up doing was what fathers have done for centuries. He did what he could. Little by little, he teased out the real story. Charlotte told him that she hated walking into school every day. She said there was a coterie of girls who took their orders from Olivia, who had for some reason turned them all against Eric's favorite person on earth.

Eric sought explanations—something he *was* pretty good at, something he *could* help with. He implored Charlotte to think, *hard*: had she done something, anything at all, to the girls? Had she said something that might have been misconstrued?

Olivia says I think I'm better than everybody, Charlotte said. But I definitely don't. She let out a little sob and leaned into him.

Eric knew he should tell Nancy about the fight. Nancy hadn't divorced *her*. Charlotte had made this argument and she was right. How did the new wiring diagram look, though? Recently, Charlotte had come to him with a question on a school assignment. She'd wondered how one designated divorce on a family tree; was there some special symbol to show a break in the connective lines? If so, where was it placed? Who got severed from whom?

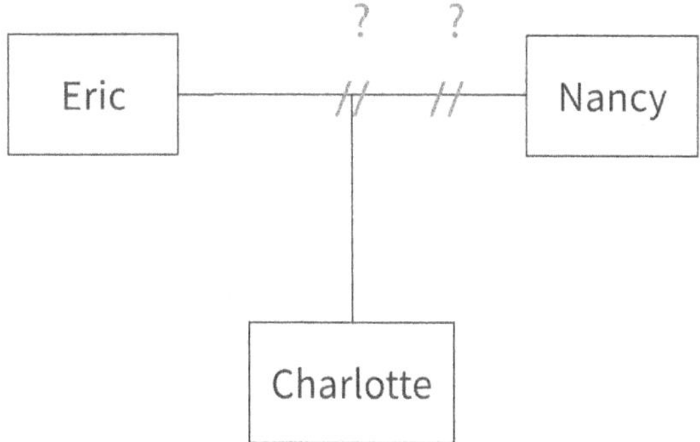

Later that night, after checking Charlotte's bandages and tucking her into bed, Eric picked up the phone and dialed his old phone number. He listened to the rings, visualizing the familiar rooms into which the phone made its plea. The rooms of his ex-life.

Nancy had started sending him a check every month. It covered nearly his entire mortgage payment. Without it, he and Charlotte couldn't afford to live where they did.

Every time Eric cashed one, he felt like the fucking babysitter.

The ringing stopped. On came the affected, chipper voice: Nancy's outgoing message.

Eric hung up before the beep.

Eric was working in the kitchen in the evening light. He was preparing his lectures and his lunches for the week. He overturned a small, three-minute hourglass and nestled half a dozen eggs into a pot of boiling water. For just a moment, he observed the white sand slipping through the slender neck and accumulating in the lower bulb, and he thought about how each grain inexorably sought the earth, and how the earth in turn sought each grain, and how earth and grain both meanwhile sought the sun, and the stars, and vice versa, and so on, the seeking shared to some decimal point among all manner of hurtling masses in the universe. And for just a moment—the transit time of a single grain—Eric comprehended it all.

Charlotte walked into the kitchen. Eric cut short his musing. Nodded at her. She'd been napping all afternoon.

He reached a hand out to her, palm up. She took it, as if accepting an invitation to dance, but that's where the gallantry ended. He grappled the arm into various positions to inspect the scars. Her stitches had come out weeks ago.

Charlotte looked away, contorting to accommodate the pivots, bracing herself against the table. *Dad*, she said. You're hurting me.

He apologized. He let go. It's healing up nicely, he said.

Can I have cereal for dinner? she said.

No, he said. It's just sugar.

So she made a show of looking in a near-empty pantry, a near-empty refrigerator.

Fine, he said. But, tit for tat, he asked: What's Mom think about your scars, by the way?

She hasn't asked, Charlotte said.

Eric was amazed. Granted, Charlotte's eyebrow had grown back in over the thin scar there, but the scar on her right hand was still quite plain to see. Meaning Charlotte had been going to some length to hide it during her stays with Nancy. So, sweatshirts at the pool? Forks held in the off hand? Envisioning it, Eric wanted to laugh (but did not). Because Charlotte had just put to rest his doubts about which side she was on. Eric wasn't the only one keeping secrets in La Jolla.

Growing up can be fun, but it's also very tricky, is it not? You have to figure out who you are. You have to sign the social contract. You have to take on debts, fiduciary and figurative. You have to find your own special way to connect to the world. (Quiet in the court, please. I said quiet in the court! We can all see your heads shaking, ladies. And yes, it is not lost on me, the irony of a man-child extoling the qualities of maturation . . . I'll hold you all in contempt if you don't stop tittering!)

Anyway. For Eric, figuring these things out started when he was eleven. It began with radio. More of a scanner buff at first, a young Eric rarely turned his TR switch to transmit. He preferred to just listen. Partly this was because the equipment was his father's. As with the old man's half-ton dually, Eric was fine riding in it, he just wasn't ready to drive it. Weekend nights, after his family went to bed, little Eric would climb the narrow stairs to the attic—see the moonlight sloping in through the dormer windows—and don a pair of man-sized headphones. And he'd be kept company for hours by weather forecasts, maritime reports, air force chatter, politics. People in basements, garages, and cluttered offices; people on bases; on boats; Australians; Arizonians. And, on rare occasions when the ionosphere cooperated, Europeans. Voices traversing thousands of miles of empty darkness in search of a single ear.

His.

Long after, on a Saturday night in La Jolla in late January, Eric was scanning the dial when he happened upon a retired couple sailing off Catalina Island. He started chatting with them, listening as they second-guessed one another's depictions of the island's breakfast buffet. He found them endearing. He mentioned that he was once married.

So what happened? the woman asked.

Her husband jumped in: That's none of our business, dear.

But their conversation was at that moment interrupted by a male voice informing them that the frequency was in use. Eric transmitted a quick apology. He invited the couple to join him on another frequency.

QSY down 10, he said. Repeat, QSY down 10, to 1-6-3.

As Eric adjusted his receiver to 7.163 MHz, he considered the wife's question. What *had* happened? It wasn't as though Eric and Nancy had agreed to an authorized version. Surely, Nancy had endured some prying at the lab. Eric knew those people—inquisitive by trade, expert data gatherers, their lives so deficient in juiciness they'd feast on a morsel of scandal like a colony of ants with a raisin. So what story was being told in the corridors of IBM? Had Eric been slandered? Did he deserve to be?

Suddenly he was all amped up. His toggled the TR switch. This is W7MPB, he said. Is the frequency in use?

He tried again. And again. Startled by his own urgency.

This is W7MPB, he repeated. Calling CQ, calling CQ. George, Mary Beth, are you here?

As he rechecked his displays, it hit him just what frequency he'd landed on. This particular slice of spectrum had *history*. It felt like he'd just dialed a high school sweetheart's number. And it was ringing . . . No answer yet though. Fuzz on the line.

No matter. The narrative forming in Eric's head gained momentum. It begged to be told. So he just pushed the button.

Opposites attract, he said.

It felt strange, talking to the ether. He released the TR switch. Waited. Gave the elderly couple more time to rejoin. And while he did, he thought about how Nancy used to come home late, undress in front of him, and slip into bed. He was the only one who ever got to see her out of her armor. Until eventually she stopped taking the armor off. Her daily transition back and forth from woman to machine (her word) apparently became more hassle than it was worth.

He'd first seen Nancy in the lab library. Books flayed open on her lap, on the table, on the empty chair beside her. She wore a red, knee-length skirt and a white blouse. Her black hair pulled back in a headband. *Cute*, Eric thought, but the look in her eye didn't match: the look was too severe. Something in Eric couldn't help but want to adjust it. To tinker. To experiment. He'd filled out a journal request form and gone to stand so close to her that she was forced to acknowledge him.

Can I help you? she'd said.

Sorry, he'd said. Do you know how to fill out these interlibrary requests?

She'd reached up and snatched the form from him. Her finger hopped efficiently through the entries he'd already made.

Okay, *Mr. Eric*, from *Electronics Research Department*, she'd read. Looks like you're pretty close here already. Let's see, you've requested *Permission to Engage in a Noncommittal Visit to a Local Eatery*, from the journal *Review of Human Anatomy*—okay, and for date you've written, *Friday?* . . .

And Eric had gotten exactly what he'd wanted: a giggle, like a hiccup.

He leaned forward to the microphone. I watched it happen, he continued. I watched her *accelerate*. And I was okay with it, just being there, to make her laugh, to be her release valve. But after a while, it just took too much out of me. It became . . . *work*.

He released the switch again. The hush he heard was hollow. As if it were seashells and not headphones cupped to his ears.

In the morning, still slouched in his radio chair, Eric opened his eyes to find Charlotte standing before him, gnawing a piece of toast.

Time for school? he asked, rubbing his whiskered chin and staring at his daughter as if he hadn't seen her for days.

It's Sunday, Dad.

Since it was Sunday, Eric and Charlotte headed to the beach. She gathered shells to make into necklaces (something she'd never do with her friends around). Eric slouched in his folding chair and graded student work. Charlotte told Eric about Pangaea. How the continents were constantly drifting apart.

Interesting, Eric said, playing dumb. So does that mean that someday they're gonna smash together again on the other side of the planet?

Probably, Charlotte said. Right?

Eric tossed a corn chip to a seagull waddling by. The bird dipped its head to the sand and jerked the offering down its snow-white throat. Eric liked seagulls. He thought them beautiful. So do I. But one must be careful with scavengers. They'll swallow just about anything you toss 'em.

I'm not sure, Eric ventured.

Charlotte changed her vote. Yeah, she said. Probably not.

And even if the pieces *did* come back together, Eric said, do you think the puzzle would look quite the same on the other side?

No, Charlotte said confidently.

Eric looked out at the ocean. He'd never done anything like he had the night before on the radio. My guess is that it was therapeutic for him in the same way writing in a journal has been for me at certain times in my life. Although Eric's version might be preferable. There's nothing left to reckon with later on. No record. His confessions were said and gone. Invisible waves loosed into the California sky, some flying past the moon, into infinite vacuum.

But, no. Eric didn't believe that.

CQ, CQ, he called that Sunday night, too. And Monday. CQ, CQ. The economical algebra of ham radio. This is W7MPB. Is the frequency in use?

There was never a reply. Each time, he talked for a few minutes to the air. The act of shaping things into something like a story forced him to try to find explanations. If no good marriage ends in divorce, what had been rotten with his? When Charlotte was younger, she was forever asking *why* when he read her books. (*Well*, he'd explain, *because Madeline has good balance* . . .) More recently, lecturing to drowsy students who rarely prompted him with questions, Eric had taken to playing his own interlocutor. He asked the *why's* so he could go on explaining the laws of physics to himself.

Such is the authoring of these, our respective midlife crises.

We fell out of love, he explained to the air.

And why was that, Eric?

. . . for many reasons, he continued.

Name one, dude.

She worked too much, he said.

That's one.

. . . and I didn't work enough.

So that's it, then?

And I guess there was the intern thing.

Go on.

This intern got assigned to me one summer. I had lunch with her in the cafeteria one too many times, I think. While Nancy was eating in her office . . .

That seems pretty minor.

And there was a vasectomy I agreed to, after our daughter was born. I resented it.

Hmm. Is that all, then?

No, Eric said to the air. What really did it was, I had an affair, of sorts—a relationship, at least.

Now we're talking . . .

Really, it was nothing. Just some conversations on this very frequency, 7.163 MHz, with a woman.

But it wasn't *nothing, was it?* She was *something*, Eric said.

Because this was no journal. Not all the waves propagated past the moon. His one-hundred-watt antenna reached every continent. And so like the anchorman who smiles into the lifeless eye of a camera lens, Eric treated the cold metal sphere of his microphone like an ear.

Her ear.

Four months it had lasted. Nothing sexual, nor even physical. It ended on the night Nancy awoke to Eric (quote) gabbing like a girl at a slumber party (unquote)—Nancy's words. At which point Nancy got out of bed. Yep. She got out of bed and she came down the hallway. She came down the hallway and she stood in the doorway. Right behind Eric. Listening. Just listening. She listened (quote) long enough to hear enough (unquote), even though the other half of the conversation was to Nancy nothing but a silent, dancing skyline of equalizer bars.

Eric hadn't known Nancy was there. It wasn't until he saw a hand reach in to unplug his headphone jack, thereby rerouting the signal to the speakers, that he'd nearly fallen over in his tilted-back chair. A woman's voice started pouring into the room, going on and on about Charlotte. This voice knew Charlotte's best friend's name. It knew Charlotte's teacher's name. Indeed, Eric himself had already begun to question just how interested the voice was in *him*—so preoccupied was it with the details of his daughter's life.

From their conversations, Eric knew the woman belonging to the voice had once competed in rodeos. But she tended to steer away from that period of her life. He knew she'd gone to cooking school. That she'd put on weight, lost it, put it back on. She'd gotten a job as a chef. Worked all the time. Loved work. She'd told Eric that all she'd really ever wanted to be was a mother. A mother and a wife. And yet she'd somehow arrived in her forties alone. The problem, she'd lamented, was men.

Never managed to find one worth marrying, she'd told Eric. Let alone one worth makin' babies with! When Eric asked her about adopting, she'd scoffed. Kids need fathers, she'd insisted. Good ones. Like you.

He'd told her there were plenty of good men in the world.

Seems all of 'em got rings on their fingers, she'd said.

But there sat such a man, in a cramped bedroom in San Jose, California, staring down at his amateur radio while his professional wife stared down at him.

Have you slept with her? Nancy asked.

Eric was so surprised by the question he didn't answer it. Nancy interpreted his silence as stalling. Eric stitched his hands atop his head, almost laughing. I don't even know what city she lives in, Nancy. I don't know her fucking name!

All the while, that beautiful Texas accent filled the room—going on and on about Eric and Nancy and Charlotte as if they were characters in a soap opera. Eventually the voice started asking questions. Eric? it said. You still listening, hon? Or'd I put you to sleep again?

Do you love her? Nancy asked.

Jesus, Eric said. No . . . He reached around Nancy, pushed the TR switch and, kindly but abruptly, signed off.

Nancy leaned against the wall. She was crying. Eric couldn't remember ever seeing her do that.

From there it only worsened. Late into the night and into the days that followed. What Eric had told Nancy was true: he knew only the woman's call sign, W7NIX. Nixie, he called her. A name that reminded him of Nixie tubes, the neon number displays on old electronic equipment. It was nothing, he told Nancy. Why, then, was Nancy inconsolable? She said she believed Eric had never slept with the voice on the radio, but that this only made it worse. For it meant their *connection*—that's what Nancy kept calling it, pronouncing the word like some disease—wasn't lust. It was something deeper, and therefore more egregious.

Eric could only shake his head. For he knew that if Nixie were to magically materialize in his radio room, he'd be unable to contain the urge to touch her. He'd entertained wild sexual fantasies. He'd wondered if Nixie had too. Whether she was as hungry as he'd become.

A woman just *knows*, Nancy said.

Yes, Nancy. A woman does.

W7NIX's rare female voice was a light about which the night bugs of amateur radio congregated. The first time Eric spoke to her, two old men were already chatting her up. They politely signed off, but treated Eric like a boy holding a corsage.

Take care of her now, one grumbled. Don't keep her up all night.

She's got scones to bake in the morning, said the other.

The men were residents of a retirement community in Texas where W7NIX worked as the country club pastry chef. Harmless duffers, she called them. They were also members of the community's ham radio club—the very organization responsible for getting W7NIX hooked during a demo day at the club. The members (all men) had even equipped her with gear from their own stockpiles.

Men on the airwaves usually adopted the same patriarchal tone with W7NIX. She was a girl lost in the woods. But, just as often, she was a woman they might—against all odds—find a way to fuck. Radio men can be lonely men. Well, *hello*, they'd say. It didn't matter that W7NIX's physical appearance, let alone physical address, remained a complete mystery. This only boosted her allure, especially when paired with the measured molasses of her voice. And, of course, that *laugh*. Eric couldn't see her naked body, but he could *hear* it, whenever she laughed. It was a sound he pined for. The harsh acoustics of a transceiver couldn't dehumanize it.

That first night on the radio, W7MPB and W7NIX traded scone recipes. W7MPB asked W7NIX if she put her butter in the freezer before adding it to the batter.

I put my *mixing bowls* in the freezer, W7NIX said, and within a month W7MPB was in love.

A week after Nancy first overheard him, Eric came home from

the grocery store to find her curled up in the recliner. She was listening to a Walkman he'd given her. The headphones looked like a headband. It held her hair back in a way she never wore it anymore, the way she'd looked when he'd hit on her in the IBM library. Her eyes were bloodshot. She was well into a bottle of wine. The end table beside the chair was littered with tape cases—"KRIC" scribbled in Eric's handwriting upon the slide-in labels. He feared the worst, but hoped for the best. KRIC was the fake radio station he'd recorded for Nancy when they were first married. It had been his way to keep her company on her work trips.

Recently, since it was often difficult to find good times to chat with W7NIX in person, he'd revived the station. He'd record five-minute sets of music and deejay chatter, and even the occasional news segment, to play automatically on 7.163 MHZ at prearranged times.

He still used cassette tapes. That's what he knew; that's the equipment he had.

Actually, Nancy said, these tapes are more recent. Mostly country music on these.

She looked right at him. He clenched his jaw and managed not to break down.

Later that weekend he voluntarily dismantled the antenna on the roof of their building, with the promise to sell all his radio gear.

Eric understood that tearing it all down was the right thing to do. But he couldn't bring himself to part with it. He'd only get a few hundred bucks for it all, when it had cost him thousands. But that wasn't it. It was that he expected it all to blow over. Nancy would get over it. She'd see she was overreacting. He'd set it all up again. He'd get over W7NIX.

Things would go back to normal.

Then Charlotte spoke the word *divorce* into an otherwise empty Thai restaurant in a quaint seaside town on Thanksgiving and "normal" changed.

Entries. That's what La Jolla Eric started calling them. The kind a ship captain might log, and often just as mundane. Meals. Morale. Once he'd exhausted his patience for, and understanding of, the topic of divorce he moved on. Sometimes if it was funny he'd share what a student had blurted at the end of that day's lecture. He talked about Charlotte a lot.

He never referred to her by name, nor shared specifics, but he couldn't help but veer toward her. Charlotte was *the* person in his life.

He cooked Charlotte breakfasts and made her lunches and walked her to school every morning and picked her up and walked her home every afternoon and cooked her dinner and watched TV with her when she finished her homework and tucked her in and talked to her if she wanted to talk and on the weekends they went to the beach and out to restaurants. But Eric had nobody his own age to chew the fat with. And so trivial things went unspoken and accumulated. They became sagas of lost sunglasses, horror stories of the DMV, grand weekend landscaping plans. Eric's entries started to serve as a minutiae release valve.

In those years, there was an eccentric man who walked the La Jolla Shores beach with a Great Dane and a llama daisy-chained on a rope. We locals loved this unlikely menagerie. They were something of an institution, really. One time Charlotte and Eric came around a corner to see the llama's head protruding regally from the rear window of the man's Econoline van. Eric handed Charlotte a 50 and told her to take it to the man.

For what? Charlotte asked.

Llama food, he said.

The man took the cash and added it to a pouch around his neck and bowed to Charlotte, palms together. He gave her a slice of apple to feed the llama.

So: *that* became an entry.

More and more, Eric found he was approaching life in a new and troubling way. It was subtle, though not inconsequential, the way things didn't seem to count until they were entered into the record. It used to be that life, x, was what one told about, y. It was: $x=y$. But then something changed. Instead of living to tell about it, Eric found himself telling about it to live: $y=x$. It wasn't the same at all. He'd disproven the symmetric property of equality.

Eric made an entry most every night. The 7.163 MHz frequency was usually free after midnight. If he happened to interrupt a conversation in progress, he'd apologize and ask if he might join in. Most folks were happy to oblige. (Chatting up strangers is the whole point, after all.) Well. *Others* had come to chat. Eric boarded the same train every day, hoping to bump into someone who used to ride it.

CQ, CQ, he called. This is W7MPB. Is the frequency in use?

He would hope for static. He'd give it a good ten seconds, then repeat: seek you, seek you. If again his call elicited no reply, he'd scoot forward in his chair, rub the bridge of his nose, shut his eyes, and depress the TR switch.

She never answered.

Maybe it wasn't like boarding a train at all. More like talking to a headstone. A one-sided conversation with a memory. Marconi invented radio in an attempt to get the dead to talk back. They did not.

Taped to the file cabinet of Eric's cramped campus office was a picture he'd cut years ago from *National Geographic*. It showed a Namibian elder hunched inside a thatched hut next to a small diesel generator. An extension cord ran across the dirt from the generator to a shortwave transmitter. The photographer had used a long exposure to make the man's hand a blur upon the Morse key into which he was furiously tapping out a message. What are these calls we broadcast into thin air, I have wondered, if not prayers? But to whom? Many of the waves escape into the heavens, sure, but the ones that bounce back to Earth were the ones Eric, at least, hoped would find a listener.

Having hit upon an effective mix of rigor and showmanship, Eric commanded his classroom for the entire fifty-five minutes. Most of his lectures had a pragmatic bent. His litmus test for what was worth teaching was a simple question: what's the *use*? This did not come easily for him. He wanted to believe he did it for his students, who would soon vie for jobs, who needed "skill sets," not grand theories. But he knew: he did it because of Nancy. As if to make her see—though she of course could not see, and probably didn't want to see—that he'd smartened up. That she'd been right, but now he was right too.

I've known my share of vengeful divorcées who'd immediately shed the weight and frumpy sweatpants that had so recently led their ex's eye to wander. In Eric's case, he wrote word problems borrowed from the "Real World." He photocopied pertinent physics-related articles about the skyrocketing cost of copper and its impact on the power grid. He moderated debates about the FCC's stranglehold on the electromagnetic spectrum. *How ya like me now, Nancy!*

Still, sometimes he couldn't help but cook up something indulgent. Something purely theoretical. Philosophical, even. Food for thought. On the Friday before finals, he decided to talk to his Introduction to Electricity and Magnetism class about wave-particle duality.

He said not a word as he made his way to the center of the chalkboard. Holding a stick of chalk sideways in all four fingers and his thumb, he dragged it downward in a thick, textured line. That's a wall, he said.

He heard notebooks opening, mechanical pencils clicking to life.

He didn't turn around. He just erased a gap in the line using his palm. That's a hole in the wall, he said.

He marched to the left side of the board and did an about-face.

He shouldered an imaginary shotgun. Pantomimed firing the gun at the wall. Bang, he said drolly.

Scattered, hesitant laughter.

Now, he said, if this were a real shotgun and that were a real wall, and I put a piece of paper behind the hole, it would show the scatter of the pellets that got through the hole, concentrated near the center.

A hand went up: an overzealous, middle-aged woman with outdated hair, about whom Eric and Charlotte regularly vented. Eric swiveled and leveled his weapon at the woman. He pulled the trigger, dramatizing the recoil.

Booming laughter: the other students didn't like her either.

He peered over his imaginary barrel at Charlotte, and found her hunched over her fold-up desk, laughing. He went on with a whole new energy.

My gun fires *particles*, he said. But they could be photons—like the ones coming out of those lights in the ceiling, or out of a radio antenna. Or they could be electrons. They could even be atoms.

Eric turned back to the board. He used his palm to erase a second gap in the wall. Now, he said. Here's where things get *miraculous*. When we shoot our particle gun at *this* wall, which has *two* gaps in it, the particles no longer make a normal pattern in the paper behind the wall. There's *interference* in the pattern now.

Silence.

So, what's that mean, he said, *interference*? Remember, we talked about it earlier in the semester? When we were discussing waves? How waves can cancel each other out if one wave at its peak meets another at its trough. Or when two waves meet at their peaks, and the combined wave is double tall. Well, the same thing happens to these particles.

He tapped the board with the chalk and lowered his voice, forcing the room to listen harder. Does that even make sense, though? he asked.

His gaze gravitated toward Charlotte. He figured he'd lost her. She made a silly face at him. He winked back. Then he clapped, once, nice and loud. Breaking what had been a captive silence. Chalk dust rising from his hands.

Well, he said. We're forced to conclude that *each individual particle* is somehow passing through *both* gaps, at the *same time*. Like they're actually waves!

He scanned the faces but couldn't get much of a read. Charlotte stared back at him as if it were only the two of them in the auditorium. That look in her eye. He'd seen it before. A hesitant look, but a volatile one, too. *Holy* . . .

Like that wall you made at the beach, she said. With the canals on both sides.

Eric stared at his daughter, registering her voice, the rend it'd made in the continuum. Heads turned, accompanied by an audible shifting of seats. Eric felt exposed, then embarrassed. *What was his class to think? That this daughter of his was allowed to just chat with him mid-lecture?* The longer he looked at her, though, the more he didn't give a shit.

That's exactly right, honey, he said. He walked over to her desk. Remember? he said. How the wave came up the beach and went up *both* canals? That was one wave in two places at the same time.

Charlotte nodded. Eric had now completely forgotten himself—where he was, what he was supposed to be doing. It was glorious. Over the years he'd attempted lots of conversations about physics with Charlotte, knowing she was only ever half listening.

Dad? she said.

Mm.

You said this happens with atoms.

I did, yes.

But *we're* atoms, she said. Our bodies. You said that.

Yes. That's true.

Charlotte just stared, like she was mad at him. Like he was a charlatan.

Think of it this way, he said. Each of us is a boat going across the water. And the wakes we send out, and leave behind, those are us too.

He watched for the telltale light in her eyes. Seeing none, he gave a diffusing smile and decided that their little philosophical sidebar had gone far enough. He turned back to the class.

Let's just say it's not easy to wrap our minds around! And that, ladies and gentleman, is particle-wave duality. Clear as mud.

A hand near the front. The same woman. Clearly unfazed by shotgun blasts to the face. I didn't see this in the homework, she said. Can we expect it on the test?

Not really, Eric said.

Not really, she repeated. She looked over her shoulder with an incredulous expression, hoping to garner support from her classmates.

Just something to noodle, Eric said. I mean, it's a terrible explanation, but it's the best we've got. Maybe one of you budding physicists will find a better one, and win a Nobel.

He looked out into a sea of distraction and apathy.

Class dismissed, he muttered. Go home. Study for finals.

Finally, change came over the students' faces. They were caught off-guard. He'd only been lecturing for ten minutes. He began erasing the board. His back was to the class as he shouted his signature signoff: *Queries? Complaints? Epiphanies?*

There were none. He gave a dejected salute and started gathering his notes. The room bustled to life. Amid the sounds of zippers and spring-loaded seats banging back to verticality, there came a voice, barely loud enough to transcend the commotion.

CQ, CQ, it said. This is W7NIX, over.

Eric froze in place. Students were side-stepping down the rows and funneling up the stairways through the double doors at the back. His arms and fingers involuntarily spread out, as if his body had been called into duty as an antenna. He ached for complete silence so as to better tune in. But the chatter only intensified.

Charlotte watched him with a concerned look on her face. Was his desperation that obvious? He'd stopped breathing. Everyone but Charlotte seemed to be on their way out. Eric's eyes flitted from face to face, winnowing candidates. Most every chair was up now. A red-haired woman leaned against the wall, midway up the stairs, a backpack on one shoulder, a purse on the other. But no: she was waiting for someone, with whom she turned to leave.

This is W7MBP, Eric managed to croak. Come in, W7NIX.

There were about a dozen people left in the room. Two young men turned their heads, but for the most part Eric's pronouncement had no effect. The double doors swung open, banged shut, swung open again. Clearly someone was teasing him. But who? Now he was eager to play along, to see this joke through.

This is W7MPB! he yelled. Come in, W7NIX!

Charlotte said, Dad, what're you doing?

Quiet, he snapped.

Two of the three remaining stragglers left. The doors clanged. One person remained. A woman. And Eric, having primed himself to wring the neck of a smartass, found himself unprepared. He peered up into the dim outer ring of the auditorium. Compelled by some reckless magnetism, he started bounding up the steps. Two, three at a time.

The woman started down them. And it was then Eric knew. It was her. *Her*.

Impossible! And yet happening, second by second, demanding that he participate. Before they said anything to each other, they embraced, right on the steps. This proved awkward: she was one step up from him, so his face pressed into a pair of pendulous and freckled breasts. Awkward too because she was, well, a complete goddamn stranger. Eric had never seen this woman before in his life, and yet he'd just run to her and taken hold of her like she was his . . . *what?*

She on the other hand seemed to be enjoying this surprise. She had the advantage of having emotionally prepared for it.

She had on perfume and a big belt buckle with a turquoise number 1 on it.

Eric could only gawk. She was a little shorter than him. Her chestnut hair was pulled up in a tortoiseshell clip. Her sparkling green eyes matched her turquoise earrings.

Eric slapped the chalk dust off his pants.

Helluva lecture, she said, *Professor.*

You've been listening, he said. On the radio.

She just stood there with her Irish eyes all a-twinkle.

C'mon, c'mon, he said. Tell me how long you've been listening.

She winced. A while, she said.

Since when?

February?

February, he said, not computing.

They studied each other some more. Eric could hardly take it. You better start talking, he said.

Right, W7NIX said. She closed her eyes. Composed herself. Well, lemme see. I hadn't heard from you since that night when you signed off and never came back. Remember?

Eric nodded.

Well, time went by, obviously, she said. A lot of time. Here I'd figured we had something pretty special, so my heart was broken. A bit. But it healed. And then, *poof*, you resurface, and you're jabbering away, and I don't know what's become of you—are y'all still married?—and so I listened awhile, and then you just stopped talking and signed off and, well, I just sat there. It felt like I'd been eavesdropping, honestly. And I didn't want to talk to you, not really, not with the way you'd dropped me before and all. But then I hear you again a few nights later and I realize there's nobody on the other side! Since then, I've been listening for you most nights. You sound so darn *lonely*. And after a while, I just knew . . .

Knew what?

That I wanted to talk to you again.

But you didn't.

I didn't want it to be on the radio.

Here, he said.

Here, she agreed. And she laughed that laugh of hers.

Eric shook his head. He couldn't take his eyes off her, this woman he'd once believed he knew. She was a complete mystery. What kind of person did this? Just showed up out of the blue, premeditated, and barged into someone's life? A psychopath, that's who.

But no. Eric could already tell: she wasn't that. Not at all. Who she was showed in her eyes. A kindness that can't be faked. It was in her hands, the way they gripped the stair railing. Something honest and overwhelmed and delighted all at once. This was the woman who knew his secret longings, his stupid stories. As he knew hers. It struck Eric then that he might know her better than he'd ever known Nancy.

Can people fall in love from the inside out? (I cannot say that *I* have, but that certainly doesn't rule out the possibility, what with my being a superficial asshole and all.) Can someone be real to you before you've seen them? Before you've touched them?

Eric suddenly remembered Charlotte. She was still sitting on the other side of the empty auditorium.

What are you doing? he asked. Come over here. I want you to meet someone.

A drawn-out moment ensued during which Charlotte made her way ever so gradually along an entire row of chairs, then up the stairs to reach her father's outstretched arm.

He tugged her like a ragdoll to his side. Charlotte, he said, gesturing with his free hand to the implausibility now standing before them, emanating perfume. This, he said, is . . . Nixie.

Amy, she said.

Her turquoise bracelets jangled as she extended her hand. Charlotte shook but kept her eyes on her dad, looking far more confused than she had about particle-wave duality.

Instead of walking home as they'd planned, Eric and Charlotte piled into Amy's dusty, bug-splattered Dodge Durango. Eric gave turn-by-turn directions to the bungalow.

Charlotte got pouty. Eric tried ignoring her, but Amy engaged her in chitchat.

I gotta know, Amy said. Has your Daddy caved? Is he letting you wear makeup yet?

Charlotte glared at Eric as if he'd put Amy up to this. How else could Amy have hit on such a sensitive topic?

A little, Charlotte muttered.

As they pulled up at the bungalow, Eric saw it as if for the first time. The overgrown lawn, the unpruned hedges, the cracking paint. The place had the aspect of a man who isn't growing a beard so much as not shaving.

Charlotte disappeared into her room. Eric envied her. He, too, could have used a moment alone to sort things out. He settled Amy on the couch and ducked into the kitchen. He found a sleeve of saltines and fanned them on a dinner plate. He sliced some cheese. He pulled the cork from a half-empty bottle of wine, smelled it, and poured it into mugs.

Fancy! Amy said as he set it all out on the coffee table.

And there it was again. That laugh.

They ate and sipped. Chewed and swallowed.

Do I get the tour? Amy asked.

Of La Jolla?

Amy chuckled. Of your place.

Oh, Eric said. Well, you can see just about all of it from where you're sitting.

C'mon, she said. She took his hand. Eric's body thrilled. They headed down the hall.

Bathroom, he said, pointing, and started down the hallway.

But Amy blocked him and forced him to expound. Well, he went on. I guess those towel racks are new . . .

He snuck peeks at her as they moved through the house. She had the air of a queen being ushered through a small-town zoo, peering politely into each modest exhibit. She offered praise not so much for the place itself, but "what y'all have done with it."

What was she seeing when she snuck peeks at him*?* he wondered. A quirky professor? A radio geek, lurker of the airwaves? Did she even *like* what she saw? She must, Eric decided, because she was flirting with him. Or was she just being nice? Was he even equipped to pick up on those kinds of signals anymore?

They stopped in on Charlotte and found her listening to music. She looked surprised to see Amy still in the house. Eric closed the door and ushered Amy into his own room. She set her mug of wine on the dresser and stepped past his unmade single bed to the radio desk. Amy brought her hand to her mouth. The silence in the room tingled with an electricity Eric had not felt in a long, long time.

This is it, Amy said, staring down at the microphone.

She turned to him and took his hands and placed them upon her ample hips as if teaching him how to hold a dance partner. He could feel the pressure of her body inside her pants. He wanted to pop her clothes open like a can of biscuit dough, watch the pent-up curves come bursting out. She cocked her head and smiled at him and there was nothing left to do but kiss her. He had not kissed like this for many years. He got lost in it—only to suddenly snap out of it.

Charlotte, he said.

Right, Amy said. She lowered her gaze and bit her wet lip. I was thinkin' . . . I'd love to make y'all dinner tonight. How'd that be?

Half an hour later, standing behind Amy in a grocery checkout line, Eric was recognized by the cashier as she scanned the carton of eggs Amy would soon transform into quiche. Where's your daughter? the cashier asked.

Pouting, Eric said.

Lane 4 just opened up, the cashier said, nodding to the adjacent aisle.

Oh, Eric said. No, I'm with her. We're together.

The cashier glanced across the check-writing desk at Amy. Amy winked back.

The cashier nodded. Eric blushed. Another thing he hadn't done in a long time.

At the dinner table, Charlotte was so cordial as to arouse Eric's suspicion. She wolfed down the quiche, then excused herself to her room, not to be heard from the rest of the night. Eric knew she needed to be dealt with. Just not tonight.

His favorite listener on earth was soon sitting beside him, on his couch, in his front room, with her legs crossed and her hand draped over his shoulder. She touched his knee. Her eyes drank him in, sip after sip. They talked for hours. Near midnight, there came a moment when the absolute quiet of the house compelled Eric to lean over and finish the kiss he'd started that afternoon. It lasted and lasted. His hands made their way around her waist and up under her blouse. They took the measure of her for the first time. Her hand found his lap, and Eric led them tiptoeing down the hall, past the closed door of his stewing teenage daughter, to his room. With its single bed. He eased the door shut.

The curtains were drawn. It was utterly dark inside. There was only Amy's voice, that tantalizing giggle. He laid the voice down, peeled off its jeans, its blouse. The voice tugged his shorts and boxers off. It slipped out of its panties and straddled him.

The voice let out a laugh, and Eric reached up and put a finger to its lips, *shhhhh.*

Even though it killed him.

Literally. It killed him. Just not right away.

Charlotte

2002

YOU'LL FIND THERE are *two* Charlotte chapters. They are sequential. Yes. But so too are the years 1928 and 1929. Any history buffs in the audience? Anyway. You might wonder, why did I break Charlotte up this way? The answer is, *I* didn't. She was broken when I found her. We'll get to that.

Let's head back to Texas first. Another car ride with Eric and Charlotte. Who'd made Amarillo by noon of the second day of a little road trip Eric put together.

Charlotte rolled down her window as they exited the freeway. Raw heat and humidity gushed in.

It's like *broth*, Eric said, laughing.

He read directions scrawled on his palm as they navigated master-planned boulevards bordered by tan and salmon stucco tract houses. He pulled up to the curb of one such house. Father and daughter stared at it from the car. The daughter had a stomachache brought on by gas station cheese puffs and strawberry milk, an amalgamation she'd been allowed to count as breakfast by the preoccupied father. Eric shut off the car engine but didn't get out. Without the AC running the car immediately started getting hot and stuffy.

They had a little chat.

Let me just say I have no idea what's happening here, Eric said. I'm just going with it. I'm hoping you can too.

I can try, Charlotte said.

That's all I'm asking, Eric said.

He patted Charlotte's knee and climbed out into the broth. Charlotte followed him across the lawn to the porch. He rang the bell and cracked his knuckles. Charlotte bent over to ease the pain in her belly just as the front door burst open. Out gushed Amy, absolutely beaming. She captured both of them in a bear hug. Charlotte straightened up just in time to have her arms pinned to her sides, her shoulder lodged in her father's damp armpit, her face plunged into a denim-clad, two-gallon bosom.

I'm so happy y'all made it! Amy said. She planted a kiss on Eric. She held his head between her hands to get a good look.

We all are happy too, Eric said. He and Amy turned to look at Charlotte, confirming this was indeed the party line. Charlotte noticed a sticker on Eric's tropical linen shirt, a column of letters:

L
A
R
G
E

She yanked it off with the same sadistic pleasure her father took in removing her band-aids.

Amy led a tour of her two-story box of a house, which she'd dubbed The Barn. The bottom floor had a huge kitchen overlooking a main room with fifteen-foot ceilings. Sliding glass doors opened onto a backyard abutting a golf course fairway. Amy's bedroom suite was downstairs, with a canopy bed and a walk-in closet that looked to Charlotte like a costume shop. So many laughable colors and fabrics, so many boots, so much big jewelry.

Upstairs were three more bedrooms. One had a battered wood desk cluttered with radio equipment. The next (where Charlotte would be sleeping) had a single bed, an ornate bureau, and a bookshelf full of old wind-up clocks, a few of which ticked asynchronously. The last featured infantile pink-and-blue-striped wallpaper. Amy leaned in to switch on a rocking-horse light fixture that dangled in the empty space. The room reminded Charlotte of the dollhouse that so bored her as a girl.

This was a nursery when I bought the place, Amy explained. I haven't seen fit to do anything to it just yet.

Mm, Eric said. He pulled open a cabinet at the end of the hallway and peered in, inexplicably captivated by linens. Amy eased the ex-nursery door closed. As Charlotte's view of the room contracted, her interest in it inverted. She got the urge to force herself back in, to swing a bat at the rocking-horse light fixture.

How 'bout some sweet tea? Amy said.

Yes, Eric said. He shut the cabinet.

Later, they all piled into Amy's street-legal golf cart.

This is The Horse, Amy explained.

Of course, Eric said.

Charlotte rode in the rear-facing bench seat. Eric and Amy asked Charlotte nothing as they rode. Charlotte said nothing. She rubbed her cramping gut and watched the road recede. She had never been to Texas. But she didn't turn around to see out the front. She already saw exactly where they were headed.

Amy's job as the pastry chef at Heritage Ranch—the "active adult community" to which she belonged—entitled her to a pair of transferable fitness club memberships that Eric and Charlotte were allowed to use. That afternoon, while Eric played sous-chef in a baking class that Amy taught to retirees,

Charlotte checked out some racquetball gear and had rally after punishing rally with a wall. That was where she found herself—grunting slurs between echoing *plocks* of the ball—when she got the disconcerting sensation of having wet herself. She dropped the racket. Left the ball bouncing off into a corner. Fumbled with the weird knob on the court's midget-sized door. Got frantic.

She speed-walked to the locker room. Took shelter in a stall. Her underwear was spotted with bright blood. She slipped them off. Held them dangling in her fingertips.

Panicked. Dropped them in the toilet. Flushed.

Problem solved.

Charlotte soiled another pair before dinner. She was helping herself to more sweet tea from Amy's fridge when she felt it happening. She slipped into the guest bathroom, cleaned herself up, and stuffed her underwear into a plastic bag to launder later, in private. She stuffed Kleenex into the crotch of her pants. This helped, but it gave her a cowboy stance she feared would get her noticed.

Charlotte generally understood what was happening to her. It had happened to other girls she knew. She had no intention of bringing it up with her father. This was not the type of attention she wanted from him at the moment. Nor would she tell Amy, knowing the joy Amy would take in playing mother. And anyway, by Thursday things had abated, though not before Charlotte ran out of clean underwear. The soiled pairs were all stuffed in a baggie hidden under her dirty clothes.

She put on bathing suit bottoms under a pair of shorts.

She found her father at the breakfast table. He was perusing the Amarillo paper as if they'd always lived there. Amy sat across from him making a grocery list. Charlotte refused to sit down—refused to assume her role in such a fake little family.

Will you please take me to the pool? she asked her father. (She avoided addressing Amy.)

Eric folded the wings of the paper together. A swim, he said approvingly. Of course. I'll run you over there in a minute.

I'll wait in the cart, Charlotte said. (She also refused to call it The Horse.)

The pool was empty but for an elderly man swimming excruciatingly slow laps, shedding sad little wakes. It was ninety degrees out. The Texas sun somehow bigger and brighter than the California one. The water was cool, though. The chlorine triggered a nostalgia Charlotte didn't fully notice. Something subconscious. She stood for a moment listening to the gurgle of the pool filter, then dunked herself, pushed off the wall, and came up swimming.

Two lengths of the pool. Then two more. She torpedoed off the walls without time to catch her breath or dwell on the image of her father and Amy using their fingers to pick bits of powdered donut off each other's lips at the grocery store, or the thought of him deferring to Amy about which words a thirteen-year-old girl should be allowed to use after stubbing the living fucking shit out of her toe on Amy's hideous turquoise sofa.

Maybe it was in the chlorine. But it struck Charlotte that her father used to be something of a swimmer. Eric had somehow injured his knee and had surgery to repair it. Then he'd started going to the pool at the YMCA for rehab. At the time, Charlotte had wondered how anyone could delight in something so dull. But in Amarillo—kicking and stroking the best she knew how, and stretching for the wall and popping up from the water with her eyes stinging and her lungs working like bellows, and checking the oversized timing clock on the pump-room wall to find she'd shaved a couple seconds off her time—Charlotte wondered if she'd been wrong about her father. Or at least about swimming.

Maybe she'd mistaken rhythm for monotony, therapy for exercise.

They lingered in Amarillo another week. Charlotte swam every day. Her limbs got rubbery from overuse. In La Jolla, her half friends Tara and Sarah sometimes cut themselves. They'd once convinced Charlotte to try it too, to savor the sting as the blood seeped out. How silly that seemed now, compared to this! Swimming felt like pain for the sake of something. For what, Charlotte couldn't say.

Never had she tested her body's tolerance for exertion. Turned out, it followed even her harshest orders. It was a body born to swim. She had her mother's narrow hips, her father's long limbs. Charlotte's mind, too, was well suited. She had her mother's perfectionism and knack for experiment. She liked making tweaks to the angulations of her hands, the straightness of her legs, and seeing if her time improved. She liked the sluggishness that came at the end of a session. She liked dragging herself out of the pool like some shipwreck survivor, too worn out to fuss much about anything (Eric & Amy) or anyone (Amy) for the rest of the day.

One afternoon at the pool Charlotte sensed she was being watched. She stopped mid-lap and wiped her eyes to look around and there stood Eric and Amy. Charlotte was mortified to have been caught trying so hard at something. She might as well have been swimming naked.

She made her way laterally across the pool, sliding over and under the floating lane lines like a weaving thread. At the pool edge Amy dangled a pair of goggles in her face. A treasure from Lost and Found, she said.

Charlotte took the goggles. The lenses were tinted a sinister reflective black. A name was written in faded marker on the band: Richard Cashill.

Dick used to be a member, Amy said. Real nice fella.

Oh, Charlotte said, not understanding.

Mr. Cashill died, Eric explained. He won't be needing those anymore.

Amy and Eric chuckled. Charlotte tightened the elastic band. Again her thoughts turned to wannabe goth girls Tara and Sarah, both of whom were already envious of Charlotte's naturally black hair and pale skin. What would they say now, to see her don the black goggles of a dead man?

Charlotte submerged, sinking through exhaled bubbles to the pool bottom. She looked out at an entirely new world. She paused to take it all in—the undulating lane lines, the stripes of blue tile converging toward the other end of the pool, the two wavy human figures on the deck above. One of the figures knelt. Its hand penetrated the surface. The man to whom it belonged remained a distortion, but the hand was crystal clear. Refraction made the wrist look horribly broken. Charlotte reached up and gripped it. For a moment a link formed between their worlds. Charlotte started to tug playfully, as if to pull her father down with her. To her dismay, his grip tightened. Suddenly the opposite was happening: she was rising. Eric hoisted her out of the water and set her down on the deck.

Goggles fit okay? he asked.

Charlotte tried not to pout. Yeah, she said—looking at her father. Thanks.

Oh, you're *welcome*, darling, Amy said.

And that?—well, that was it. Charlotte decided she had to do something. The bullshit hunky-dory charade could not go on. Not on her watch.

That evening, while Eric and Amy were fixing dinner, Charlotte took the cordless phone to the back patio. Above her, a radio antenna like the one in La Jolla was strung between two poles in Amy's yard. A pair of twilight golfers wandered up the fairway.

Charlotte dialed San Jose.

Nancy sounded surprised to hear from her. (Usually Nancy called Charlotte.)

So, how's the road trip going? Nancy asked.

It's not really a road trip, Charlotte said.

Oh? So, where are you guys?

Amy's house.

Who's Amy?

Nixie, Charlotte said. Then she waited.

Honey, Nancy said calmly. Would you mind putting your father on the line?

Not at all.

Inside, Eric sat on a kitchen barstool, shucking corn. Amy stood before an open refrigerator. Charlotte walked in with the phone held to her chest. Um, Dad, she said. Phone's for you . . .

Eric looked up. For me? he said.

It's Mom, Charlotte explained. She crossed the kitchen and handed the phone over like a live grenade.

Eric stared at it. Charlotte almost pitied him. Almost regretted it.

Nancy? he said into the phone.

Boom.

Charlotte watched Eric listening hard to whatever Nancy was saying. His face was the picture of unpreparedness. He excused himself through the sliding glass door. Charlotte watched him wandering among the cacti, gesturing with his free hand.

Can I help? Charlotte asked Amy.

Amy showed her how to tear away the stringy corn husks.

Thanks again for the goggles, Charlotte said. My eyes don't sting anymore.

It's important to see where you're going, Amy said.

Charlotte nodded.

Do you know what I mean by that? Amy asked.

Charlotte nodded again. You used to be in rodeos, she said. I saw that *big 'ol belt buckle a yours*, she added, putting on Amy's accent.

I'll be damned! Amy said. Texas rubbin' off on you already!

Did you win it? she asked.

The buckle? Yeah, I s'pose you could say that.

Sounds like you were good.

I was.

Why'd you stop?

I got sick of rodeos, Amy said. And my mom.

Really?

Well. I hated that I hadn't *picked* rodeos. I wanted to be a chef, and a mother, and—well, that's a long story. Let's just say, I went after what I wanted and I got it.

Because you're a chef now, Charlotte said.

That's right.

Just, not a mother.

Charlotte stopped ripping at the corn long enough to look up and see how her comment had landed. She found Amy smiling.

Why didn't you? Charlotte asked. Have a kid.

You make it sound like it's just a matter of picking one outta the catalogue, Amy said.

I know how it works, Charlotte said.

That so, Amy replied.

Neither of them spoke for a time and then Amy broke the silence. I was running a load of wash for your father this mornin', she said. Figured I'd toss in whatever you had. And when I grabbed up that pile of clothes on your floor . . .

Oh my god, Charlotte said.

Amy winked at her.

Why don'cha follow me for a sec? Amy said.

Moments later, in the upstairs bedroom, Charlotte looked on as Amy slid open a closet and took out a small, pink and blue box of maxi pads. These are for you, Amy said. She handed the box over like a bomb.

Boom.

Now, now, Amy said, patting Charlotte's arm. It's no big deal. Well, it *is* a big deal, but it's not a *bad* one. It's *wonderful.*

I don't need these, Charlotte said.

Of course you do.

It stopped, Charlotte said.

Amy gave a knowing smile.

Does my dad know? Charlotte asked.

Don't worry. This is just one girl looking out for another, honey.

Charlotte stared at Amy, then hustled off to her room and stashed the box. She came back out to find her father coming up the stairs. Amy came out of a bedroom.

What're you two up to? Eric asked.

Oh, Amy said. Charlotte was helping me make up a bed. Did you and Nancy have a nice chat?

Eric smiled and handed the phone to Charlotte.

She put it to her ear. Hey, Mom, Charlotte said.

There was no reply. The phone was dead.

She's not there, Charlotte said.

I hung up on her, Eric said.

He winked at Amy, who let out a sound like a whoop, only to cut it short.

Charlotte recognized and immediately resented this little act of sportsmanship—the victors trying not to rub it in. She stormed back to her room and strangled to death a Texas-shaped pillow by its Panhandle neck. For the second time in her life—the first being the divorce—Charlotte hated both of her parents equally. Her hate swirled about the room. It fixed on her black, felt jewelry bag. Tucked inside was the Omega watch her father had given her. Charlotte had never worn it, but she had always considered it precious. It had after all been her mother's. Then her father's. Neither of them wanting it, in the end.

Charlotte could relate.

She put the watch in her left-front pocket. She nabbed Amy's silver belt buckle off its Plexiglas stand and put it in her right-front.

She could hear Amy and Eric whispering in the kitchen. She could only guess at the smug looks on their faces. She slipped outside through a side door and jogged barefoot to the end of the block. The horizon was the bruised colors of sunset. She followed a cart path around a hill dappled with sagebrush.

She emerged at the edge of a large pond. A boy was making weapon noises in a backyard abutting the path. He poked a rubber-band rifle through a wrought iron fence. Watch out, he warned. There's bats.

Charlotte clutched the watch as if to crush it, then cocked her arm back and threw it as far as she could out over the pond. A small bird (or perhaps, in fact, a bat) darted toward the watch, then curled away. Charlotte and the boy were sole witnesses to the ripple made in the water.

Nice throw, the boy said. What was that?

Charlotte took the buckle from her pocket. She winged it too. Side-arm, the way Eric had taught her to skip rocks. The buckle kissed the water near the shore, took a giant hop, and, spinning wildly, careened away to slice into the pond with a *plip*.

Charlotte started walking back the way she'd come. The boy shadowed her on his side of the fence. It was a watch, huh? he said.

Charlotte acknowledged him. What do you care? she said. You gonna go get it?

No way, the boy said. There's barracudas.

The next morning Charlotte took a thoroughly exhausting swim, then availed herself of one of the club's loaner bikes. It had a suspension seat post and a cushy saddle. It made the road feel smoother than it really was. Charlotte drifted along the cart paths, half conscious. She came to the big pond, where she found the boy wearing a feather headdress. He was staring out at an older boy who was snorkeling around in the pond. Charlotte could hear the older boy panting. He teetered in the water, head-down like a feeding duck, legs kicking air. Charlotte dismounted and set the kickstand. What the hell, she said. Who's that?

My brother, the boy said.

"Finders keepers, losers weepers" can feel, to a weeper, most unjust indeed. Suddenly Charlotte saw the watch for what it was: the sole remaining relic of her normal life. She stepped out of her shorts and pulled her T-shirt off. The bathing suit underneath was still damp. She grabbed her dead-man's goggles from the handlebar basket and rushed the pond like a triathlete starting a race.

The shallows were mucky. Silt squished through her toes. She swam toward where she remembered the buckle splashing in. The boy in the water changed course in a single stroke and casually kicked toward the far side of the pond, as if that had been his destination all along.

The pond was about six feet deep in the middle. Sunlight filtered down through the greenish water. Charlotte could make out dozens of golf balls on the bottom. Faded soda cans too. She took a breath, then dove. The deeper water was cooler. With her belly against the pond floor, she contorted to peer in all directions. But the debris she kicked up made the water murkier. Her limbs brushed ropy plant life. She came up for air. Dove again. This time she kept her motions minimal and didn't stir up as much silt.

On her fourth dive, she found the buckle. This came as a massive relief. The theft hadn't been detected yet. If it had, Charlotte could see now, her father could have rightfully aligned himself with Amy. Charlotte refused to let that happen.

She headed out to where she thought the watch might be. Again and again she dove, finding nothing. She started to feel stupid being in the pond. She decided to cut her losses.

While she was deciding this, she continued to dive. And dive. And dive. And on one such "final" attempt she spotted a glimmer among some yellow weeds and swam toward it. When she saw through her goggles that it was just a bottle cap—when she had the tiny folded crown of aluminum in her fingers—she snarled a string of curses, and bubbles poured out her lips.

She followed them back to the surface.

Rode back to The Barn.

Set the stupid buckle back in its stupid Plexiglas stand.

Fumed.

On the Sunday they left Amarillo, Charlotte lay in bed, unwilling to make an appearance at the breakfast table. Eric came looking for her. He described the bounty awaiting her downstairs. Amy had prepared them a farewell brunch: crepes, sausage, eggs, fresh-squeezed Texas Ruby-Red grapefruit juice, et cetera.

Not hungry, Charlotte said.

Eric glowered at her. His grip on the doorknob tightened. The knob creaked. Charlotte could still piss him off like no one else. But as soon as his eyes darkened, they cleared up. More for me, he said, and he was gone again.

Charlotte listened for repercussions of her defiance coming from the kitchen. She wasn't disappointed.

It's mainly just *rude*, she heard Amy say. What, with all I do for that girl . . .

Then she heard her father say, I guess it's to be expected. Let's just leave her be.

And leave her be they did.

For about a year.

It worked both ways, though. Charlotte let them be, too. She became an eighth grader, a fourteen-year-old, a La Jolla Junior High Vaquero. Mostly, though, she identified as a La Jolla Swim Club Seahorse. Nancy covered the club's hefty membership fees. The coaches tried Charlotte out at all the strokes, but she'd known what she was ever since her seminal laps in Amarillo. She was preternaturally comfortable not seeing where she was going.

She was a backstroker.

She learned that water is unforgiving. (She had no idea how unforgiving it would prove.) That it has a knack for finding fault with a body, that a head becomes a dragging cannonball if held at the wrong angle. To hone her form, Charlotte's coach made her swim while balancing her signature black goggles atop her forehead.

Eric and Amy's courtship took the form of a long-distance relationship. There were alternating "road trips" to La Jolla or to Amarillo every month or so. But eventually Amy moved into the bungalow with Charlotte and Eric and started a new job as a buyer for a San Diego restaurant. This had her dashing off to fish markets and specialty shops in her Durango, still sporting Texas plates. Eric took on the teaching of a summer lab course. Both of their radios went unused. Amy rented out The Barn, having failed to sell it despite lowering the asking price three times.

With school out for the summer, Charlotte's swim practices shifted from afternoons to mornings. Meets were on Saturdays. One weekend, after she won the two-hundred-meter backstroke, Amy and Eric filed down the bleachers to the pool deck to congratulate her.

I'm so proud, Eric said, hugging her. Sometimes I wish your mom could see you race.

Charlotte was surprised by this. Me too, she said.

Eric headed away to the snack bar.

Amy turned to Charlotte. I've wondered, Amy said. What *does* your mom have to say about your swimming?

Charlotte shrugged. Not much, she said. She pays for it.

Amy put a hand to her own heart, hearing that. Undulating reflections danced around the indoor complex and over Amy's annoyingly serene face.

Why? Charlotte asked. Because it saddened Charlotte, actually—the token interest her mother allotted to swimming compared to, say, report cards. Nancy told Charlotte it was good to have "hobbies," just not to go overboard.

There's different kinds of moms is all, Amy said. Some put the "mother" in "smother." I'd say your mom seems to have things in *perspective*.

Amy usually danced around the topic of Nancy. But if that

door cracked at all, Amy could be trusted to slip a boot in. Strangely, she often came down on *Nancy's* side of things.

Amy claimed to understand Nancy.

You've never met my mom, Charlotte said.

It's true, Amy said. But I been outnumbered by y'all long enough to feel I know the woman pretty well.

What's that mean, she has things in perspective? Charlotte asked. Like, because swimming isn't very important?

Not as important as *you*, Amy said. That *you* chose it. It's a good thing, especially at your age, to have some things that're yours.

Charlotte wanted to be angry at this. She knew Amy was wrong, but couldn't find the angle to prove it.

Whatever, Charlotte said. You barely know *me*, either.

Well it ain't from lack of trying, darling, Amy said.

Anyways, Charlotte said dismissively.

I know what it's like being young, Amy persisted.

I'm *fourteen*, Charlotte said.

Right. I've walked in those boots. I know what it's like.

What's it like, then?

Hard.

Eric returned. He handed Charlotte a Gatorade and Amy a coffee. Both women thanked him while continuing to stare at each other.

In June in La Jolla, day after day, hot inland air rises, sucking the marine layer in off the Pacific and smothering us in a gray blanket. June Gloom, we call it. Still, our beaches fill up. Still, kids fly kites in the fog. I like the break from the sun. Not everyone does.

During that particular June Gloom, Charlotte stewed, but Eric was giggly and eager to please (Amy). Night after night, Charlotte was tortured by the sound of flirty voices in the front room. Like a grumpy spinster, she'd climb out of bed and shout down the hallway that it was late, that she had practice early in the morning. They'd apologize and switch to whispering. This, of course, was even worse.

It was enough to make Charlotte pine for San Jose. She'd spend a weekend there with Nancy once or twice a month. Just as her father had come to enjoy the artificially heightened emotions of his own long-distance relationship with Amy, Charlotte savored her intense overlaps with Nancy. Charlotte's childhood bedroom had been converted into a guest room, with high-end furniture and décor that lacked personality. It felt like a nice hotel. Charlotte liked it. Though she'd never had a sister, the relationship Charlotte settled into with Nancy was a skewed approximation. Nancy played the protective older one, Charlotte the unprotectable younger one.

Charlotte liked forcing her mother out of her comfort zone. Getting pedicures together, Nancy would pick a demure red polish, only to let Charlotte goad her into a showy pink. The divorce had toppled the infrastructure. They were no longer mother/daughter as much as they were Nancy/Charlotte. Charlotte could see Nancy now as a separate person, where before her mother had been something integral—an extension of herself, always there, taken for granted. Just: *Mom.*

During Charlotte's latest visit to San Jose, she and Nancy had been milling through a street fair when Charlotte nudged her mother into the chat-you-up zone of a sidewalk busker. Minutes later, Charlotte took the photograph now pinned inside her locker at the pool—Nancy in a dreadlock wig, balancing spinning plates on manicured middle fingers.

Charlotte wished Nancy would actually flip her off sometimes. Get real. Get pissed. It always bothered Charlotte the way Nancy hadn't put up a fight to win back her husband, nor for custody of her daughter. She'd just pulled the plug. As if her family were some failed research project. Maybe that made Nancy an empowered woman. Charlotte wasn't ready to make up her mind about that.

Theirs was a shallow sisterhood, though. Even Charlotte

could see that. She was careful to share only enough about herself to keep the line connecting La Jolla and San Jose from going completely slack. She volunteered basic details about swimming and school, and didn't understand, let alone care, about Nancy's work at IBM.

They did gossip about Eric and make fun of Amy. Charlotte did an impression of Amy that Nancy couldn't get enough of. They secretly called Amy "The Horse" (Charlotte having repurposed Amy's own nickname for her golf cart). Amy was to them a caricature, her rough edges stretched to comic proportions. Nancy took to using the nickname as if it were plural, and infinitely more insulting. For example:

Charlotte: Dad's been wearing a lot of v-necks. It's gross. They show his chest hair.

Nancy: And what do The Horse think about that?

Charlotte: The Horse love it.

Why don't you ever let me in? Amy asked Charlotte one morning.

Eric had just kissed them both goodbye and left to teach class. Charlotte was pouring herself a third bowl of Cinnamon Toast Crunch. She was a calorie furnace.

Mm? Charlotte said, chewing.

You don't want my help. You don't want my advice. I try so hard for you, honey. You don't have much of a mother figure, and I—

Are you serious? Charlotte said.

C'mon, honey. You know what I mean. I'm only sayin' I wish you'd let me into your life a little. I feel like I'm failin' you.

You live here, don't you? Charlotte said. You're in pretty far, I'd say.

From the reaction on Amy's face, Charlotte could tell she was being unfair. Cruel even. She couldn't help it. Bitchiness had been plaguing her. Sometimes she lost her leash on it, and it possessed her. She'd been learning to use it to her advantage, though. During a race, her body could be made to run on concentrated spite. Charlotte relied on this more and more, which left her feeling conflicted: she knew who she'd inherited it from.

Charlotte's biggest problem was deciding who to resent the most.

It was mostly high schoolers on the swim team. Still a middle-schooler, Charlotte tended to linger just outside their locker-room huddles. Overhearing their jokes, she kept her smile to herself. She looked up to the older girls. She'd seen them clambering from the pool, dripping and pale, to vomit in the trashcan. She aspired to that echelon of masochism. It therefore came as a shock to her when, gathered in a cramped hotel room after a meet in Bakersfield, these older girls offered Charlotte one of the mini bottles of gin they'd stolen from a restocking cart.

Hangovers, it turned out, were the real reason one puked at practice.

I wonder: if Charlotte had overdone it on that first night, in the hotel—if she'd gotten so drunk she deemed the stuff poison—whether she'd have avoided alcohol for a long time, or altogether. Instead, the single mini of Beefeater delivered a perfect buzz. Her guard came down. She helped choreograph a suggestive dance routine to Shakira's "Whenever, Wherever." Later, after lights-out, she performed this routine with a select few of the girls for a select few of the boys, unbeknownst to the parental chaperones. Charlotte's role entailed crawling across a bedspread like a sexually depraved cat.

Her reputation reversed overnight. Soon seniors were sharing swim lanes and gossip and beers with her. By the time she arrived at La Jolla High School, Charlotte was already *somebody*. The boys treated her like a tomboyish little sister; the girls treated her like a protégé. Charlotte was a natural in both roles. She wore swim team sweats to school most days. She let her hair get wiry and chlorine-damaged. She stopped painting her nails, stopped wearing makeup.

She drank. She got laughs. That was the real buzz. Alcohol answered something in Charlotte. Ashamed of her past and afraid of her future, she lived in the moment. It didn't take much—a couple beers—and out came the girl she'd spent years suppressing. *That* girl was confident, raunchy, and unpredictable. *That* girl sardined herself in between boys in the backs of speeding pickups. *That* girl partied.

Her schoolmates hailed from some of America's wealthiest families. They didn't have their own rooms, they had their own floors, their own *wings*. To be at these girls' houses with their parents home was to be home alone—with a full bar kept stocked by a staff of disinterested, overworked immigrants. The rich make wonderful enablers.

Eric and Amy were never suspicious. If anything, Charlotte thought they seemed relieved by her new friends, all of whom *did* look convincingly wholesome in their speed suits. Charlotte's hangovers went undetected. She had always been grumpy and lethargic in the morning.

One night at a beach bonfire, Charlotte pointed to a couple making out under a lifeguard tower. Well, I *declare!* Charlotte cried. Like cows at a salt lick . . .

Thus was born a *persona*. The juxtaposition of Charlotte's spot-on, syrupy, Texas drawl and her Asian facial features . . . it killed. When it came to getting laughs from teenagers, Charlotte discovered the bar was set nice and low. All she had to do was channel a woman she hardly knew. And, really, why would Charlotte make an effort to know Amy better? All Charlotte needed were silly surface details. Her impression was a veneer.

Also: where better to get fresh material than directly from "The Horse" mouth? (See how it could be made possessive as well as plural? Said aloud, "The Horse mouth" can't be distinguished from "the whore's mouth." Wicked fun.) The best Amy-isms didn't even make sense—*now that's two different buckets of possums!*—nor were they hard to come by. Charlotte had merely to sit for a minute and watch TV with Amy (who was partial to police procedurals) and before long Amy would announce that the ugly district attorney character *musta been in the outhouse when lightnin' struck . . .*

For Halloween, Charlotte bought a pair of Wranglers and a ten-gallon hat from a thrift shop in Pacific Beach. A sophomore loaned Charlotte a pair of ostrich-leather boots, insisting she didn't even need them back. Charlotte was prepping in her room for the party when she looked up to find Amy standing in the doorway.

Yeehaw? Charlotte said.

Stay right there, Amy said.

Amy disappeared down the hall. She returned with a belt bearing the very buckle Charlotte once stole, submerged, and salvaged from the holding pond in Amarillo. Amy helped lace the belt through the loops of Charlotte's borrowed Wranglers and set the hook into a hole too perfectly ovular to have ever been used. (Further down was a hole that appeared to have put up quite a fight before eventually relinquishing duties to its neighbor.) The top of the buckle jutted into Charlotte's belly.

What a sight, Amy said. The turquoise matches your blouse.

Charlotte studied herself in the mirror. I'll give it back tomorrow, she said.

No, no, Amy said. It's yours. It's just collecting dust. It's meant to be worn.

I *reckon*, Charlotte blurted.

Amy looked at her sideways. I'd say it suits you fine, she said.

Everyone'll get a kick out of it, Charlotte said.

I bet you'll make sure of that, Amy said.

Charlotte looked questioningly at Amy. By the unblinking way Amy looked back, Charlotte could tell: *Amy knew.*

So, Charlotte wondered, *why is she helping with the costume?* Like the guest of dishonor at a roast, The Horse seemed to be getting the biggest kick of all out of this. *Did she see parody and think it homage?*

Whatever the case, Charlotte was left no choice but to go all in. Darlin', she said. I'll make *damn* sure . . .

The party was thrown by a pair of brothers from another high school whose parents were out of the country. Charlotte quickly lost track of the girls she'd come with. A tray of green Jell-O shots came her way. She had one. The house was packed with people she didn't know, none of whom therefore realized her costume was more than just an outfit, that she was actually brimming with pearls of Texan insight. No circles would form around Charlotte tonight, egging her on. She was nothing but a conservative-looking cowgirl. And The Horse couldn't compete with *The Whores*: that is, the prostitute-looking witches, or the team of prostitute-looking cheerleader zombies, let alone the girls dressed as prostitute-prostitutes.

Charlotte made her way to the kitchen, where a chubby surfer was using salad tongs to stir a peach-colored concoction. This is the stuff, he told Charlotte.

She took a red plastic cup from a leaning stack. Held it out.

Charlotte stumbled around the house, nodding to the music, fixated on her inability to feel her teeth when she clacked them together. She gravitated outside to the pool. Her element. She tugged off her belt, her jeans, her shirt. Feeling eyes on her, she went barefoot in bra and panties out onto the diving board. No hesitation. She sprung headlong over the illuminated pool. Tucked her head and curled into a ball, having decided in midair that she'd do a front flip.

She didn't so much splash *into* the water as *onto* it. A horrendous back flop. A group of girls stood poolside with hands over their mouths. A gorilla with a boy's head looked ready to dive in, but Charlotte backstroked confidently to the side.

That looked hella painful, said the gorilla, helping her out.

Charlotte caught him sneaking peeks at her cleavage, and her morale recovered a little.

She locked herself in a bathroom and tried to regain equilibrium. Things only worsened. She was unsettled by her own reflection, the detachment she felt from it, the blankness of the eyes looking back into hers. The wallpaper whirled. She wanted her bed. And this helped: to have a goal. She snapped up the pearl buttons of her blouse, wrestled herself back into her Wranglers, and pulled her hat down over her wet hair. She had to sit on the toilet to yank her boots on.

In the front yard, a gang of trick-or-treaters were coming up the street—middle schoolers carrying pillowcases, wearing hoodies and scary masks. They eyed the party as they passed. Charlotte could detect their envy, their desire to be grown up and party like *that*. She in turn wished she could join their crew. Oh, to just be a trick-or-treater again.

Anyone going to La Jolla? she shouted. Nearby partygoers turned to look at her.

I am, said a boy in a rainbow wig, smoking a clove.

Now? she asked.

In a sec, he said.

I'll wait over here, Charlotte said. She sat down on the lawn against a boulder. She shut her eyes. Her chin settled against her chest. And when next she looked up, the front yard was empty. Cans and empty cups were strewn across the lawn. She stood up, hoping to feel magically sober, but . . . no. She was chilled, her hair still wet. She remembered her mission: get home.

The front door was open. A ripe aroma of beer and sweat wafted out. It repulsed her. One of her teammates was coming down the stairs.

Hanna, Charlotte said. Help.

Charlotte! Hanna said. We thought you left!

Soon they were all back in the car, arguing about where to go for food.

Can you please just take me home? Charlotte begged.

The ride became a blur of headlights, streetlights. Her head teetered at the curves. The car was claustrophobic. Finally, the rear hatch rose. Charlotte spilled out onto the sidewalk. The only thing left to do was succumb to sleep. She slipped in the bungalow's front door—not opening it enough to make it creak—and found herself awash in flickering blue light. Amy looked up from the couch.

You're home late, cowgirl, Amy said. She turned off the TV and the room plunged into darkness.

The party was in, like, I don't know. We carpooled, but . . . Yeah. I'm zonked. Charlotte started down the hall.

Hold on, honey, Amy said. She got up and clogged the hallway. How'd it go? she asked. How'd everyone like your getup?

No one gave a shit, Charlotte wanted to say. However, from the sound of it, Amy seemed willing to overlook the curfew violation.

Everyone loved it, Charlotte said.

Amy smiled. Is that chlorine I smell?

There was a pool, yeah.

Actually, Amy said, I smell more than chlorine.

Charlotte cocked her head, wondering: *Would this be the night, then?* How many times had she come home drunk and slipped into her bedroom for twelve hours? And, actually, *would it be so bad to be noticed, not just left to your own devices?*

Are you drunk? Amy asked.

Charlotte let the accusation linger, unrefuted.

It ain't the first time, Amy said. Is it?

Charlotte continued to say nothing.

I've figured as much, Amy said. Your dad wouldn't believe me, but I—

Wait. You told him? Charlotte said.

I haven't told him anything, honey.

Charlotte got a warm feeling, thinking of her father, asleep down the hall. Delusional or not, he trusted her.

Charlotte said, You stayed up to catch me.

No, it ain't like that. I couldn't sleep is all. So I poked my head into your room to check on you, but you weren't there, so I came out here to wait. Make sure you got home safe.

Are you gonna tell him?

Amy crossed her arms and leaned against the wall. That depends, she said. Do you think I should?

Charlotte was thrown by this. It *depended*? She tried this thought out, gave it space to breathe. Tossed it back at Amy. Do *you*? she said.

Probably, Amy said.

But . . . ?

Well, I'm just not so sure what *good* it'd do, Amy said. It'd certainly upset him. Is that what you want?

No.

Neither do I. See?

Not at all, Charlotte thought. She could play Amy. She didn't *get* her, though.

I'm not saying this is okay, Amy went on. I'm upset with you, young lady, but I get it. It's Halloween, and you're in high school. But it has to stop. *Tonight*. I might be willing to keep this our little secret—but only on that one condition. And don't you dare test me.

Alright, Charlotte said—just to keep Amy talking. The more Amy talked, the better things seemed to be getting.

Damn it, Amy said. You're a smart girl. It'd kill your dad to know you're being so damn irresponsible. He thinks too much of you.

Charlotte nodded, drunkenly proud of herself.

Go to bed, Amy said. Let's put this little episode behind us. For your father's sake.

Amy cupped her own hand and pretended to spit in it. Charlotte did too. They shook.

In the morning Charlotte had a headache and a sore back. She gulped ibuprofen, showered, and headed to the kitchen. Eric and Amy were at the table. They looked up at Charlotte together.

Howdy, *partner*, Amy said.

It was then Charlotte saw what she'd gotten herself into. Something tantamount to treason—to be on Amy's side, aligned against her father. *Our little secret.*

It was nothing short of blackmail. Charlotte would have to play nice now, as Amy'd wanted it all along, or else Eric would find out that his daughter was not the one he saw now before him, whisking eggs in her swim-team sweats. No. She was in fact the one who, two weekends ago, sipped Corona while a boy she barely knew took a Sharpie to her bare midriff (where her swimsuit covered) and, per Charlotte's request, drew a disturbing, bikini-clad dolphin with huge tits and puckered lips.

Charlotte cut a pad of butter into the frying pan.

Who drove last night? Eric asked in his serious tone.

Hanna, Charlotte said.

Weren't there eight of you?

Seven.

Honey. There's not enough seatbelts in Hanna's car for that many people.

Yeah, I had to ride in the way back, Charlotte said—feeling relief to admit *a* wrong, if not *the* wrong. I'm sorry, she added. It won't happen again.

It's unacceptable, Charlotte. Why couldn't you guys just take another car?

Because then another person couldn't drink, Dad, Charlotte thought. She poured her eggs into the hot butter and glanced at Amy. Amy sipped coffee noncommittally.

And you came home an hour past curfew, Eric said. I know it was Halloween, but we didn't give you special permission.

Charlotte pushed eggs around with a spatula, searing the transparency out of them, and thought: *we?*

Amy tells me she's already talked to you about it, Eric said.

So I have nothing to add except: you come home that late again, you're grounded. Are we clear?

Yes, Charlotte said.

Eric looked across at Amy with a look that said: *See what I'm dealing with here?*

You were such a hot mess! Hanna said. I heard you did a belly flop in your underwear!

That's bullshit, Charlotte said. It was a *back* flop.

It was a Sunday swim meet, and Charlotte's first chance to gossip about the party with her teammates. She'd expected laughter, but something was amiss. The girls didn't seem in the mood.

Hanna explained: Carrie got busted. Her mom caught her super drunk.

Shit, Charlotte said. Sorry, Carrie . . .

Later, Charlotte came in third in her best event—the two hundred backstroke. Emerging from the locker room afterward to rejoin Eric in the parking lot, she shrugged, waiting for his you'll-get-'em-next-time embrace—but he just stood there, examining her.

I just had a horrible conversation with Carrie's mother, he said.

Oh, really? Charlotte said.

Don't play dumb with me, Charlotte.

He was seething, but covering it over with a terrifying calmness. He went on: She told me that you and your friends were drinking on Halloween. And that it wasn't the first time.

Charlotte looked around the parking lot. She wished he'd waited until they were in the car. Teammates passed, waving. *Did they all know? Was she the only one who didn't see this coming?*

You lied to me, he said. You lied to Amy.

Well . . . , Charlotte began.

Well *what*?

Charlotte—grasping for purchase on the tilting slope where she now found herself—saw only one option. It would mean taking a fall, but she refused to fall alone. She would grab somebody on her way down. Somebody who stood to fall much farther.

I was going to say . . . Charlotte stopped herself. She needed to think. It seemed too simple to be her best move: tell the truth.

Eric crossed his arms.

I never lied to Amy, Dad.

You never lied to Amy.

No.

What's that even mean? he asked, but Charlotte could see his expression warping, his hands retreating to his pockets.

Amy knows, Charlotte said.

Knows what?

About this.

She knows you got drunk at the party?

And before that, Charlotte said. Other times.

Impossible, Eric said, laughing. There's no way she'd keep that from me.

When I came home on Halloween, we talked, Charlotte said. We promised we wouldn't tell you.

Why would Amy do that?

Charlotte moved her bag from one shoulder to the other. Shrugged.

She couldn't help but feel relief, getting this out in the open. She could feel Amy's grip on her loosening. Charlotte would be punished, no doubt—punish away!—but she could no longer be blackmailed by *The Horse*.

Get in the car, Eric said. I don't want to hear another word. Not until I've talked with Amy.

Okay, Charlotte said. That's fair.

Eric looked at her through his sunglasses. Charlotte couldn't see his eyes, but she knew there was disgust in them.

On the car ride home, Charlotte sat with her bag in her lap and stared out the windshield. She felt that to look out the side window would suggest her mind was wandering. She wanted her father to know that she was right there, ready to meet him halfway, to get what she had coming. (And to witness whatever Amy had coming.) That evening Eric and Amy left Charlotte in the house and went out to the car, to "go for a little drive," but the Saab never left the curb. They sat in the front seat for over an hour. When they came back in, Amy's mascara was streaked and Eric looked shattered. Charlotte had readied herself for a talking to—the most severe of her life—after which she'd get to apologize profusely, to begin making amends. She never got the chance. Eric came to her bedroom, opened the door without knocking, and stated simple facts: Charlotte was grounded. Two months. No going anywhere except school and the pool. Period.

Got it, Charlotte said. What about Amy?

Eric made a confused face. What about her?

Just, you guys were talking a long time.

Eric's eyes sparkled with tears. He looked out the window into the night. Charlotte turned to look out the window too, as if to see whatever sad thing he was staring at. When next she looked to her doorway, he wasn't there at all.

So began Eric's complete disappearance.

From that day forward the house was a different place. The first time they were alone again together, Charlotte tried talking to Amy. I just want to say—

You don't say anything, Amy said. I was trying to protect him, but—well, I guess you couldn't see that.

Carrie's mom's the one who . . .

Charlotte, stop. Just stop.

I'm sorry.

Jesus Christ. No, you're not. This isn't even about you. Not everything is.

I didn't say it was.

You didn't have to.

Charlotte let that one be. False as it was. For she knew this *did* have something to do with her. That first trip to Amarillo, Eric had begged Charlotte to give this new woman a chance. Charlotte had promised she'd try.

She never did.

Instead she'd taken Amy's best quality—her appreciation of Eric—and used it against her.

Charlotte wondered: *Had her father been waiting all along for a signal? Some kind of daughterly swing vote as to whether Amy would be allowed to become—what?—a second-string mother?* I feel like I'm failin' you—that's what Amy had said, thinking she'd come up short in that department. But how could Amy have failed? She wasn't Charlotte's mother.

Charlotte already had one of those.

Everyone already does.

Christmas Eve. Amy had been cooking for two days. She poured herself and Eric flutes of champagne, both quickly downed and refilled. For dinner, there was honeyed ham *and* a roast turkey, plus truffle mashed potatoes, artichoke casserole, homemade croissants, prosciutto-wrapped asparagus, and pregnant pauses.

How scrumptious. Charlotte went back for thirds.

She hadn't realized it had come to this. Having spent unprecedented amounts of time at home with the two of them over the past few months, Charlotte had noticed Amy asserting herself in unprecedented ways. When ordering pizza, Charlotte and Eric would want sausage and olive, but Amy would have a hankering for Hawaiian. Father and daughter would be fine using paper napkins; Amy would insist on cloth.

Father and daughter would crack open a few windows on hot afternoons; Amy would insist Eric buy a swamp cooler, then install it.

Now, Charlotte sensed something desperate in Amy. Charlotte tried to lock eyes with her father across the table, to corroborate this, but there was no need. He was watching Amy with a look of sympathy—as if dinner were a gift *for* her, an act of Christmas charity. Over peach cobbler, he suggested they all go for a drive to look at Christmas lights.

Amy clapped like a preschool teacher. Wonderful idea, she said. Do y'all have some Christmas music we could bring?

Charlotte was thinking the same thing—conversation avoidance—and mentioned a radio station that played holiday tunes 24/7. In unison, Amy and Eric said, *Perfect.*

While piling into the Saab, Amy stepped in front of Charlotte and squirmed into the back seat. Charlotte could not remember Amy ever once riding back there, making the gesture all the more theatrical. And Charlotte felt a sudden sadness for this woman who had never been anything but nice to her.

Eric turned the key. The engine did not respond. He tried again. *Click*, silence. The battery warning light came on. Amy started investigating, seeking an explanation—a vanity light left on, a door left ajar . . .

Charlotte? Amy said. Be a doll and check if that cigarette lighter somehow got pushed in . . .

It didn't, Eric said bluntly, before Charlotte could check.

Later, Amy's Dodge and Eric's Saab kissed bumpers, electricity traveling from surplus to deficit, resuscitating. The Saab started. They drove around and looked at lights.

But the battery didn't hold its charge overnight, and the next morning—Christmas Day—Charlotte walked with Eric to a gas station to buy a new one.

I'm just so sorry, Eric said out of the blue.

For what? Charlotte thought, but didn't ask. Nor did Eric explain.

But, it'll get better, he went on. Maybe we should go back to how things were. When we got here.

Charlotte nodded carefully, and said, Except with Amy.

Eric turned to his daughter. Is that what you want? he asked.

Charlotte was reminded of her late-night negotiation with Amy. Amy, too, had wondered what *Charlotte* thought to be the best course of action. But Charlotte had always preferred influence over voting rights. With nothing to be counted, no public record.

She turned it back to him: Is that what *you* want?

I'm not in this alone, Eric said.

They crossed the gas station parking lot. Eric tugged on the door to find it locked. Because, you know, it was *Christmas*. There was a hand-written sign.

Oh, Eric said. Right.

Maybe you liked her better on the radio, Charlotte said.

Eric looked at her for a long moment. Charlotte couldn't tell if she had impressed or depressed him. He gave a sad little chuckle, and two days later on an overcast morning Amy loaded up all her stuff and drove back to Texas and Eric shut himself in his room and Charlotte was left in the kitchen alone to wonder if she should rejoice or repent.

By late afternoon Eric still hadn't shown himself. Charlotte tapped on his door. Dad? she said.

A horrible silence. Charlotte realized he'd slipped out of the house without her knowing. No, worse: he'd . . .

A noise from within.

Charlotte pressed her palm to the door. Do you need anything? she asked. I could fry some eggs.

She heard the creaking of floorboards. The door opened. Her father stood there hunched, squinting out from the gloom. Charlotte could only gape. Impossibly, he seemed to have already decayed. The shine in his hair was duller, the lines of his face deeper. He patted her shoulder as he passed. She followed him down the hallway to the kitchen.

You gonna do the cooking around here now, then? he said. He went into the pantry and got out a bottle of wine.

I can try, Charlotte said.

He fished a corkscrew out of a drawer. You can try, he said.

Standing at the edge of the gaping hole she'd made in his life, Charlotte said the only thing she knew to be true at that moment: I wish this hadn't happened, Dad.

He opened the wine as Charlotte watched. He seemed to sense her wanting.

It's okay, honey, he said. It's not your fault.

Charlotte

2010

I HAVE TROUBLE with this part. I almost wish we could just skip it. But to where?

For one thing, it is here we first encounter my character. Or lack thereof, I don't know. At least mine's a mere bit part at this point. Hard for me to watch though.

When I moved to La Jolla I did as one does and took up golf. Which is to say, I signed up for a private lesson at Torrey Pines. The pro showed me some things. He filmed my swing with his iPad. He held it up for me to see the way a barber holds up a mirror to show you the back of your head.

That's what I look like? I said.

Have you heard of the observer effect? A universal, unavoidable truth that the act of observing something—a monkey, an electron—will affect the thing being observed. So that we can never observe something in its true state. Perhaps my golf swing is actually a thing of beauty until said swinger is filmed. Which causes him to swing self-consciously.

Such that he looks like he's not so much *taking* a stroke as *having* one.

I took no further golf lessons. I switched to Frisbee golf. No one takes *that* seriously enough to think of filming it.

The observer effect, though, is often conflated with Heisenberg. Who in 1927 proved what has to me always seemed a sad truth: the better we know a particle's position, the worse we know its speed. And vice versa. To see where an electron is, for example, we might shine a light at it. But when the light hits our little electron, it changes the little thing's course! So, sure: we knew where the electron *was* when the light hit it, but now we're not so sure where it went skittering off too. Nor how fast it's skittering. Damn it, right?

I mention this tough truth of physics in the context of Charlotte's second chapter because I fear that my collisions with her in those early months may have altered her course for the worse. Our first encounter was tiny, momentary. I shined a light on her as she traversed the darkest place she'd ever gone. We talked for just a minute. I figured out who she was (Eric's daughter). Then I lost track of her again. And I've wondered whether what I said to her that night put her on a more dangerous tangent than she might otherwise have traveled? Over time, I got to see her more often. We did a lot of drinking, a lot of kvetching, she and I. My impact was small, sure. But nonzero, nonetheless. Change the course of a ship at sea by half a degree, see if it reaches the right port a few days later.

I mean, *hell*. The fact that I'm a writer and constantly trying to find the story in everything and everyone . . . am I *changing* everything and everyone around me in the process? And for the better, or the worse? Does everything I touch turn to theater? I hope not. But I know better.

Mom . . .

Charlotte?

I'm at Scripps.

The pier?

The hospital.

Sorry, I'm not hearing you all that well, honey. They keep making announcements—all these delayed planes. I'm stuck in Philadelphia. Can you hear me okay?

Mom.

Yes?

It's Dad . . .

Charlotte, are you okay? It sounds like you're crying.

Charlotte said nothing, only made little sounds.

Charlotte? I'm right here. What is it?

No you're not, Mom. You're not right here. You're in fucking *Philadelphia.*

I know. Just, please tell me what's going on.

Dad . . .

Yes? Dad what?

Another reason I have such a hard time in this part of the story is because "finders keepers, losers weepers" floods me with guilt. Me being the "keeper" in this case. The biggest—no, probably the *only*—unqualified gain in my whole life has been made possible by the biggest loss in others'.

Charlotte climbed the porch steps. She turned the same key she'd been given the privilege of turning the first time she and her father unlocked this door. The lights inside the bungalow were off. She entered. Hung her father's backpack on the coat rack. Where it belonged. She started toward the recliner but crumpled to the hardwood floor halfway there.

Charlotte was by this time twenty years old. A child of divorce, a collegiate swimmer. She'd been away at college for a year. A big girl. She had shed her share of tears, collapsed more than once from exhaustion. But never once had she let herself go, not completely.

Nor had she that day. She'd kept it together. From the moment she knew something was wrong—when her father slipped from her periphery and she cut her stroke short to roll over and tread water and take in a breath and peer below the undulating ocean surface and see him, dangling there, just above the deeper, darker water—she'd kept it together. She took hold of his limp arm and lifted (as he'd once done to her, pulling her out of a pool). She did it at first in reflex. Then she tried again in disbelief. Then in shock. Then in sheer terror. Because each time she tried to lift him it was in vain. Since that moment, she'd felt like *she* was the one underwater. The world's sounds damped, its motions decelerated.

When confronted at the cove by lifeguards, then EMTs, and later at the hospital by nurses and finally by her own reflection in a hospital restroom, Charlotte had just kept nodding. Accommodating. A doctor and a social worker had greeted her in the waiting area. They'd asked her to follow them into a quiet hallway. She'd nodded at them, too, but didn't follow them like they'd asked her to, not at first. If she didn't step aside with them and hear what they had to tell her, nothing could happen. Nothing could change.

They wouldn't let her leave the hospital. But that's all she wanted to do. When it became clear they had no legitimate hold on her, she left. The Saab was still parked back at the cove, so she got into a taxi at the hospital's front curb. She muttered the address, then became a statue. The taxi squeaked and rattled its way down the bluff. The driver didn't try to make small talk. For this kindness, Charlotte folded an extra $10 bill in half the way her father did and handed it forward with the fare. She made her way up the porch.

The house was too quiet. It didn't sound anything like home. It didn't feel that way either. It felt to her more like she was breaking in. Curled up on the floor, she screamed once into her hands. She started to cry. And for the first time in her entire life, Charlotte fell apart completely.

She spent the night in the recliner. In the morning, the sunlight was unfettered and angular. For a few seconds after she woke up she didn't yet remember. Precious seconds.

She cinched the drawstrings of her hooded sweatshirt and curled up. Her mind returned to the unreal phone call the day before. To the long moments after she'd spoken the word *dead*, during which neither Charlotte nor Nancy spoke. Just as neither Charlotte nor Eric had been able to find words right after Charlotte first spoke the word *divorce*.

The chair's leather was cool to the touch. Charlotte inhaled its smell. She conjured snippets of her father napping through a Padres game, or peering down through reading glasses at her homework.

She hadn't eaten for a day. In the refrigerator she found a Styrofoam clamshell containing a lone triangle of Texas toast and a Chinese takeout tub clotted with fried rice. The pantry offered bags of microwave popcorn and three bottles of merlot. The freezer, a half bottle of Smirnoff.

She walked to the grocery store. She bought two frozen pizzas and a gallon jug of orange juice. She passed a familiar contraption in the store's breezeway. When Charlotte was younger, Eric would give her a quarter to drop into this contraption's slot. Together they'd watch it roll down the ramp and circumnavigate a big, parabolic cone, the radius of the coin's path diminishing with every orbit until it reached the tubular outlet and became entrancingly centrifugal, describing tight little circles until, finally, dropping out of sight into the donation bin below: *plink*. Eric would of course make a physics lesson out of it. Charlotte would beg for more quarters. Then put them in the soda machine.

The one and only person Charlotte needed around, to talk her through this—to explain it to her—was *him*. She wanted him back more than she'd ever wanted anything. She would have taken any version of him: the docile-but-content father she'd known before the divorce; the down-but-rebounding one she'd known after; the chubby, happy one he'd become with Amy; the chubbier, depressed one he'd become after Amy was gone.

Now he was gone. For the rest of Charlotte's life.

And no matter how many times Charlotte retold herself the

story of how that happened—asking *why* at every twist, the way she used to do during bedtime stories—the answer was always the same: *because of me*. There was no escaping that drain. *Plink*.

Nancy's flight into San Diego was delayed. She called from Chicago to tell Charlotte not to wait up; she'd just take a taxi to a hotel.

Charlotte could see it was different for her mother. It had been a decade since Nancy had rinsed Eric's whiskers from a sink. Nor was Nancy encountering him now. She hadn't stepped around the hamper of his laundry in the hallway, hadn't faced the oscilloscope on his radio desk, a phosphorescent sine wave still burning its ghost into the display.

On the call, her mother had listed logistical necessities that would never have crossed Charlotte's mind. Charlotte couldn't help but feel relieved by this. For one thing, Nancy was arranging to have Eric's body cremated. It was what he'd told her he wanted. Once. Before. But Nancy didn't know or remember what he'd wanted done with his ashes. The remainders, she'd accidentally called them before correcting herself: the *remains*.

Still, there were things even Director Nancy Chu couldn't, or wouldn't, handle. There was a call to be made, for one.

Charlotte slid a pizza into the oven and set a timer. She rummaged through the junk drawer and found what she was after: a little leather book. The pages emitted the faint phosphoric stink of the matchbooks also stored in the drawer. Charlotte didn't find the name she was after.

There was a small hourglass in the drawer, too. Charlotte held it up and watched unthinkingly for a moment as the grains of white sand tumbled though. She could actually hear and feel them tinkling against the glass.

She poured some of Eric's vodka and some of her orange juice into a big plastic cup. The drink was as harsh as she liked, and she downed it while she ate the pizza in front of the TV. The laugh track ebbed and flowed.

She mixed another drink and headed to the backyard. The night was cloudless. She leaned against the chimney, methodically crushing ice in her teeth and recalling the sight of her father repelling down the bricks. Her eyes were sore from crying.

Evening, someone said.

Startled, Charlotte peered down the alley. Then a rustling came from the other direction—the neighbor's yard, where she noticed now a man standing near the fence. She remembered someone moving into that house about the time she was moving out. The man grinned. He, too, had a drink in his hand—a tumbler that tinkled with ice as he raised it in salute. To what he raised it, Charlotte could not guess.

You're Charlotte, right? he said.

Yes, she said, composing herself. Sorry. I didn't see you there.

Having been watched for a moment unguarded, Charlotte felt exposed: this man somehow knew her, and had just seen her reckoning with her darkest thoughts. There seemed no need, then, for introductions, only conclusions. He seemed of similar mind.

It's sadder at night, he offered. I think because we can see so much further.

Charlotte thought about that. Yeah, she said. Maybe.

The man took a drink. He studied her.

I'm Z, he said. I know your dad a little bit. A wonderful guy . . .

Charlotte didn't care to correct the tense of Z's verbs. Not that night.

Z prattled on. He talks about you, he said. Hell, you're practically *all* he talks about.

Sorry about that, she said.

No. It's great. I don't have children of my own. So I like keeping up with how you're doing.

Charlotte nodded.

Z said, I guess that makes me a long-time listener, first-time caller. He laughed.

Charlotte stared at nothing.

Your dad around? Z said.

Charlotte shook her head. It was too much. She forced a wave, politely bid her nosy neighbor goodnight, and escaped back inside the bungalow.

Leaving me in the dark.

Charlotte was lying on the single bed in Eric's room that he'd bought when he and Charlotte first moved to La Jolla. The better part of his room had been conceded to radio equipment. The room was spinning. She had a thought. She climbed out of bed and slipped down the hall to the kitchen. Went back to the junk drawer. Got the leather book out again. She opened the microwave door to get some light, then flipped to the N's. And there it was, in all caps, two lines below "Nancy": *NIXIE.*

Before Charlotte could reconsider, she dialed the ghost of Christmas past.

Hello?

Charlotte was startled by the voice—that of a young girl.

Sorry, Charlotte said. I think maybe I dialed wrong? I'm calling for Amy . . .

A rustling on the line, then a muffled shout: *Maw-awm!*

Seconds later, a different voice. The one Charlotte knew all too well, having used it as her own many times to get a laugh. Hello, it said.

Amy? Charlotte said.

Yes, ma'am. Who am I speaking to?

It's—this is Charlotte.

Charlotte . . . Eric's Charlotte?

Yes.

Well, I'll be!

Sorry, Charlotte said. I just realized. It's probably kind of late there.

Oh, it's no trouble, honey! Me and Francine here are up watchin' a movie. Matter of fact, I been meanin' to email you. I found some pictures the other day . . .

Is that who answered—Francine?

Right. Yes. She's my daughter.

Adopted, Amy explained. Maybe a year after I left La Jolla? Yeah, I guess that's about when.

Wow, Charlotte said, trying to regain composure. Good for you.

She's my little angel.

Amy, Charlotte said flatly. I'm calling . . . I need to tell you something.

Shoot.

My dad died.

A gasp, then silence. Lasting longer than Charlotte could bear, so she broke it. It was a heart attack.

Oh my god, Charlotte. Oh my god . . . When?

Yesterday.

Charlotte teetered on a ledge. She steered toward the lesser of two regrets. I'm sorry to be the one to tell you, Amy. I know you and I didn't—that I wasn't very fair to you. Before.

Oh, you poor, poor thing. My heart's just beatin' out of my chest for you. How are you doin'? Are you doin' okay?

Yeah, Charlotte said. Not really.

No. Of course . . . I just, I can't even fathom it, honey.

Charlotte was knocked off balance. It was impossible just how *nice* the woman was, and had always been. What a beautiful thing, to be kind to someone you had every right to hate. What a strong thing.

I'm supposed to ask, Charlotte said. Did he ever say anything, you know, about what he wanted . . . like, with his ashes?

Oh, Amy said. Well. I think we did talk about it once. *Hell.* You know, just a silly thing people talk about in the dark. As if it'll never happen.

Do you remember what he said?

I wanna say he thought to leave it in *your* hands. For you to decide.

Me?

No one knows him better, honey.

Charlotte's first reaction was to deny this. She searched her mind for names she might list off, people better suited to the task, old pals who *really* knew her father.

But . . . *who*? Nancy?

Charlotte felt an unexpected tingle of pride, of solidarity—her first dose in days.

Amy started whispering away from the phone.

You need to go, Charlotte said.

No, no. I'm right here.

It's fine, Charlotte said—though she did have something more on her intoxicated mind. She said, Can I ask you something first?

Of course, dear.

Do you hate me?

Charlotte. Absolutely not. You know that.

I didn't, actually. Because, well, you *should.* You know *that*?

People change, Amy said.

The past doesn't, Charlotte said.

Thank you for calling, darling. It's big of you.

But Charlotte had never felt so small.

Charlotte woke with a pounding head. Her bones ached. She threw cold water on her face in the bathroom, then headed down the hallway, steadying herself against the wall. In the kitchen, documents and folders had been sorted into piles on the counters, on the burners of the stove. Nancy leaned against the sink. She was staring out the window the way Eric used to. She'd helped herself to some of Charlotte's orange juice.

You're here, Charlotte said.

Nancy crossed the kitchen and Charlotte let herself be held

for a moment. Then she pulled the junk drawer out so far it drooped. She started to rummage.

What're you after? Nancy asked.

Pain medicine.

For what?

Pain, Charlotte muttered.

Nancy produced some ibuprofen from her briefcase. Charlotte held out a supplicant palm. Nancy shook the bottle over it. A pill tumbled out, then two more. Nancy reached out to take the third one back, but Charlotte closed her fingers over them. She uncurled her fingers, twice: *more*. Nancy hesitated, obliged. One more. *Plink*.

Charlotte washed down the pills with orange juice straight from the jug. The taste was reminiscent of the screwdrivers and made her cringe. And crave.

Talked to Amy, Charlotte said.

Oh? Nancy said.

She said Dad wanted *me* to decide.

Nancy went rigid. Charlotte headed back down the hall to take a bath. She saw herself in the bathroom mirror. At one time, her biggest trouble had been deciding who to resent the most. That was no longer a problem. She was looking right at her.

The raging sadness she saw in her own eyes was autocatalytic. She chased it deeper, and deeper.

She felt the same bottomlessness half an hour later when looking across the kitchen table into her mother's crying eyes. By then Charlotte had no tears left. They'd all gone down the drain. Charlotte's head was wrapped in a towel. The ibuprofen had kicked in. She felt numb, drained, and slightly more human. It's Sunday, she realized aloud.

It is, Nancy said.

And what a normal day it appeared. Blue sky when it ought to have been black. Sometimes, when your mood is wrong, nothing can be more callous than Southern California sunshine, forecasted to stick around into the coming century.

Nancy weighed in about Eric's desire for Charlotte to handle his ashes. The word Nancy used was *appropriate*. Charlotte could see that Nancy, too, had just lost the man of her life. Charlotte resented that a little. She felt she should bear this weight, this invisible enormity, alone.

I've been looking at his finances, Nancy said. He was always so disorganized, but . . . Well, it isn't as bad as I expected. I've emailed Fred Rhodes. You remember Fred, he handled our divorce?

I wasn't really involved with that, Charlotte said. Not the finances, at least.

Well, I'll get it sorted. You just focus on the ceremony, okay?

That must be it, Charlotte thought: this was her mother's way of coping—reducing Eric to numbers. A solvable problem. A "remainder."

Are you hungry? Nancy asked.

I don't know, Charlotte said.

Me neither.

The two women remained at the kitchen table, neither of them taking action.

I made him go out there, Mom, Charlotte said. I made him get in the water.

He had a heart attack, Charlotte. That is not your fault.

I turned him into what he was. I ruined him.

Please, Nancy said. Nobody ever made that man do anything he didn't want to do.

He loved Amy, Mom. He wanted to be with her. He just kept waiting to see if I could love her too. But I didn't even try. I made him stop loving her. *Me*. I did that.

Relationships are complicated, Charlotte. Look at your parents. We didn't last, but that wasn't because of you.

Charlotte got up and stared into an empty refrigerator. This was different, she said. After Amy left, Dad was a wreck. You didn't see him. You have no idea.

Oh, I've seen him that way before, Nancy said.

Not like this, Mom. He *gave up*. He started drinking all the time. But he still taught. He came to my meets. People saw him, they thought he was fine, happy—but he was happy for *me*.

Charlotte could still see Eric at the pool, smiling down at her from his spot atop the bleachers. At the beach he wore his UCSD Gilligan hat, but at meets he wore a ball cap with her school's seahorse mascot on it. He found it amusing that the school had adopted such a tiny, vulnerable creature for a mascot. Once, during a visit to Scripps Aquarium, Charlotte and Eric had stared, mesmerized, into a tank of seahorses bobbing on invisible currents. Charlotte had read aloud from the placard about how the males carry the babies in pouches on their bellies.

Kind of weird, father and daughter had decided. But kind of cool, too.

Nancy unspooled a square of paper towel and blew her nose into it.

Charlotte nibbled a fingernail. Maybe being away at school helped me see it better, you know, when I came home. Dad looked *fat*. He was wearing those grubby sweats . . .

Not the orange Broncos ones, Nancy said.

Charlotte nodded.

I hated those, Nancy said.

I went into his room, Charlotte said. I actually went into his drawer and got out his bathing suit. I *brought* it to him, Mom. I said, *Let's go swimming, right now*. And he said, *Let's*.

Nancy reached across the table and put her hand on Charlotte's. What you're feeling is perfectly natural. I've been reading up on this.

Of course you have, Charlotte said. You think you can *manage* it.

I don't, Nancy said, calmer than Charlotte would have liked. I'm trying to get some sense of the process is all. Don't you think it's better if we understand what's happening to us?

Us, Charlotte scoffed.

Yes, *us*. Don't act like this is only happening to you.

I don't believe it *is* happening.

And because Charlotte had not yet caught up to the present, she was able at that moment to stare right through her mother and out the window into the mercilessly blue sky. She could still see her father's body sprawled across a boogie board as she and a pair of Filipino boys paddled him awkwardly back to the beach, Charlotte screaming over and over and over for a lifeguard. Charlotte would never forget her father's eyes. His pupils were big and black and empty. Death already in them.

Nancy spent Sunday night at her hotel. Monday, she was back with bagels by the time Charlotte woke up.

A small, nondescript white box had materialized on the kitchen table.

Charlotte kept an eye on it as she ate a bagel. Nancy read aloud names listed on a yellow pad. Charlotte's job was to say yea or nay as to who should be invited to the small, nondescript, (not entirely white) memorial service slated for the coming Sunday. The details of this service remained hazy.

Tony D., Nancy said.

He's a grad student, Charlotte said. Probably a no.

Tony R.

Wait, there's two Tonys?

Charlotte expected her ignorance in these matters to piss her mother off. But Nancy didn't get angry. Charlotte was reminded of just how good her mother could be at cutting out emotion, at concerning herself solely with The Data. It was as comforting as it was frightening. It made it easier for Charlotte to pose this question: What about Amy?

What about her? Nancy said.

Just, she knows about Dad. Not the memorial, though.

Nancy set her pen in her teeth. I defer to you, she said. I've never met the woman. But—well, I can see how she might be considered.

Charlotte rubbed her eyes. She'd hoped Nancy would outright object, making the decision simple. Maybe she won't want to come, Charlotte said. It's pretty short notice.

Very short, Nancy agreed.

Charlotte had no idea what to do with the ashes. Maybe they belonged back in Colorado, where Eric had grown up. Or maybe San Jose. Nancy told Charlotte to give the matter *appropriate* consideration. Also, that they needed an answer very soon.

Meantime, the little box made its way to the mantle, where it sat like a polite, waylaid traveler.

On Tuesday, Nancy took Charlotte to an Ann Taylor in the La Jolla Village mall.

Charlotte tugged at the three-quarter sleeve of a taupe blouse. The air in the fitting room was bitter with perfume.

What if we have to hike a little? Charlotte asked.

Oh? Nancy perked up. Does that mean we've decided where the memorial will be?

Bass-less pop music seeped from unseen speakers.

It just means, Charlotte said, these clothes rule out some options.

That's a one-inch heel, Nancy said. You'll be fine.

Why do we have to dress up like it's church? Dad hates this kind of thing.

Nancy assessed Charlotte in the dressing room mirror. Turn to the side a little, she said.

A waifish attendant arrived and cleared space on a rack with her forearm—hangers rasping along the metal rod. She added the charcoal-gray, calf-length skirt Nancy had sent her to fetch. Charlotte could hardly look at herself. Even bathed in the flattering light, her skin was pale, her eyes sunken. Cool air blew from an overhead duct, and yet beads of sweat crept down her side beneath the fine fabrics.

Her grief arrived in rogue waves. It would come from out of nowhere and wash over her, hold her down. Her throat would tighten, her breathing shorten.

You look so nice, Nancy said.

I look like *you*, Charlotte said.

Charlotte had not gone this long without swimming in months. Two nights earlier, she'd managed to keep from drinking by taking a long jog to Pacific Beach and back. Last night she'd ended up scrubbing, vacuuming, and dusting the entire bungalow. She'd come upon the white box and forced herself to peel back the flaps. She'd believed it was her duty to familiarize herself with the stuff inside before bereaving eyes fell on her. She'd lifted out the little plastic sack.

So paltry, almost sacrilegious. A *plastic sack*.

It was tied shut in a knot, and weighed less than Charlotte had expected. The man of her life was now a handful of gray powder. Her fingertip had glanced against . . . something hard. A bone? A tooth? *My god* . . . She'd kneaded gently at the bag to get the object against the translucent plastic and discovered that it was a metal pin about the size and shape of a golf tee. It had a matte, bluish tint. Charlotte realized what it was. When she was young, her father had hurt his knee. He'd had surgery to repair the ligaments. She'd seen the scars every time he wore shorts. He'd brag when they roughhoused: *Beware: I'm part titanium!*

She'd put the bag back in the box and the box back on the mantle and tried to pretend it wasn't there.

At Nancy's insistence, Charlotte composed an email to each of her professors and her swim coach to explain her ongoing absence. This forced Charlotte to type, *My father passed away on Saturday*. It was surreal to see on a screen. The cursor blinked with the surety of a heartbeat, waiting for her to go on. Clicking *SEND* each time felt like throwing a rock through a window.

Two days later, on Thursday, Charlotte walked to a coffee shop to meet Nancy.

I'm going to be all over town today, Nancy said. I'll be with the lawyer, two accountants . . . Nancy looked up from her menu. So, she said. What's our plan?

Working on it, Charlotte said. She rose from the booth and said, I'll call you.

Wait, you're leaving? You just got here . . .

Also, Charlotte added, I let Amy know.

Know what?

About the memorial.

What is there to know at this point?

That there is one.

Nancy folded her hands and looked out the window. She said, We need a site, Charlotte. *Today*. What if we need to reserve something?

I know.

Should we just call it off? We can.

No.

Nancy sat with that for a moment, then said, You need breakfast.

I'll call you later, Charlotte said. She gave Nancy a curt hug and walked out of the restaurant. She found herself yet again bombarded by unrelenting sunlight. Traffic washed by. People hurrying places, life being lived. Charlotte had no destination in mind. Still, she walked with apparent purpose past the window of the restaurant just in case Nancy was watching.

Charlotte started northward. She wandered her old neighborhood until, eventually, semiconsciously, she rejoined the route her father had walked twice a day for years—many times with Charlotte along. She picked her way up through the Scripps campus. Up the steep paved roads and railroad-tie staircases. She emerged atop a bluff. The trail continued across a field to the UCSD campus, where Charlotte had once sat through

Eric's lectures. She left the trail and walked through a grove of eucalyptus to a promontory. She sat in the windswept grass.

She had sought perspective. Well, she'd found it. Panning left to right from where she sat, one can see the green, mansion-bedecked hills of La Jolla. Rising from the ridgelines are the tall radio antennas. The large white cross atop Mount Soledad looks like an antenna, too, actually.

Charlotte's eyes contoured down to La Jolla proper, with its buildings and palm trees and crooked streets, its coves and cliffs, then back along the shoreline to the Shores Beach, the thousand-foot Scripps Pier, and finally out into the hazy coastal juttings to the north. Sun bathed her skin. Gulls cawed and quarreled above the bluff. She inhaled the onshore breeze—the air rich and brackish and tangible—and stared out at an undulating belt of kelp a few hundred yards offshore.

She'd been thinking lately about the young man who used to wander La Jolla with his Great Dane and his llama. How the trio had been something of an institution. We locals had thought of the man as one of our own, a happy-go-lucky knockabout.

We hadn't known him from Adam. When he handcuffed himself to a buoy anchor twenty feet underwater at La Jolla cove, news had spread quickly. A surprisingly thorough obituary had run in the *Union Tribune*. We had expressed our shock and dismay. Kids at Charlotte's school had wondered aloud, *What'll happen to the dog and the llama?*

Charlotte decided: she'd definitely known her father. He was *Dad*. But *Eric*? Well, *he* was a stranger. *Eric* had worked and fished in Alaska. *Eric* had fallen in love with a barrel racer from Amarillo. So how could Charlotte possibly intuit what *he* would have wanted?

Sitting together in the bungalow's front room one Sunday morning, watching sunlit motes drift past the front window, her father had explained how waves of light are forever bursting from a fiery speck—a sun—and traversing a vast emptiness at the speed of time itself to arrive mere minutes later at an even smaller speck—a planet. And Charlotte had been asked to take all this in, to think it over, but it left her feeling small and sad and she'd thought about other things. That day, as she stared out at the Pacific, she saw more waves there, arriving from all over the world. Every few seconds another one made landfall, just below her. The Scripps Pier intercepted them; they resonated the pier's concrete pillars. The waves crashed against the coast, patiently pulverizing an entire continent to bits of sand. The sand itself was made of even smaller bits—too small to see—which never ceased to vibrate, and in so doing, to make waves. To broadcast their infinite, infinitesimal messages.

Who could possibly parse it all?

Her father had been more of an asker than a teller when it came to teaching. So many things he'd taught her. Almost everything.

How to swim out of a riptide.

How Earth's atmosphere lets only a thin band of frequencies through—the radio window.

On nights when she was young, Charlotte had joined Eric at the radio desk after her bath. He'd introduce her to whomever he was talking to. Often, she'd coax him into singing with her. Always the same song. Charlotte hadn't known who Mother Mary was. Nor, at five years old, had she yet experienced a single hour of darkness. Not true darkness. She'd just liked the Beatles. But it struck her then that those radio waves were still out there somewhere, hurtling across space, countless miles away. A father and daughter harmonizing for whoever cared to listen.

The father Charlotte knew would never stand for some awkward gathering: *Nancy shaking hands with Amy for the first time; a Colorado family Eric hadn't seen in years pretending to feel the same sadness Charlotte did; finger food . . .* The father she knew, the one she'd called Dad, was the only person she could ever hope to please, retroactively. *Eric* was on his own.

And Charlotte knew then what she *didn't* want. She didn't

want people around, staring at her, saying comforting things, when she knew all of them blamed her at least a little for what had happened. As she believed they should. Not because she'd taken her frail father swimming in open water. But because she'd not let him be happy on his own terms. Only hers.

She stood up from the grass and brushed herself off. She was decided.

She walked back down the hill to the bungalow. The place was empty. She went to the bookshelf in the main room. There was a framed photograph there. (It is there still.) A close-up of Charlotte from before she and Eric moved to La Jolla, before the divorce. Charlotte has on a pair of big, goofy sunglasses in which a figure is reflected: Eric. Holding up a bulky, flashing camera. The look on Charlotte's young face is one of certainty. Maybe that's what Eric liked about the picture. It shows a girl who still trusted the world, who believed it would stay whole, who believed in *him* like she believed in the very ground she stood on.

Her father was in many places at once, yes. But also only in a single place: the small white box. Charlotte took him down off the mantle. She held him in her hands. She located the backpack hanging in the entryway, right where she'd left it a week ago. He was her weight to bear. She nestled him back inside the bag and zipped it shut.

This was what he'd want.

She walked out of the house, down the porch and up the sidewalk. She walked quickly lest her doubt catch up to her. If everyone chose to blame her from afar, fine. Charlotte hoped they did. She welcomed it. They couldn't hate her any more than she hated herself.

And, how do you get out of a riptide, honey?

Swim sideways to the current.

Good girl.

Charlotte reached the beach. Nothing there had changed. There were wheeling seagulls. People were folded into folding chairs. Pigeons pecked along the promenade. Children held quivering kites earthbound. A biplane struggled up the coast, all but flying in place, burdened by the banner it towed. Charlotte kicked off her sandals and marched across the white sand. The tide was high. She headed north. As she passed under the pier she was compelled to lay a palm upon one of the mussel-ensconced pylons. She hoped to feel some faint shudder in the concrete, but could not.

Reemerging in sunlight on the opposite side, she knelt and unzipped the backpack. She took out the box, peeled back the flaps, and tugged out the sack. She worked her fingernail into the single knot and loosened it.

She left the backpack on the dry sand and waded out into the water. The crashing waves stirred the sand up into a liquidy, churning amalgamation. The sea coursed around her knees, wetting the cuffs of her shorts. She hadn't been absolutely sure until this moment. This was what her father would have wanted because it's what *she* wanted. As sad as that made her.

She upended the bag. The ashes and pieces tumbled out. Some of the gray dust lifted on the breeze and was carried off, but the bulk spilled into the foaming water and dissolved into the next wave as it rolled through. And it was done.

He was gone.

Charlotte wiped her eyes and her nose on the sleeve of her sweatshirt.

It had not been a weight she'd had to bear, she realized. It had been just the opposite, and would always be. It was an emptiness through which waves could move. This was her father's final lesson.

I'm sorry, she whispered. I miss you.

Charlotte stood knee deep in the sun-spangled Pacific. She closed her eyes and he was standing right in front of her.

I love you, she said.

Goodbye, she said.

Arriving home, she hung his backpack on its hook and went to the kitchen and poured what remained of the vodka into what remained of the orange juice in the plastic jug and went back outside to sit in the undying California sunshine and await the coming storm.

Zhiyu/Jerry

2010

WE RETURN NOW to Zhiyu/Jerry. Why?

Good question. I've heard it said that we do not understand the truth of something unless we can track it back to its core by asking "why" seven times. How about eleven:

1. Why did Nancy end up on my porch that night? Because her daughter Charlotte needed help.
2. Why did Charlotte need help? Because her life was a wreck.
3. Why was Charlotte's life a wreck? Because she blamed herself for her father's death.
4. Why did she blame herself? Because she hadn't let her father keep Amy.
5. Why hadn't she let him keep Amy? Because she wanted him for herself.
6. Why had she wanted him for herself? Because she loved him so much.
7. Why did she love him so much? Because he was her father.

8. Why was Eric her father? Because Eric and Nancy made love.

9. Why did Eric and Nancy make love? Because Nancy decided he was the one.

10. Why did Nancy decide Eric was the one? Because her father, Zhiyu, said so, in not so many words.

11. Why did Zhiyu say so, in not so many words? Because of a *plink*.

Care to hear it? Let's keep listening . . .

Zhiyu had a favorite chair. He'd found it years earlier in the gutter by his bus stop. He'd looked up and down the street, hoisted the chair upside down over his head, and carried it back to his store, where it stayed for over a decade.

It was a mahogany swivel desk chair. At its max height setting (and using a blanket for a seat pad) it put Zhiyu high enough to comfortably run the register. Running the register was really all he did by then, in 2010. He had stock boys to carry the things he and his wife, Fei Yen, could no longer carry. He'd hired clerks to work the shifts they no longer wanted. The chair was not dual-purpose like the step-stool/chair combo thing they'd kept behind the register for years, and which was now solely a step stool, used for reaching items stocked high behind the front counter—the pricier liquors, the electronics. Zhiyu's favorite chair had caster wheels on two of its four feet. The other two feet rested, respectively, upon a white-pages-only phonebook and a can of expired Vienna sausage.

Zhiyu could not carry any type of chair over his head by then, in 2010. His doctor had explained that the inside of one's lungs is supposed to look like bunches of grapes.

What do my lungs look? Zhiyu had asked.

Like raisins, the doctor had said.

In Zhiyu's lungs, fresh air got pulled in, lingered, grew stale.

In fact, regular, ambient, fresh air no longer sufficed for Zhiyu in 2010, but leave it to the Americans to solve that! Zhiyu now breathed 100 percent pure oxygen, piped to his nostrils from a tank. The oxygen could be a fire hazard though. So he left the tank behind the counter when he went out on the sidewalk to smoke.

Having lived in the U.S. since before 1972, Zhiyu was in 1996 eligible to become a naturalized citizen. Which he did. His correctly bubbled Scantron and his sincere pledge of allegiance entitled him to Medicare, with all the oxygen of government-assured purity he could breathe. *What a system!* Zhiyu thought. He also thought this: *Get what you can get, while you can get it.* Life being surprising, life being short. Two weeks ago, Zhiyu's former son-in-law, Eric, died in the arms of Zhiyu's granddaughter, Charlotte, while they were swimming—something both of them were very good at. But the store could not shut down out of sadness.

So Zhiyu was back in his favorite chair.

It was an exceptionally sunny, almost hot, October afternoon in South San Francisco. A trio of teenagers came in. They went straight for the ICEE machine and were soon dispensing more of the bright red slush into the dome-lidded cups than the cups could hold. They were laughing and licking at the little eruptions, tracking stickiness across the checkered linoleum with their flip-flops, when a woman in a wide sunhat and sunglasses came in. No one came or went from Zhiyu's store without his notice. He had caught dozens of shoplifters without the use of cameras or mirrors. He relied upon old-fashioned vigilance. The stink eye.

The sun-hatted woman lingered at the refrigerated display cases in the back. When Zhiyu first opened the store he'd had three such cases—one for soda and beer, one for dairy items, and one for frozen foods. Now the cases ran the full length of two walls and displayed increasingly tall, increasingly caffeinated, increasingly sweet drinks. That's what the people wanted, so that's what Zhiyu sold. *Such a beautifully simple system!*

The kids paid all separately for their ICEEs using debit cards. They talked to each other as if Zhiyu were not there. As if they were sliding their cards into a vending machine, not a calloused, tendony, smoke-yellowed human hand. The store was empty again by the time the woman glided up the aisle and set a box of almond cookies and two bottles of water on the worn Formica counter. She lifted her hat. Black hair tumbled out. Zhiyu tilted his head, suddenly welling with recognition, suddenly lacking oxygen.

Hi, Dad, she said.

Zhiyu inhaled from his tubes. He managed to say his daughter's name.

She came behind the counter and planted a kiss on his head. How you feeling? she asked.

Good, Zhiyu said. Good!

Mom tells me you're off at 3:00.

You see Mom? You go to house?

Your doctor said you shouldn't be here.

He say cut back.

Nancy nodded, plucking a tiny bottle of energy drink from a display and studying it. And? she said. Have you?

A little, Zhiyu said. He looked out the window. Oxygen hissed gently and coolly into his nostrils. It not so simple, he said.

Nancy ripped into the bag of cookies. She took one out and bit it in half. Let's get you out of here, she said. I want to show you something.

A surprise!

I guess, Nancy said. Yes.

Zhiyu was confused: a hint of disdain had crept into his daughter's voice. When Nancy was in high school, there had been days—weeks!—during which this particular tone was the only one she ever took with Zhiyu and especially with Fei Yen—even when asking for money! But that was so long ago he'd forgotten its timbre and the bile it stirred in his gut. He glanced at a clock radio. A pudgy but trustworthy nephew of a family friend would be arriving momentarily to start his shift.

Where your car? Zhiyu asked.

Up the street a little.

I meet you outside, five minutes.

Nancy took a wallet from her purse and peeled it open. Zhiyu shooed it with both hands. His daughter had never paid for anything in his store.

Nancy nodded at the top shelf. What's your doctor say about Hennessy? she asked.

Same as for work, Zhiyu said. Same as for cigarette.

Can you even reach those bottles? she asked.

You want something? What you want?

I do.

Go get car, Zhiyu said with all the authority he could.

I don't want you . . .

Go!

Nancy shrugged. She stuffed the cookies and waters into her purse. Situated her hat back on her head. Did as her father told her.

Zhiyu waited until she was out of sight before he detached his oxygen and fetched the step stool.

Zhiyu settled into the taut leather passenger seat. *Lexus*, he said in a reverent sort of way. He glimpsed its sleek reflection in the glass of his storefront as they passed. He toggled the electric window down. Smells of the city flowed in.

Wanna drive? Nancy asked.

I don't know where we going.

True, Nancy said. Well, we're going south.

San Jose? I seen your condo, Zhiyu joked.

We're not going to my condo.

Nancy closed Zhiyu's window from her control panel while accelerating up the 101 onramp. Zhiyu considered reattaching his oxygen tube, but didn't: it would have been louder than even the engine in the sound-sealed cabin. What's more, it made him feel weak. When here beside him was one of two women on earth who'd ever thought him strong.

How Charlotte? Zhiyu asked, tangentially addressing the elephant in the back seat—her recently dead ex-husband, her daughter's ex-father, her father's ex-son-in-law.

She's, ah . . . she's still kind of a mess, Nancy said. You remember I went down there a few weeks ago, right after it happened? To be there with her and try to put things in order . . .

Your mom, she still not happy you cancel funeral.

No, Nancy said. But in the end, Charlotte and I decided it was best to just have a private little gathering. Just family.

We family.

Immediate family, Nancy said. Plus, it would have been very difficult for you to make the trip. Are you cool enough? Do you have enough air?

Zhiyu fiddled with an air-conditioning vent. Nancy adjusted some virtual dial.

I fine, I fine, Zhiyu said. He rubbed his sore knees. He could tell that Nancy wanted to leave the subject of Eric behind. But Zhiyu had not said his piece. His daughter had now lost Eric twice: first in divorce, and now in death. But she did not seem adequately defeated by this. She was acting *more* resolute, if anything. Zhiyu found this concerning.

When he met Fei Yen, he had tried to impress her with his potential. Potential was all he had to offer. Once he'd gotten his store, he'd slaved away to make her proud, to prove her right about him. Who, then, did Nancy have left to impress? Certainly not Charlotte, whom Nancy hardly spoke to. (Charlotte would have been more impressed if her mother *quit!*) Nancy and Fei Yen were more like gossiping friends now—and mostly they gossiped about Zhiyu. No. Zhiyu realized that it was he alone—her father—that Nancy remained determined to impress. This warmed his heart and it also ruined him. He was soon to be gone. She would be very much on her own. Didn't she see that? Shouldn't she face it?

Eric was very good person, Zhiyu said. Very good father. For Charlotte.

Yes, Nancy allowed. It'll be a long time before she gets over it.

She never get over it.

Right. Yes.

What about you? Zhiyu asked.

Nancy gave a rapid-fire answer about all the things on her plate: international travel, company politics, a company Tai Chi class she'd recently funded. Zhiyu turned in his seat to watch her drive. To really just look at her. She must have felt his gaze. She became a different person right before his eyes. Her younger self. Her shoulders hunched ever so slightly, her hands slipped from 10:00 and 2:00 on the wood-grained wheel and came to dangle together at 6:00.

I'm still processing it, she said. It'd been *months* since I'd spoken to Eric. A year since I'd *seen* him. Our lives went very different ways, Dad. So, when I got the call from Charlotte—well, it wasn't like I had time to dwell on it. There were all the logistics, the legal stuff. I didn't want Charlotte to have to deal with any of that. I've been very busy, and I just . . .

Zhiyu gave her a moment. Then he said, It good to be busy.

It is, Nancy said.

Everyone sad their own way.

Nancy didn't seem to hear him. She stared blankly up the road. The weekend traffic was light. She slipped out of the fast lane to pass a car not keeping fast-lane pace, apparently. The pressure in the cabin ticked up ever so gently.

Dad, Nancy said.

Mm.

Do you still think we were right for each other?

Who?

Eric and I.

How you mean.

Just, you told me that. Remember? The night you met him.

We ate duck.

Yes. We ate duck, and then you told me Eric was a good pick.

He was.

Yes. But for *me*?

Zhiyu closed his eyes. He was getting lethargic without his oxygen. Had this been a normal day, he would have fallen asleep against the bus window on his ride home from work, then resumed his nap when he reached his couch. An eight-hour shift now sapped him to the bone.

I'm serious, Nancy said. Do you think he was the right one for me?

Is that why you come get me?

No.

Zhiyu didn't want to say what he truly believed, and what his daughter seemed to believe as well, for saying it would be slanderous and unnecessary and not make things turn out differently. But he had to say something. Maybe not everyone have perfect match, he said.

Maybe not everyone needs one, she said.

Maybe, Zhiyu allowed, as he had all those years ago on his front stoop, telling Nancy what she most desperately needed to hear, true or not.

She settled back into the slow lane. The conversation died. By the time they reached San Mateo, Zhiyu was asleep. He was awoken as they exited a freeway he didn't recognize. They turned west into the low mountain range separating San Jose from the ocean.

Sorry, he said, stretching. I get sleepy.

Nancy petted his bony, arthritic knee, then returned her hand quickly to the wheel to steer them along a sharpening set of curves. Almost there, she said.

He was about to drift off again when she said, You're right

about Eric and Charlotte, by the way. What they had. It *was* special.

Mm.

Actually. I do think it's because of Eric I came to see you today.

I like surprises.

No you don't, Nancy said with a chuckle. Anyway, time is short. Right? Everyone says that, but you kind of just forget it's true. I've been at IBM *twenty-seven years*, Dad. And it's gone by like *that*. Nancy snapped her fingers.

Zhiyu nodded. He knew what time travel felt like, too.

I've been director for a year already, Dad, Nancy said. And you've never—never *seen* that. Don't you think that's a little strange?

At Zhiyu's store, sweet-and-sour candies were big sellers. Nancy's words had that flavor to him: sugarcoated resentment. Suddenly his window came halfway down, as if of its own accord. The road pitched upward, traversing yellow foothills. Zhiyu knew where they were going now. It should have been obvious to him all along. They rounded a curve and there it was. The complex tucked into the hills like some secret base. It was the size of two high schools. The parking lot took up acres. Manicured lawns, mature trees, water features, glass and steel, a trio of flagpoles—company, state, country.

Big, Zhiyu said.

Nancy pulled into a parking space with a sign bearing her name and title. The handicapped parking pass Zhiyu kept folded in his wallet wouldn't have gotten them any closer to the entrance. But it was a Saturday. The lot was mostly empty. Nancy got out and grabbed the oxygen tank and the Hennessy. Zhiyu groaned as he gripped the doorframe and eased himself out.

I no need, he said, pointing at the tank.

We have to walk a ways, Nancy said. Don't argue with me.

Okay. You the boss. Sign says!

Exactly, Nancy said.

Zhiyu situated the oxygen tube around his ears and below his nostrils, then trundled along behind his daughter toward the complex. She held her credential badge up to doors. The doors unlocked. They rode an elevator to a wood- and glass-adorned executive suite. A thick IBM logo was set into the wall above a desk with two large monitors on it.

Nice, Zhiyu asked. This your office?

That's the receptionist's desk, Nancy said. This way.

Their footfalls were lost in lush carpeting bearing fresh vacuum swaths. The squeaking axles of the oxygen cart made the only sound. Zhiyu searched his mind for a time he'd been inside a nicer office—some San Francisco bank, maybe?—but he could not think of one. This embarrassed him. He felt he should not be allowed here—with his ratty shoes, his yellowed collar, his silly English. His disgrace deepened to realize Nancy could tell he was impressed. Just not impressed in the way a man of the world is impressed. Not because he has seen grandeur and therefore recognizes it. He was impressed in the way a child is impressed. And he knew it in the way an old man knows something.

Nancy paused at a door and turned to wait. Zhiyu waddled down a hallway wider than his living room. Sorry, he said. I slow.

Nancy swung the door open. Reached in and flipped a bank of switches, illuminating the space with copious, tasteful lighting. Zhiyu approached. According to the placard, they'd finally reached the office of the director. The one Zhiyu once taught to walk. And count. And do calculus. But he hadn't taught her *this*.

Zhiyu felt about as meek and out of his element as he ever had.

Still, he could tell: Nancy wasn't angry with him for never

having been here. It was partly *her* fault, too, after all. Yes, he should have asked. He should have begged her to bring him to this office. While she had it. For Zhiyu knew that jobs could evaporate. He'd seen it happen many times to hard-working people. He'd never taken his store for granted. Humble as it was, it was his. It had paid for everything he'd ever needed.

Did Eric see this? he asked.

Eric? Nancy said—her voice a little off balance. Well, I guess. I'm sure he saw this office. Just . . . not while *I* was in it.

I think you wrong, Zhiyu said. I think he saw you in it, long time ago.

Nancy set the bottle of Hennessy on an end table but kept her hand on its neck. She looked to be steadying herself. Her eyes had a vanquished look. Zhiyu went to her. She let him wrap his arms around her.

The embrace didn't last long. Nancy stepped out of it, and Zhiyu noticed her wipe away a tear. He gave her a moment, turning his attention to the bookshelves. They were crammed with textbooks and plaques and photographs of Nancy with people Zhiyu knew from TV. Except for two photos: one of a young Charlotte at a lake, and one of Zhiyu's storefront. Zhiyu wondered if the lack of personal photos was purposeful. Sappy family shots might remind visitors they were dealing with a person, someone with a life, with a family, someone soft on the inside, someone they might take advantage of, a woman.

Who take this? he asked, pointing at the picture of his store.

I did, Nancy said. In college. I'll get you a print if you want . . .

No, it fine, Zhiyu smiled. I see store enough.

Nancy pulled a box from a cabinet and tore into it. Inside were IBM-logo mugs in bubble wrap. Please, she said. Have a seat.

Zhiyu unhooked himself from the oxygen tank. Crossed the carpet to the pair of chairs facing the desk.

No, no, Nancy said. Other side.

Zhiyu did as he was told. He walked around the desk to the big chair. It was formed from some futuristic, tautly stretched netting. He sat. Gingerly at first, but then he let his forearms settle along the armrests. He pulled his shoulders back. Raised his chin.

Obviously his daughter had sat in this chair and thought to herself: *If my father could see me now*. She had finally acted on that impulse. She had plucked him from his puny life and driven him here to see what a splash she'd made in the world. And he would go along with that, because—again—she was right.

He'd believed his favorite chair at the store was perfect because it had been free—its comfort-to-cost ratio was infinity. But he wondered now about his calculus. Perhaps a chair that comes at an extraordinary cost is more comfortable *because* of the price paid. A throne won through battle.

He swiveled to face the big window. The view encompassed the company campus, the hills beyond, the lowering sun. True: he'd never been to see Nancy's office. But *his* own parents had never seen his *country*.

And suddenly Zhiyu was traveling backward through time. To a muggy summer night in the kitchen of a ramshackle farmhouse. He was seated to his father's left, across from his mother. The rest of the seats full of brothers, sisters, uncles, aunts, cousins, grandparents, neighbors. Zhiyu's voice, if he cared to raise it, merely contributed to the clamor. Zhiyu's father—who sat in his own favorite chair, a Spartan wood thing—greedily scooped the rice they'd all planted and grown and harvested and cleaned and cooked into his gaping mouth, directly from his bowl. He twisted up his face and peeled back his lip to pinch a pebble off his tongue and drop it onto the table—*plink*—and then went right on eating. Fully accepting that pebbles could and would be found in one's hand-harvested rice. And settling for that truth, even as the sound waves from that infinitesimal collision of stone and wood sent a ripple through a young Zhiyu. A ripple that swelled to a wave, a wave that carried him away for good. To here. This office. Lightyears from the farmhouse, its crowded table.

Zhiyu missed the din of the voices. He missed his mother tongue. But he had traveled too far. Too much time had passed. There was no going back. Nor was there any way to get a message to his boyhood self to let him know what would become of him. To say to him, Don't worry.

Nancy poured two mugs. She handed one to Zhiyu. He took it, and they clinked in cheers. It felt a little stilted: they had never toasted like this before, nor would they ever again. Zhiyu would be dead by year's end.

Zhiyu sipped. The cognac burnt his throat and warmed his belly.

So? she said. What do you think?

If I could only see me now. That's what Zhiyu thought.

Amy

2011

YOU MAY RECALL: when we met Amy she was readying herself to trace the cloverleaf pattern known to barrel racers the world over. Indulge me then as we recap her life since then in the form of that well-trod trifecta. You may also recall: her first barrel nearly tipped (got knocked? . . .)—Amy narrowly avoiding an unplanned parenthood and, in so doing, altering the trajectory of her life to a direction *she* chose. And off she went! See her shooting across the arena to reach her second barrel, a love affair with Eric. They rode off together toward what Amy thought would be a sunset. But a third barrel lurked: Charlotte. Next thing poor Amy knew, she'd been turned around, and she was headed right back to the chute from whence she'd emerged: Amarillo. Tail betwixt her legs.

But, whether the run lasts seconds or years, no barrel racer returns to the chute the same as she left it.

To keep herself from helping, Amy cuffed her right hand in her left behind her back.

Francine—now eight, going on eighteen—tapped an egg on the rim of a steel mixing bowl. The crack she created in the shell was too subtle. She brute-forced it apart with her thumbs. Severed yolk spilled through her fingers. Fragments of shell rained into the bowl. She was left clutching a collapsed and shattered thing. Her head dropped by a degree only a mother might measure.

It's *fiiine*, Amy said (stretching, as she did, monosyllabic words into multi).

Amy released her hands from their bind. With her finger she pinned one of the bits of shell against the bowl and dragged it up to the bowl's lip. Using its wetness against it, she extracted it upon the tip of her finger and held it up for Francine to admire. Francine set to fishing out the rest this way.

Good girl, Amy said. She crossed the kitchen to confer with Zach. They discussed the three dozen *other* cakes, plus the twenty dozen cookies and fifteen dozen cupcakes, scheduled for delivery today.

When's Samantha getting here? Amy asked.

She told me 8, Zach said.

She and Zach glanced at the clock on the wall above the row of commercial ovens—ovens in which the forms Zach had filled with batter during the dark hours were now rising with the Texas sun outside. An aroma that Amy had always equated with hope was filling the kitchen. She was wont to joke that her tombstone would read: *I was told there'd be cake.*

It's 8:22, Francine said from across the kitchen.

You worry about your cake, honey, Amy said. Mommy'll worry about hers.

Zach took out his phone and tapped furiously.

Have you *talked* to her? Amy asked.

Like, called? Zach said.

Right. Exactly like that.

We text, he explained.

That's not talking, said a woman who'd talked herself into love twice—the first over the phone to a boy who broke her heart when she thought she was pregnant, the second over the radio to a man who broke her heart after she thought she'd become a mother.

Francine had by now removed from the bowl most of the shell bits along with much of the egg.

We gotta get our butts in gear, Amy told her. Your cake needs to be in the oven.

You said I could do everything, Francine said.

I know, sweetie. But at this rate, you won't be frosting the thing till the cows come home.

What cows, Francine said.

Touché, young lady. There were no cattle there, nor horses for that matter. Not anymore. Amy only rode herd on her family, such as it was, and her two millennial employees.

Lemme just help you get your batter goin', Amy said.

Francine stepped away from the table and wiped her hands on her jeans. Amy slipped into the working space thus vacated. Ten minutes later, two amateur cake forms went into the oven among the many rows of professional ones.

How about we go in and pick out a pony? Amy said.

Francine took off her apron and hung it on her allotted hook.

Zach held out his fist. Francine pounded it with her own.

I'll be here, Zach said.

Amy made no reply to this worthless statement of the obvious. Zach's very "here"-ness, in this kitchen, on time, every day, was his sole value-add. This was not to say Amy thought any less of Zach for that. "Here"-ness was Amy's purpose by this point, too. It's why she'd returned to this property to convert a stable full of horses into a kitchen full of ovens. A transformation made possible by Amy's sweat equity, plus her father's *equity* equity, and minus her mother's ability, in absentia, to veto it all. Amy refused to accept her father's money as anything but a loan. She cut him a check every month, chipping away at the balance. The debt Amy felt to her mother was not so easily repaid.

Amy and Francine crossed the driveway to Amy's childhood

home. Now Francine's. In contrast to the heat of the kitchen, the autumn air was brisk and windy. The Texas sky big as ever. It was Amy's "something old, something new, something borrowed, something blue."

In the months that became years that Amy spent waiting for an adoption to come through, she'd found the only thing to make time pass at a tolerable clip was work. When she'd moved away from Texas to be with Eric and Charlotte in California, she'd given up her position as pastry chef at Heritage Ranch. Upon her return to Amarillo, she'd queried her replacement for work. He'd given her the name of a club member in desperate need of a cake. (The club didn't do wedding cakes, and the single high-end bakery in town had refused the job upon learning the cake would be topped by two tuxedoed figurines.) Amy reached out to the mother of groom #1 and asked what she'd pay. Amy was grateful the conversation was conducted over the phone—allowing Amy's mouth to gape, her eyes to widen, but her voice, when she finally spoke, to sound nonchalant: I believe I can help y'all.

Amy had baked that first cake in the top-and-bottom wall ovens of her home. She'd baked it three times before she was happy enough with the result. She went on to make hundreds of cakes and thousands of cookies in those ovens. Amarillo's gentry were willing to pay, and pay well, to signal status via pastry. Amy filled a niche. She convinced her clientele, and later herself, that she was capable of something approaching artistry. She had a way of elevating flour, eggs, butter, and sugar into creations exponentially more valuable than the sum of their ingredients. The secret ingredient was labor. Which came cheap. She'd been glad for the distraction work provided. Eventually, demand outstripped throughput. Also, Amy learned she wasn't zoned for Amarillo's better schools. Though her adoption was still nowhere in sight—she was stuck on a long waiting list—she'd sold her house and moved downtown.

Things had progressed quickly after that. She'd leased time in a commercial bakery. She'd hired Zach. Bought a used sprinter van and wrapped it in her logo—a woman turning a horse adeptly around a huge, tiered cake—and her new company name: BARREL QUEEN CAKERY. Amy had the logo designed gratis by a graphic art student at the community college. That student was Samantha. Amy hired Samantha.

Amy came from entrepreneurial stock. Her parents, Doreen and Hank, had built a construction company from nothing. Later, Doreen had turned an underutilized stable and corral into a going concern, teaching riding lessons to some of the same families Amy now catered for. Still, Amy had never pictured herself as an entrepreneur, let alone an employer. Now that she'd undeniably become both, it surprised her to realize that her biggest inspiration wasn't her parents. It was a woman she'd never met: Nancy Chu.

Eric had described his ex-wife (a hint of irrepressible pride in his voice) as a shrewd and confident woman. A true *professional*. And so, did it not stand to reason that Eric had a *type*? That he'd recognized in Amy, and been attracted to, an inner *Dr. Chu* that Amy had been reining in all her life? Amy had decided to believe that story. She'd also come to believe that her life was done bucking.

Then the adoption came through.

Amy followed her adopted daughter into their adopted home—one zoned for Amarillo's better schools, though it was a bit of a drive to reach them. Amy's father, Hank, was away, hunting pheasant in Nebraska. With his wife gone, he was always finding reasons to be away. Francine led them back to Amy's old bedroom. It was preserved in more or less the state it was on the day Amy moved out in 1977. Francine went to the bookcase. It burst with trophies and medals and plaques and photographs. Plastic horses stood flank to flank across the bottom shelf. Francine got on her knees on the shag carpet. She took a horse out.

Amy smiled: *Is she after the one she likes best, or least?*

Francine didn't have many friends. All the hours she spent at the cakery had disposed her to the company of adults. Amy worried about that.

Think she'll like a paint? Francine asked.

I do, Amy said.

Maybe the Arabian.

Take your time, sweetie.

Amy headed down the hallway to her eldest brother's old room. Amy had taken to crashing there last year, after long days and nights helping Hank tend to a decaying Doreen. A disappearing Doreen. Francine had taken Amy's younger brother's old room. Of course, Francine had *wanted* Amy's old room, with its pink wallpaper and four-poster bed and plastic ponies, but Amy drew a line. As Doreen had once put it to Amy, for Francine to follow so literally in Amy's footsteps would mean stepping over Amy's dead body.

Amy took off her baking garb (Carhartt overalls, clogs). She pulled on black stretch pants, a denim polo, and a belted, knee-length cardigan that accentuated her curves while concealing her bulges. She pulled on a pair of riding boots. She clipped her hair up in a bun, applied lipstick, and stood in front of a mirror.

Honey, she thought to herself. *Who the hell you tryin' to impress?*

Amy helmed the sprinter. Francine rode shotgun. They drove the same road, past the same barbed-wired fields and lonely power lines, as Doreen once drove Amy to see a pediatrician who told Amy her life *wasn't* about to change forever.

Francine re-secured the red bow taped to the chosen horse's back. Her cake was in a special cubby in the back of the van, among many other cakes for which Francine's would never be mistaken. Francine had borrowed from Zach's already-made batch of frosting. She'd added a few drops of blood-red coloring to turn the frosting a light pink—another trick Amy had taught her that she now performed without assistance or attribution. (Cruel, is it not? How Mother Nature transforms mothers so completely into teachers only so their children will learn to do everything *without* them, even *in spite* of them?) Amy would have killed just to wipe jelly off Francine's chin again. To be needed, without an ounce of resentment, or even so much as recognition, of that need.

For *my* birthday, I'm going to make red velvet cupcakes, Francine said.

Well, you've still got a few months to decide, Amy said.

Francine gave her current favorite reply: I know.

The doors swished open automatically. Amy smiled hello to a bored, middle-aged man wearing a polo shirt embroidered with a setting sun. Francine headed straight to an interior security door. Amy set the cake on the reception desk.

Look at *that*, the man said. I wonder who made it.

I did, Francine said. With my mom.

There's another one for y'all in the van, Amy said. I'll bring it in later.

You shouldn't have, said the man.

Amy shooed his remark, but he was right: both cakes would be squandered on their recipients.

The door at which Francine waited gave a buzz. She shoved it open and held it for Amy.

I'll let Jimmy know you're here, Francine, said the man.

Francine waved her thanks as she and Amy started down a wide hallway. A few of the doors were open, granting glimpses into geriatric oblivion—TVs on low volume; child- (or self-) made art taped to windows; a potpourri of odors: broth, urine, disinfectant.

Francine raced to the door and looked back. Amy nodded permission. Francine knocked.

Who is it? came the voice of someone both bothered and frightened.

Us, Francine said.

The man at the front desk gave a thumbs-up through the security window. Francine turned the handle.

The room was small and plain. A reclining bed with rails and a chair faced a TV. There were bookshelves lacking books and a table with three chairs. Standing in the doorless doorway of the railing-equipped en suite bathroom was a stranger.

Who are you? the stranger asked.

Your daughter, Amy said.

Doreen looked unconvinced, then uninterested.

And here's Francine, Amy said. Your granddaughter.

Doreen appeared even less acquiescent to this fact. She knotted her brow. But she's—, Doreen said, held in check by some vestige of decorum in her shattered mind.

Francine had helped Doreen pluck this particular shell fragment from the bowl before.

. . . pretty? Francine prompted.

Doreen shook her head.

. . . tall? Francine said.

Doreen kept shaking.

. . . *black*? Francine said—magnanimous as an ambassador.

That's right, Doreen said. You can't be my blood, honey.

Bless your heart, Francine said.

Months earlier, Francine had learned about DNA in school. This had led to a conversation over spaghetti that ended up at Amy's laptop, where a query revealed that the DNA of Amy and Francine and everyone else on earth—Doreen included—was 99.9 percent identical. Francine later offered this fact to Doreen. *Dee and aye?* Doreen had said. Leaving Amy to wonder just what percentage of *reality* Doreen still shared with everyone else on earth.

By that point, Francine was more Amy's daughter than Amy was Doreen's.

God knows, though (as did Amy), that without Doreen,

Francine would never have let herself be loved as deeply as Amy wanted to love her. Nor would Francine have been able to return such love. For it had been Doreen who'd broken through Francine's emotional scar tissue—a reticence to form connections. Doreen had done the only thing she knew to do: she'd set Francine astride a horse. The effect had been gradual, and undeniable. Francine had begun to *trust*. The heavy animals hadn't tried to kill her, they'd obeyed her. They'd trotted over to the fence to greet her. They'd nibbled mini carrots from her mini hand. As months went on, trust in the world fostered for Francine a confidence in herself. By the time Doreen began to founder, and to forget Francine, Francine had learned poise enough take it all in stride.

Already Doreen looked exhausted by Amy and Francine's arrival and their subsequent revelations. She let go of the doorframe like it was a pony wall at an ice rink and skated in her slippers to the recliner. She sat. Facing away from Amy and Francine.

Francine went to her and presented The Pony. Doreen took it.

Palomino, Doreen muttered, as if being quizzed. (The stuff she remembered! She'd recently explained to Francine, out of the blue, about the distinctive height at which the Texas flag could be flown relative to the American one.) She held the little plastic horse as if it were a wet and repulsive thing, a stillborn foal. Her expression changed to concern. Who's tendin' the horses? she asked.

The horses are just fine, Mom, Amy said.

They're with Zach, Francine explained. He's new. And he's *fantastic*.

Doreen didn't even try to catch up. Her shoulders slumped. The horse fell with a plunk to the floor. Doreen stared at it, unseeing.

Look, Grandma! Francine said.

Francine brought the cake to Doreen. She lit up a little, seeing it. She reached out and dredged a finger through it. She managed to get some cake into her gaping mouth and sat there chewing it. Frosting on her lip and chin, crumbs in her lap. She frowned like a food critic, then started into "Happy Birthday," sweetly and gently. She addressed the song to Carole, her own mother, long dead.

It's *your* birthday, Mom, Amy said.

Doreen's surprise was cartoonish. How old am I? she asked.

Seventy-one, Francine said.

Bullshit, Doreen said.

You can have more, Francine said, holding out the cake for her. Doreen shook her head.

Francine set the cake on the table and shot Amy a look. Amy winked. Francine went to Doreen and planted a kiss in her frazzled hair. Doreen reached out to Francine with a trace of familiarity.

Love you, Grandma, Francine said before slipping back out into the hallway in search of Jimmy, with whom she had a long-running game of gin rummy.

Once she was gone, Doreen wistfully confided: I had a daughter, once.

That so, Amy said.

Doreen nodded. Kids are what it's all about, she said. Especially daughters.

Amy could only stand in shocked silence.

Don't tell my sons, Doreen said, winking just the way her daughter did.

Amy drew an imaginary zipper across her lips. A tear pricked at her eye. Doreen's eyes, meanwhile, stared out into a different, darker space. Amy would have to find her again on a different frequency. *Seek you, seek you . . .*

Though Amy had given away all her radio gear after she'd returned to Amarillo from La Jolla, she thought often of Eric. Such thoughts were no longer tainted by the anger she'd felt in the immediate aftermath of their dissolution, nor by the sadness that settled in soon after.

The last time Amy had spoken Eric's name aloud was on a phone call with Charlotte. One of two such calls in the span of a few days—coming after years of radio silence. The first call had been to inform Amy of Eric's death. The second had been to cancel the memorial service Amy had been planning to drive halfway across the country to attend. For Charlotte's sake, not Eric's. (Just as Doreen's birthday party was not for Doreen's sake.) And so Amy could never think of Eric without hearing Charlotte's voice, apologizing again, for letting Amy down, again.

You gotta stay strong, honey, Amy had told Charlotte on the second call. Keep moving forward.

I'm trying, Charlotte had said. But I can't.

Tell you the truth, Amy said, I ain't exactly been fixin' to find Eric's replacement.

Well, I ain't fixin' to find a new dad, neither.

Of course, Amy had said. I wasn't meaning to compare. What you're going though, honey, it ain't the same thing at all.

It was only months later, as Doreen's mind began to truly slip away, that Amy wondered whether losing someone incrementally might in fact be the more excruciating.

As if it matters, though. As if our suffering is scored. As if we could win at loss . . .

What y'all decide to do, then, Amy had asked Charlotte on that second call, with the remains?

What I wanted, Charlotte said.

Attagirl, Amy thought.

There had been a silence on the line. Amy had thought Charlotte was about say goodbye.

I still have your belt buckle, Charlotte said. I wear it all the time. It pisses my mom off.

I reckon she hates me.

Maybe, yeah. She's jealous.

That makes sense.

Not of you and my dad, Charlotte said. Of you and me. What *we* had.

Amy had gone speechless at that.

But anyway, Charlotte had said.

Amy had wanted desperately for Charlotte to go on—to gush to Amy about all the little ways she'd been a mother to her. Charlotte didn't go on. But with just three words—*what we had*—she'd given Amy the one thing she'd been seeking, above all else, all her life: proof she had it in her. Because with Francine in those early years, Amy hadn't yet been sure.

Amy had thanked Charlotte for calling.

Charlotte had said goodbye.

That was in 2011. In the year since, they have not talked again. Both have spoken to the other—only, neither one held down their transmit button when they did.

Amy stared at the cake on the table. She tore a chunk away with her hand and ate it, sucking her fingers clean. *Delicious.* More delicious, somehow, without a fork.

Excuse me, ma'am? Doreen said. Can I have some of that?

Of course, Amy said. It's yours.

Amy brought the cake to her mother. Doreen helped herself to another handful. She smiled as she chewed, lost in some primal, pleasurable meditation.

Daughter wiped pink frosting off Mother with a party napkin.

Nancy/WMDL

2012

A CORRECTION, if you please. That night, tonight—when Nancy arrives on my porch? I told you that I brushed aside my curtain to peer out my window at just the moment Dr. Nancy Chu—"my neighbor, my unrequited love"—put her own face to the glass as if we were about to kiss, if not for the pane between us. Well, all of that was and remains true, save the name. Dr. Nancy Chu. Well, that is her name. Just, that's not my *neighbor*, nor my unrequited love. *That* woman is WMDL. I can explain. Let's rewind a little.

Dr. Chu, you see, was a woman. That tended to surprise people. A Swiss ambassador once gifted her cufflinks. A KTVU reporter she'd corresponded with via email once referred to her as a "he" when the story aired. No surprise, then, that the limo driver with his whiteboard gazed right past her, to watch for Dr. Chu among the other arrivals at San Diego International Airport on the day I was to meet her for the first time.

I'm your man, she told the driver with a smile, presenting herself.

The driver's eyes tracked back, took her in.

Miss Doctor Chu! he said, laughing in a happy and—to Dr. Chu—enviable way. The driver was amused by his tiny failure.

Nancy, she said—extending a hand.

The driver was correct, now, though: It *was* Miss. It *had once been* Mrs. And it *would always be* Doctor, yes. But it *had very recently been* Director. Dr. Chu's failures were not so tiny. She, unlike the driver, was not laughing.

The driver piloted them up the coast. Through the limo's tinted windows, Dr. Chu observed people pedaling bikes and zipping around on jet skis. On a work day! She opened the mini fridge, stocked with beers and sodas and single-serving bottles of champagne. On a work day! The driver came over the intercom: Something specific you're looking for? Maybe some Scotch? You drink Scotch, Dr. Nancy?

She assessed her reflection in the tinted glass. Cognac, she said. On occasion.

Namely, if she was celebrating. She was not celebrating. She'd been fired the week before. Before that, she'd been the director of the IBM Almaden Research Center in San Jose, California. She liked to joke that she'd worked at IBM for so long they'd turned her into a fellow. The title had come with an Omega watch. It hadn't fit her wrist. She'd given it to her husband.

She'd lasted as director for three years, which was longer than her predecessor but about half as long as she'd expected. She'd worked as hard as she ever had. But the corporate office hadn't judged her by that; they'd judged her by Key Performance Indicators: the number of new patents licensed, the research dollars netted, the technologies productized, et cetera, et cetera. She had always stood on metrics. *You are the sum of your data.* Before she became director, she'd chaired the committee that coauthored the very criteria by which she was later judged inadequate.

But a fellow doesn't get demoted. (Back to what?) No, a fellow "steps down." So said the press release. There had been a small severance package.

Since then Nancy had received emails of condolence from people who'd called her horrible things behind her back. She'd received regular work emails, too, from people who hadn't gotten the news right away—a request from a senator, an invitation to chair a conference. She'd also gotten normal replies to the dozens of normal emails she'd sent in the oblivious hours leading up to her final one, during which everyone she worked with was still working with her. When no one yet knew, least of all Dr. Chu, that her world was about to implode. It was these emails in particular that had since been keeping her awake.

Her mind could not, or would not, switch off. It was still trying to solve all those problems. Her mind had not achieved *severance.*

She missed all the problems. She had no idea who she was without all the problems.

She was her only problem now.

They reached a bluff with panoramic views of the ocean. Nancy put down the window. The air had a tang to it. The hillsides were stacked with glass houses. Kids were riding skateboards in flip-flops. A silver-haired woman ducked into an art gallery carrying a mini Doberman in her purse. Nancy put her window back up, lest someone catch her gawking.

The limo arrived at a single-story, brown brick bungalow with white upper siding and a large picture window facing the street. White concrete steps, a porch, a Spanish tile roof. In the backyard, an antenna was strung between the chimney and a palm tree. Last year, Nancy had finally paid off the balance of the mortgage.

Still, she felt the place owned *her*.

The driver left the limo idling. He started tugging luggage out of the trunk. He'd had to double park, funneling traffic on the narrow street into a single lane. A man in a Mercedes convertible honked. Nancy raised her hand in apology. The limo driver switched from a walk to a jog and fetched another set of bags. Nancy grabbed a load despite his insistence that she do nothing. Nancy was incapable of that.

Charlotte materialized on the porch. She stood peering down at them. Nancy climbed the stairs and they embraced, but it was cut short as the driver cut through with more bags. He wiped his forehead on his coat sleeve and promised to be out of the way momentarily.

Limo didn't fit in the driveway! he explained to Charlotte.

A taxi would've, Charlotte muttered so only Nancy could hear.

When the driver was done unloading, Nancy tipped him. She followed Charlotte back inside. The luggage clotted the entryway—five large bags and two medium ones. Mother and daughter found themselves trapped between a coat closet and a futon. How do I have so much stuff? Nancy asked.

Packing had been discouraging. Dr. Chu's wardrobe was ill-suited to leisure. Most of it was dry-clean only: slacks and blouses, long skirts, high heels. In the end, she'd packed bedding sets, lots of towels, pillows. Some of the bags contained only smaller bags. One of the bags contained Dario. Dario was a vibrator. He/it took its name from a tallish FedEx man of indeterminate race who'd delivered it in a discreet package to Nancy's doorstep a few months after her divorce, and whose face she cannot help but picture whenever she cannot help from using him/it.

. . . Mom? Charlotte was saying.

Mm? Nancy said.

I said your hair is long.

Charlotte plucked a sleeping bag off the futon and started cramming it into a sack. Empty beers and a halved honeydew in the kitchen lent an oversweet stench to the room.

How long you staying? Charlotte asked.

Didn't you get my email? Nancy asked.

Charlotte made an amused face, as if email were funny.

Nancy used to get irritated when colleagues didn't reply to her emails within an hour.

Charlotte un-velcroed the side pocket of her garishly patterned board shorts. Took out her phone and thumbed a message.

Charlotte was twenty-two. She told Nancy less about her own life with every passing year. When the bungalow's most recent tenants' lease had ended two months earlier, Charlotte had asked them to leave and then moved in herself—thereby cutting off her sole source of income. (Nancy had been letting Charlotte keep the rent money in exchange for "managing" the property.)

Nancy asked Charlotte what she'd been charging for rent. The number Charlotte gave was almost double what Nancy expected. Nancy raised her brow, impressed. Charlotte rolled her eyes.

The house was mostly bare. Rectangles of unfaded hardwood showed where furniture had once been. To Nancy's surprise, Charlotte followed her down the hallway. Charlotte played a casual docent through the echoing spaces, calling attention to the dates and height marks etched into the hall closet doorframe, the burn mark on the floor from a soldering iron tip. The bundles of wire snaking up the wall of the master bedroom went unmentioned.

I should just get a hotel room, Nancy said. You stay here until I can buy a bed.

Charlotte pretended offense. It's *fine*, Mom, she said. I'm gonna stay with Carter.

Nancy could not remember Charlotte ever mentioning a Carter, but was afraid to ask, in case she (Nancy) just hadn't been listening well enough.

You can crash on the futon, Charlotte said.

Nancy had never "crashed on a futon." She had never "crashed." At all.

There's some furniture in the storage unit, Charlotte said.

Carter's got a truck. I'll bring it by tomorrow and we'll go. Cool?

Okay, yeah, Nancy said. *Cool.*

They were standing in the hallway, forced to stand close. Before she could stop herself, Nancy slid Charlotte's wayward bra strap back under her tank top. Charlotte reached up to finish the adjustment. Their hands touched, electricity in the connection. Charlotte, repulsed, excused herself to finish packing up her things. Nancy stuffed her hands into the pockets of her pantsuit as if to punish them. Charlotte threw away the beer cans. With a quick hug, she left Nancy alone.

Nancy stood in the middle of the kitchen for a few minutes. She took a slice of melon from the cutting board and walked out back, chewing it. She wiped at her chin with the back of her fist.

The lawn looked dry and neglected. A pigeon was pecking its way up the alley.

Find anything good? Nancy asked it with her mouth full.

Having secured shelter, Nancy set about securing sustenance. She walked to a grocery store she'd seen on her way in. Upon her termination, IBM had given Nancy the choice of buying her company car. Nancy had refused this offer. On principle. She wasn't sure which principle. But she was going to try going without a car for a little while.

On her way back from the store, an elderly couple glared at her from porch chairs. Seagulls crisscrossed overhead, cocking their heads to peer down at her as if collecting recon. Nancy set her bags down to pet a cat that offered up its belly as if to test Nancy's character.

Back at the bungalow, she sat on the futon and ate potato salad out of a plastic tub. She took out her laptop and gravitated to the IBM Almaden website. There was a headshot and accompanying welcome message from her successor. He was a glad-handing German Nancy hated for his un-hate-ability.

She searched "chu." According to the internet, the most important CHU was a radio station in Canada that broadcasted nothing but a tiny time signal—bleeps, calibrated to atomic clocks. There was a link. Nancy clicked on it and listened: *Bleep. Bleep. Bleep*. She could feel time passing. She was not used to that feeling. Nor was she used to the sounds she heard outside. Weed eaters. Kids. A wind chime.

There were no drapes on the big front window. Nancy kept the lights off. Otherwise she felt as if she were living inside a zoo exhibit. People peering in at her little nest, reading her placard: *Lesser Chinese American Female International Business Machine. Age—fifty-three years. Weight—105 pounds. Diet consists primarily of takeout and Starbucks. Male partner rears offspring. Skills—micromanagement, experimental design, strategic budgeting, schmoozing. Outside interests—unknown.*

Later—standing tiptoe on a shifting phonebook atop a stool in a failed attempt to swap out a nine-volt battery in a beeping smoke detector—Nancy started to cry.

The next morning, she could not open a jar of peanut butter. She ran the lid under hot water and tried using a towel for grip. Nothing. She took the jar out back. While tapping the lid against a concrete step to try to budge it loose, she noticed a man standing behind a hip-high chain-link fence. She straightened. The jar felt like a tampon in her hands: evidence of a feminine difficulty, and absolutely none of his business.

The man was tall. Late sixties, with deeply (overly?) tanned skin. Sun-bleached gray hair sprouted from his visor. In *his* hands: a pair of long-handled pruning shears. At his feet: their handiwork.

He tipped his visor brim. Morning, he said.

I didn't see you there, Nancy said.

Charlotte told me you'd be moving in.

Oh. Yes. Well, we'll see. Taking some time off.

That's what I told myself, too, he said.

Nancy wandered toward the fence.

The man set down his shears. My first few months, he said, shaking his head. The sheer number of choices! What to cook, who to call, where to *go* every day! *Paralyzing*, really. I spent an entire summer doing pretty much nothing. Nothing! It took time to learn that that was okay. To slooowww dooowwwwn . . .

How long ago was that? Nancy asked.

Oh, he said, I guess it's been two years now.

Well, I'm not *retiring*, Nancy said. She then asked a sequence of questions about retiring.

As he answered them, he reached across the fence and casually wrested the jar from her. It got swallowed up in his leather gloves. His face contorted, relaxed. He handed the jar back, lid rattling.

Thank you, Nancy said. She felt she owed him something in exchange. My dad . . . , she started to say.

He waited.

He just, Nancy continued, well, he had this little store. In South San Francisco. Worked there until the day he died. Every time I'd go home to visit—even a few years ago—he'd pull me aside and ask, *Still have job?*

Her impersonation earned Nancy a small laugh. However, the helpless feeling that had brought her outside in the first place came rushing back. Suddenly there were tears in her eyes, unsummoned. She wiped each one gone as soon as it emerged. Apologized.

It's fine, he said. Really. He reached across the fence and laid a hand on Nancy's elbow. She was dying to go back inside.

She held up the jar and smiled her gratitude.

Pleasure, he said.

Safely back inside, spooning peanut butter straight from the jar, Nancy realized she'd failed to get the man's name.

Though they'd arranged to meet at 10 a.m., Charlotte still had not shown by 10:20. Nancy checked her phone, saw she'd failed to notice a text: "lets do afternoon k?" The message was time-stamped 3:56 a.m.

Afternoon? Nancy thought. *What's that mean?* Was Charlotte out late or up early? Was she okay? Nancy started to dial her daughter, then decided against it. She didn't want to come off as overbearing, or worse, dependent.

She plunked down on the hardwood floor. Flipped idly through a pop culture magazine she'd bought the day before. The kind of magazine she'd always seen in checkout lines and wondered, *who has the time*?

Her buttocks went numb against the floor. She stood up and tried to remember things from her IBM Tai Chi class—one of the "wellness modules" she'd let HR implement after they'd claimed it would reduce healthcare costs. But a year later, no one had been able to prove that claim to Nancy's satisfaction. She'd cut the funding.

It was after 2:00 p.m. when Charlotte finally knocked on the door as she came through it, saying, Looks like we've been robbed!

Together, mother and daughter surveyed the riffled state of Nancy's luggage. Nancy was heartened by the "we." Her instinct was to start interrogating Charlotte. But she refused to sabotage whatever this was. After all, Charlotte *had* shown up. With a truck. Wearing mannish board shorts and a tight white tank, tucked behind a huge belt buckle—silver, with a turquoise I on it.

Such an interesting buckle, Nancy said.

Amy's, Charlotte explained.

The Horse? Nancy said.

Charlotte corrected her. *Amy*, she said. Charlotte's tone was polite, but Amy's name would only ever sound like a threat to Nancy.

Nancy watched Charlotte readjust her shorts. By pulling them further *down*.

You hungry? Charlotte asked.

Starving, Nancy said.

Carter's pickup was an oversized toy: huge tires, huge bumpers, huge shiny dual-exhaust pipes. A sticker reading OVERKILL was plastered across the rear window. (*A band?* Nancy wondered. *A brand? A philosophy?*) Mother and daughter climbed in. As Charlotte pulled away from the curb, Nancy could feel the individual tire treads upon the road.

On the freeway, the tires gave off a relentless hum. It was hard to have a conversation. Charlotte shouted out the names of nearby drive-thrus in an exhausted tone, as if to impress Nancy with the sheer number of options—there was an In-N-Out and a McDonald's and a Burger King and a Jack in the Box and a Fatburger. Unless Nancy felt like Mexican, then there was . . .

Fatburger! Nancy shouted. She'd only ever heard of it.

They rode along, cocooned in noise.

I remember you always used to drive, instead of Dad! Charlotte shouted. My friends thought it was weird!

Dad was in charge of the radio! Nancy said.

Charlotte looked over to read her mother's expression. But Nancy refused to have an expression. She looked dead ahead.

As with the name *Amy*, the word *radio* would always be a loaded one to them both.

Nancy took a bite of cheeseburger while standing astride the concrete v-channel between the storage buildings. She watched as Charlotte fiddled with a padlock, then heaved the door upward with a screech. Nancy set her burger on the truck's high tailgate. Together the two women squinted into the darkness. There was no obvious place to start. It looked like the removal of any one item might topple them all.

Nancy recognized things—the breakfast table and chairs from her and Eric's San Jose condo, their first TV/VCR. She smiled to see their old recliner mounted upon the sectional. It was upon that very furniture that she and Eric once mounted one another, during a movie playing on that very TV/VCR, in the days before Charlotte. Eric had always had an *appetite.*

Nancy rooted around. She found a stack of three-ring binders filled with lecture notes. She had wondered before if she, too, might try teaching. But she knew she would need patience. What she had instead was persistence. They were not the same thing. They were almost opposites.

Like she and Eric.

Way in the back—behind a partition created by bookshelves—Nancy found The Boxes. As if no one would ever find them there. As if the past could be kept hidden in storage. Nancy was surprised to realize that the sight of them was not the real blow. It was all the other stuff in the unit, the stuff she *didn't* recognize. The mothballed remnants of the life Eric had lived *after* her. Of appetites satisfied without her.

There was a beard trimmer. *Did he grow a beard, then? A goatee? Not a* mustache . . . Nancy plucked a Gilligan hat out of a bin. Embroidered on it was the UCSD mascot—Triton, messenger of the sea, lofting a trident. She put it on. Looked to Charlotte for a reaction. Charlotte didn't notice. She was on her cell.

I guess we just get started, Nancy muttered to herself.

Half an hour later, she was urging an uncooperative mattress toward Charlotte, who was tugging on it from the bed of the truck, when the rope handle on the mattress ripped out. Charlotte fell backward against the cab. She was slow to get up and inspected her wrist. Nancy noticed a faint but lengthy scar running down Charlotte's hand from wrist to pinky. Nancy didn't remember this scar. Charlotte grabbed the mattress with her other hand, steadied it between her thighs, and—momentarily using even her forehead—manhandled the whole thing into place before Nancy could help.

Careful, Nancy said.

It's already ripped, Mom.

I meant *you.*

Charlotte wiped her brow. Will you *please* take that off, she said—meaning the hat.

I like it, Nancy said.

It's Dad's.

Nothing's his anymore, Nancy thought.

Can we go? Charlotte asked.

In a sec, Nancy said—reasserting herself. For the same reason, she kept the hat on.

She poked around in the things that remained. There was a dresser she liked, but there wasn't enough room left in the truck bed and she wasn't about to ask Charlotte to make a second trip. Nancy nabbed a toolbox, a set of lamps, two beach chairs, and a surge protector. She sandwiched a folding table between the mattress and the box spring.

The heck is that? Nancy asked, pointing to something that, were it not for its many switches and knobs, might have been mistaken for a weed trimmer.

Nancy brushed the cobwebs off it and carried it past Charlotte's critical gaze to the truck. There was a perfect spot left for it above a wheel well.

All set, Nancy said.

Nancy knocked on the door three times, nice and hard. Followed for some desperate reason by two more knocks, gentle and arrhythmic. Now she was committed. She had to stand there until the door opened. Unless of course it didn't. In which case, fine—*better!*—she'd tried. A wind chime on the porch tinkled to life. So that's the one she'd been hearing . . .

She waited as long as seemed casual, then retreated hastily back down the steps and along a path bisecting thick twin palms.

She wheeled at the sound of her name. Her neighbor had materialized in his doorway, naked but for the towel wrapped around his waist. He waved, and Nancy was struck dumb. She'd called on him to apologize for having droned on for so long last time that they never got each other's names. *Wrong.* He'd just shouted hers.

His wet hair was plastered back. Only the skin of his underarms and between his toes and fingers showed signs of paleness. He was once white, it seemed. But now his face and body were a deep, dark chestnut.

Another day in paradise, he said. He opened his arms to encompass La Jolla—or perhaps California, or America. I was headed to the beach for a stroll, he said. What're *you* doing today?

Nancy laughed. This somehow seemed all the answer he needed.

Stay right there, he said.

He disappeared back into his house. Nancy snuck back up his steps. She peeked inside his mailbox. Found a catalogue addressed to a Mr. Peter Zemeckis. Who, when next he showed himself, had on an untucked Tommy Bahama shirt, cargo shorts, and some obscenely green Crocs. His combed-back hair shimmered in the sun. Shall we, Nancy? he said.

We shall, *Peter*, she replied.

This caused him to laugh. Nor did he stop laughing until, finally, Nancy—surprising both of them—cupped her hand over his mouth. She felt the stubble on his face.

Dear lord! he said. No one's called me Peter in, let's see . . . He wiggled a finger in the air to suggest the handling of large figures.

Nancy came clean about snooping through his mail.

That's illegal, you know, he said.

Damn it! What's your *name*?

Z.

That's not a name. That's an initial.

I, Z, stared her down through mirrored aviators.

Okay, fine. Mr. Z.

Z, I said.

I took her hand.

We walked south for one block, then we turned west and walked three more. And there we were. The rumbling shore. The onshore breeze. People shouting, people eating, people throwing things. Gulls and pigeons waddling among a patchwork of towels. Inland, scattered clouds were pierced by vectors of midday sun, but it was gray and cloudy over the Pacific that day. Down by the pier, surfers carried boards like ants lugging leaves. Nearer, scuba divers shuffled backward in their flippers into the surf. Beyond the beach the green hills were topped with antennae and a towering white cross. The hills sloped down to the promontory of downtown La Jolla, and below it were the sandstone cliffs dotted with purple flowers, and tucked into the cliffs was a little cove.

Nancy hoped the happiness she felt was written across her face for me to see.

I had my cell phone to my ear, on a call. Still, I saw it. I smiled back at her.

This place has been here all along, she thought. *All my life.*

A paper pusher from HR called Nancy. He asked her a series of questions as if he were reading them, and probably he was. Nancy did her best to be polite, though it perturbed her not to be speaking to the HR director herself—the one Nancy had hired. Talking to IBM felt to Nancy like an umbilical cord reattaching. It put her back on the campus . . . walking at sunrise along the greenbelt, past the picnic tables to the biosciences building . . . stooping at the door to use the keycard clipped to her blouse . . . the curt clicking, granting her access. Nancy's keycard had looked like everyone else's, but hers had been magic. Any door, any time. It was the first thing they'd taken back when they fired her.

The young man from HR spoke about large sums of money using the same tone of voice as the cashier at Fatburger. And why not? Both young men had very basic questions. What did Nancy want? How did she want it? And where? Yet such things were not so simple. These were the hardest things for Nancy to figure out.

The previous Christmas, Nancy had forced herself to stay a few extra days in Maui after a conference. She'd tried snorkeling. She'd bobbed along, blissfully watching the colorful fish. Then a current deposited her at the edge of a shelf. She'd found herself staring down into unfathomable, blue-black depths. She'd thought about Charlotte, who—before she went away to college, and before her father died—had trained by swimming from La Jolla cove to the La Jolla Shores beach and back. Wearing her black-tinted goggles. Nancy had told Charlotte that this sounded terrifying, waiting for a gaping oval of teeth to lunge into view! Charlotte had explained that there was nothing she could do about that, and so she just gave herself over to it. Or, as Charlotte put it, she "just kind of let go." She'd told Nancy it felt *serene*.

Nancy hadn't believed that. Still didn't.

I came to pick Nancy up for our third walk in as many days. I nodded at the gadget leaning in the entryway. With Nancy's Gilligan hat draped over its handle, it had the look of an aloof boyfriend—someone I ought to acknowledge.

I recognize that thing, I told her.

Really?

Eric was quite the *tinkerer*.

I pronounced the word like a slur, knowing Nancy would not disagree.

The sheer number of hours Eric had spent soldering, probing, futzing . . . And, long before I'd met him, there had been his swimming. And his cooking. Nancy would get home late and he'd foist a muffin or a bite of quiche on her before she could even put down her things. She'd resented his spare time. Or, really, his knack for filling it.

When Eric and Nancy had started dating, she hadn't owned a Walkman. Eric had bought her one. But, of course, she hadn't had any tapes. So he'd made her some. He'd record them like radio shows, playing the role of deejay. (*Alright, alright! You're tuned to KRIC. This next one's kinda sappy—a request and dedication from Eric in San Jose, who says he misses his hard-workin' wife. So . . . here's Prince with "Irresistible Bitch!" . . .*) More than once, Nancy had laughed out loud on a redeye flight.

Shall we? Nancy said.

I stepped aside like a matador. She charged through.

Our little outings already felt to me like a long-standing tradition. They were the event around which I scheduled my days. During that day's walk, though, I told Nancy I couldn't do lunch. To IBM Nancy, this would have been a pebble dropped in an ocean. But La Jolla Nancy's ocean was a teacup.

I got a thing, I explained. (There was no such thing: I was just worried I was already getting in a little too deep.)

A thing, she said.

Right, I said.

Nancy had told me: she wanted to learn from me. For I drank beer at lunch. I listened unapologetically to Yanni and Enya. I Frisbee-golfed. I read fiction. I kept journals. She was especially intrigued by my gleaming, capsular, Airstream trailer, which I towed behind my Jeep, disappearing for days into the desert. To Nancy, I'd attained the thing she yearned for: *lifestyle*. Though both of us hated that word. To Nancy, it screamed stay-at-home mother, indulging in some fat-free yogurt after a spiritually gratifying yoga session. But I have to say, she'd been making an effort. She'd started setting her watch ten minutes slow to force herself to be habitually late. Like me. Problem was, Nancy always did the math in her head. She remained woefully punctual.

Arriving back upon her porch, Nancy pecked my cheek. You know. To show she was cool, carefree.

I left, for the same reason.

Inside, she peeled a banana and considered calling Charlotte. Except, what then? Chat?

That's when she noticed the introvert leaning in the corner. She took hold of its skinny waist and headed to the backyard.

Nancy was startled by a figure at the edge of her vision. The figure was standing on the back stairs, pantomiming. Nancy lifted her headphones off and stood in the backyard she owned now, surrounded by the dozens of holes she'd just dug. She looked like she'd been pulled from central casting to play some kind of mad rodent scientist.

You need to go look in the mirror, the figure said. The figure being Charlotte.

How long have you been standing there? Nancy asked.

Go, Charlotte said.

As Nancy passed Charlotte on the porch stairs, Charlotte put a hand to her mouth. Moments later, Nancy, too, saw the reddened skin on her nose, her arms, her legs. And, more conspicuous, the pale disks around her ears where the headphones had been, the pale ring on her forearm from the wrist strap. A geek tan. (But a tan nonetheless!) Which hadn't hurt until she'd seen it. She was suddenly dying of thirst. She chugged a glass of water. Her shoulder and arm were starting to cramp. Her feet ached. *What a glorious feeling*, she thought.

She returned to the backyard. Fished a dime from her pocket. Handed it to her daughter. Play fetch with me, Nancy said.

The indignation on Charlotte's face . . . Nancy refused to let it kill her buzz.

C'mon, Nancy said. She went so far as to pant like a dog. This surprised both of them. They were alone in a backyard, and yet Charlotte was embarrassed. Nancy was able to tell because it was how she (Nancy) had felt for much of her childhood.

Charlotte chucked the coin to the very back of the yard. It vanished as if into a pond.

Nancy gave a gleeful little bark. She reequipped and hustled to where the coin had disappeared. She swept the antenna back and forth across the grass. She'd left her headphones inside, so the signal issued from a speaker on the detector. She walked forward, backward, forward again. She strained to hear a bleep in the tone.

The first thing Nancy had found with the detector that afternoon was this same dime. She'd promptly reburied it at various depths, to figure out what to listen for. At some point she'd realized the detector's boom was adjustable. She'd shortened it. This had made it easier for her to keep the antenna flush with the ground. It had also brought to mind Eric's long arms and body. Nancy had then readjusted it, adding back an inch—a tiny tribute. Since then she'd unearthed two pennies, a nail, a rusty hinge, and the real treasure among the trash—a watch with a simple white face and a black band, its hands long stilled. She couldn't wait to show it to me. To say to me: Look . . . *here* is a watch conducive to leisure . . .

Ba-bleep . . . Ba-bleep, went the speaker. Nancy knelt. Parted a tuft of lawn with her sunburnt hand. Pinched out the dime. Crossed the lawn, handed it over. Curtsied.

She was rewarded with a sarcastic golf clap. Charlotte looked worn out, too.

What's wrong? Nancy asked.

Nothing, Charlotte said.

Nancy nodded—disappointed. They stood looking at the yard.

Carter and I broke up, Charlotte said. She faked a smile.

Oh, no, Nancy said. I'm so sorry to hear that.

Yeah, well.

Do you need to stay here, with me? I mean, are you . . .

I'm staying with Amber.

Amber. With the, um . . . all the . . .

The piercings. Yes, Mom.

Nancy placed her aching hand to her aching heart. She managed to catch Charlotte's eye. I have not been the mother you needed, Nancy said. I know that. All these years and . . . I missed my chance.

Charlotte's expression didn't change any more than did the flat-line buzz now emanating from the detector.

Wait, Charlotte said. Now *you're* gonna cry? Is that what you want me to do?

No, Nancy lied.

Well, let it out, Mom! I'm not angry. You're just a little *late*. And . . . well, whatever. I remember feeling that way, too. Like I'd missed out on something. Like *we* had. But that was ten fucking years ago.

Nancy wiped her nose on her sleeve. Carter, she said. Was he a good guy?

He's still with us, Mother. He didn't die.

You know what I mean.

Charlotte stared back as if the question were an insult. But she shook her head, *no*.

Maybe it's better, then? Nancy ventured. That it's over?

Charlotte remained unreadable.

A little? Nancy said.

A little, Charlotte allowed, looking away.

Nancy hefted the detector and waved it over Charlotte's waist. The tone shrilled with each pass of the hooped antenna over the silver buckle—*ba-bleep . . . ba-bleep*. The same sound we all listen for when a doctor is trying frantically to revive a flat-lining patient.

Fever brought on by sunburn kept Nancy up half the night. In the morning the mere lifting of a spoon hurt. She took ibuprofen and lay down in the breeze of the swamp cooler. This cooler remained a mystery to Nancy. Eric had always hated air-conditioning.

Nancy settled into her soreness, relishing it. Closed her eyes. Fell asleep.

Awoke to the bleating of her phone.

Where are you? I asked. I just came by . . .

Nancy plucked at a tendril of drool connecting her chin to her shoulder. I guess I was asleep, she said.

Progress! I said. Sleeping in *and* barking! I told you retirement's weird.

I'm being gossiped about, Nancy thought. *Progress indeed.*

I'll be by again in half an hour, I said. We're taking your new toy to the big leagues.

Clouds of flies arose territorially from the piles of kelp as Nancy passed. She gave wide berth to the scraggly mob of seagulls standing with their beaks to the breeze. Everybody and everything at the beach seemed to her to have been there first, to have already staked claims. She was not welcome. Which hadn't slowed her down. She'd so far dug up half a dozen nails, swollen with rust. I'd told her to move away from the bonfire pits, where nail-ridden wood pallets are the fuel of choice. She'd given me all the nails she found.

They look like Lincoln Logs, I said.

What are Lincoln Logs? she asked.

You poor thing, I said. You never had a childhood.

Nor you an adulthood, she said.

I set to constructing a little cabin on the tide wall. She unearthed a toy monster truck. She wanted to give it to Charlotte as a joke, but wasn't sure if her daughter was ready yet to laugh about Carter.

Two weeks earlier, Charlotte had butt-dialed Nancy at 4 in the morning. Music thumping in the background. Charlotte could be heard yelling to someone. She'd sounded too happy to be sober. Then the call cut out. Nancy had called back. No answer.

Nancy rinsed the little truck off in one of the public showers. She held her head under the stream to cool off. Her white T-shirt got wet and her bra showed through. She caught me peeking. I offered to buy celebratory piña coladas on the promenade.

I'm okay, thanks, Nancy said. She slurped at the drinking fountain.

I hope you realize, I said, I'm trying my best here.

Nancy turned to look at me.

A fellow waits on you half the day, I said, the least you can do is let him buy you a drink.

I see, Nancy said.

Do you? I asked.

Nancy's hair was tossed about in the wind. My eyes followed it.

She asked what had gotten into me. But she could surely read the answer in my eyes. She'd seen me open the passenger door of my Jeep for sharply dressed women. Heard the staccato clacking of their high heels on my walkway. She knew what I was. I was a man.

But she was a woman. Sometimes that was a surprise to her, too, I think.

While she was metal detecting she'd missed a call from a former IBMer. Some fellow fellow she hadn't seen in years. He'd become the CEO of a biotech firm in San Diego. When he'd heard the news about Nancy's firing he'd reached out to see if she had any interest in a seat on his board of directors. He'd invited her to dinner to discuss, suggesting he'd also heard about her divorce. It was an offer Nancy would have jumped at a month ago. Now it felt to her like an interruption.

That night, more angry than aroused, she reached for Dario for the first time since arriving in La Jolla.

Nancy learned that Charlotte didn't have a computer. She left Charlotte a voice message saying she was taking Charlotte to get one, no arguing, with a ladies' lunch afterward. A full day went by before Charlotte called back.

Where have you been? Nancy asked.

Out, Charlotte said. And about.

What's that mean?

It means, I'm not on your fucking schedule, Mom. You don't get to just come down here and expect we're gonna lock arms and skip down the beach. You know that, right? That's never going to happen.

I'm only trying to help, Nancy said. *I found a bottle of vodka under the bathroom sink*, she didn't say.

I'm not doing this right now, Charlotte said. I'm going to bed.

It's 3:30 in the afternoon, Nancy didn't say.

I don't need you, Charlotte said, to buy me a computer.

This isn't charity, Charlotte. It's an *investment* . . .

Yeah, well. I'm a bad bet, Mom.

Nancy bought a long-handled scoop. She kept it clipped to her belt so it would drag behind her while she raster-scanned the beach, indicating where she'd already looked. When the beach was crowded, she looked like a janitor trying to wax a basketball court in the middle of a fucking game.

People were always coming up to Nancy. They were always asking her if she'd found anything good. Nails, she'd tell them. But also: foil wrappers. Yogurt lids. Aluminum cans. Flip tops. Lots of coins—some so oxidized as to be unrecognizable. Motel keys. House keys. Car keys. Toys. Buttons. Padlocks. Fingernail clippers. Fishing weights. Rings. Bracelets. Odds. Ends. A cute little dog collar with a tag bearing the name *Leviathan.*

She bought a canvas vest from an army surplus store. Most days she ended her session by emptying this vest's many pockets into a trashcan by the boat launch. This ritual was not disappointing to Nancy. On days when she had Nothing, it was Something.

One day she came across a small dead shark that had washed ashore in front of the La Jolla Beach and Tennis Club. There was a hook lodged in its gills and weighted fishing line tangled around its body, slicing into its fins. Its black eyes were wide open. Nancy let it be. Soon a small crowd gathered around it. Lifeguards arrived in their orange pickup and took the corpse away.

Two days later, Nancy was at the south end of the beach by the tide pools when she got a hit. Her scoop glanced off something rubbery below the surface. She dug down to find it was the shark, still wearing its necklace of fishing weights. The lifeguards had buried the corpse. (Why? Neither Nancy nor I could tell you. Some sort of shark-rights thing, perhaps: this being California. We don't eliminate a problem here so much as make it someone else's.) Nancy reburied it.

Of the animals on the beach—humans included—Nancy loved the sanderlings most. The way they ran in and out with the surf, pecking treats from the liquefied sand. They had a ferocity belied by their tiny bodies and twiggy legs.

She loved the sand crabs, too. They, like her, sidled along, pausing here and there before carrying on.

Another day, she was at the drinking fountain when a very tanned old man (not me) glided up on roller skates. He waited his turn, smiled at her, then took a few slurps. She'd seen him before on the promenade. Everyone had. He was there most days, making super slow strides on his skates, zoned out on his headphones, slaloming pedestrians. His T-shirt read SLOW-MO. He'd sweated through it.

That any fun? he asked, nodding at her detector.

Is *that*? she said, nodding at his skates.

He launched into a description of the euphoric state one could achieve by constantly accelerating. Something about the inner ear reorienting oneself with the gravitational core of the Earth, et cetera. Nancy smiled politely.

I used to be a neurologist, he volunteered.

That so? Nancy said.

I also used to be an asshole, he said, winking.

Nancy raised her hand. Recovering asshole, she said.

Nancy started going to the beach at night. By day, too much is covered up by We The People and our things. At night the beach was all hers. The sand cool underfoot. She could walk long swaths with her eyes closed, just listening to the tone.

For our eyes see only the surfaces of things. And surfaces lie.

One night in early August Nancy arrived at the beach to find people gathered at the waterline, stepping carefully among countless small, silvery fish littering the sand. A pack of young boys were gathering them up in buckets. Each wave deposited more onto the beach. The fish flopped about, suffocating.

Nancy approached a man and his daughter. The man was kneeling, pointing at a fish as it excreted a gooey cluster. Those are the eggs, he said.

The fish arched its sleek body, then went completely still.

Did it die? the girl asked.

Let's give it a sec, the father said.

A little boy with a bucket ran up. He reached for the fish but Nancy swung her detector out over it, blocking him. The boy gaped at her. So did the man and his daughter. They hadn't noticed Nancy there before. The boy ran off.

Boys, Nancy lamented. She shook her head in hope of diffusing the tension she'd inadvertently created.

Look! the girl said. She pointed at the fish. It was wriggling back toward the water.

That fish is the mom, said the father. So, her job is done now. The eggs will stay here until they hatch.

Who takes care of 'em? the girl asked.

The father shot Nancy a knowing smile, adult to adult. Fish aren't quite like people, honey, he said. When the babies hatch, they'll just swim out into the ocean. They can take care of themselves.

The little girl seemed okay with that explanation. Or just bored by it. She slipped her father's embrace and hustled away to join the other kids.

The father eyed Nancy's detector. Find anything good? he asked.

School began again. We La Jollans donned our pants. The crowds at the beach thinned out. I had by this time tired of what I'd begun calling (to Nancy's face) her "obsession." I'd stopped accompanying her. Nancy, in retaliation, had started leaving on my fucking doormat all the nails she dug up. She put them in the blue doggie-doo baggies from the dispenser on the promenade.

Meanwhile, I'd started disappearing more often. It'd be a Tuesday evening and Nancy would notice the Airstream hitched to the Jeep. By the morning, both would be gone, and my house would stay dark for days. One afternoon, Nancy was looking out her window when my little train pulled up alongside the curb, the Jeep and trailer dusty and bug splattered. I started unloading empty jugs of water, propane tanks, plastic tubs of gear. Nancy came outside and yelled to me from her porch: Where you been, dude?

Wouldn't you like to know, I thought. I smiled. I was unshaven and, impossibly (possibly!), even tanner. The desert! I said. *Dude . . .*

I did not elaborate. Nor did I ever offer to take Nancy along. I *did* invite her over for frequent barbeques in my backyard. Charlotte usually showed up too, usually late. Nancy and I took what she could get from Charlotte. It had crossed Nancy's mind to offer the San Jose condo to her daughter as a place for her to get clear of the accumulating debris of her life. I thought it was a good idea, too.

At one barbeque, waiting for Charlotte to show, Nancy asked me what separated a "party girl" from a "drunk." I shrugged. For I'd wondered whether drinking was any worse than other forms of coping. I asked Nancy whether a recovering workaholic had the right to point that particular finger.

A mother has the right, Nancy said assuredly.

I agreed. However, this was Nancy's main problem. She was not allowed to suddenly act like one of those (a mother, that is). Charlotte had made this quite clear.

Nancy found it very hard not to hate herself.

She had by this time bought herself a nice bed and a nice couch and a nice coffee table. Otherwise, she preferred just to wait until she couldn't live without something—a Phillips screwdriver, say—and then, if it wasn't within walking distance, she'd borrow my Jeep. Which is to say, Nancy was "managing." Just not in her former definition of that word.

And so it came as something of a shock to Nancy when, over grilled portobellos, I asked her what, exactly, she was trying to prove. My tone was a little cagey, I suppose. And Nancy couldn't tell: it sounded to her like I was *angry*. (Ding ding ding!) Just before this, the conversation had veered into politics. Nancy had jokingly threatened to register to vote in La Jolla just to cancel out my more liberal picks. Neither Charlotte nor I had laughed. The ground had shifted under Nancy's feet.

Or so it seemed. She sat looking across the table at us, two co-conspirators. And she wondered whether this was actually the same ground she'd been standing on since the barbeque started. No: since she'd first arrived in La Jolla.

I'm not trying to *prove* anything, Nancy said.

Charlotte jumped in. What he means is, you're kind of just playing at all this, Mom. Like you're on vacation. Like that house is a timeshare or some shit.

I'm sorry, Nancy said. Am I disappointing you two?

Both Charlotte and I started to speak, then deferred to each other like a married couple deciding who knew a story best, who should tell it. This must have been when Nancy put it together. How, at these dinners, Charlotte and I tended to linger at the table while Nancy did dishes (her side of the bargain, having been banned from cooking). How Charlotte and I would chat and refill each other's wine glasses, laughing louder and easier with Nancy out of earshot. Now, Nancy knew the joke.

Charlotte started in: That beach isn't safe at night, Mom. People get mugged.

I can't believe this, Nancy muttered.

I'm sixty-four, I went on. You're what: fifty?

Fifty-three, Charlotte answered when Nancy wouldn't.

I said, Isn't that a little early for someone like you to . . .

Someone like me, Nancy said. What's that mean?

Of course, she knew full well. But the thing was—and Nancy knew this, but Charlotte and I didn't yet—we were disappointed in the wrong person. We were disappointed in *Dr. Chu*.

We love you, I said. We want what's best for you. We don't want you to languish.

Nancy laughed.

You're such an *able* person, Charlotte piled on.

Nancy tossed her napkin on the table. And you're both *drunk*, she said. (Ding ding ding!)

This of course incited me. Tell us, I ventured. When was the last time you got laid?

The question sideswiped Nancy. Charlotte, too, by the look on her face. Now I had both of them sneering at me.

I doubled down. It was my only option. Sorry, I said. But I don't think it's healthy, pretending she's above all that. Above *us*.

Fuck you, Nancy said.

I felt sorry for her. I really did. I'd gone too far. I reached a hand across the table. *Nancy*, I said. *C'mon*.

She picked up my wine glass and dumped its contents into my lap.

I was certain at that moment that she'd permanently ruined my shorts and our relationship. I was half right. Par for my course.

Two weeks later Nancy stood barefoot on the La Jolla Shores beach. It was just after 11 p.m. on the last night of September. She consulted a tide booklet. Over the next few hours, the beach would experience an unusually large negative tide. Big swaths of beach usually hidden underwater would be dry—swaths where people might have, in their respective pasts, mistakenly divorced themselves from precious things.

She spent three hours canvassing an area the size of a football field. Insects swarmed in the lights along the promenade. A teenaged couple stole away from a nearby beach bonfire and wandered into the darkness beyond the fire's aura. When they saw Nancy they giggled, swerving off to find privacy elsewhere.

That's right, Nancy thought. *The wacky metal detector lady was here first.*

Wacky Metal Detector Lady was Nancy's first and only invention since leaving the lab. It was with *WMDL's* eyes that Nancy more often preferred to look out upon the world. WMDL had proven a blessing and a comfort to occupy. *She* gave Nancy moxie. It had been *she*, in fact, who'd lunched with Nancy's CEO pal, *she* who'd made jokes about their mutual acquaintances, *she* who'd scavenged beef broccoli off his plate when he was done, *she* who'd felt no compulsion to pick up the tab.

I hope you'll consider my offer, he'd said. Our board needs someone like you.

I'm a bad bet, WMDL had said—quoting Charlotte.

IBM made a huge mistake, he'd said. They should never have fired you.

Didn't you read the article? I wasn't fired, I *stepped down*. To *spend more time with family . . .*

The man had laughed at this. The Nancy *he* knew—the one he'd wanted on his board—and in his bed—was neither a quitter nor a mother.

I know, WMDL had said. That Dr. Chu's kind of a dick, huh?

At this, the man had stopped laughing. Their lunch date had ended soon thereafter. As they were leaving, WMDL had pocketed all four fortune cookies.

As a matter of fact . . . WMDL now reached into one of her vest pockets. Found one of these cookies. She tore open the wrapper and cracked the shell in half. While munching away, it dawned on her that this character she'd assumed wasn't entirely of her own invention. It was not even entirely female.

It was some version of her own father, Zhiyu (not Jerry).

Jerry worked at the store. *Zhiyu* rarely emerged. They'd be at a park, and Zhiyu would take the swing next to a young Nancy and make airplane noises; he'd run *up* the slide to meet her at the top; he'd get on all fours and chase her around, barking—just to hear Nancy laugh. Zhiyu didn't give a shit what any of the other people at the park thought. Zhiyu had crossed an ocean and traded most of his own dreams for his children's dreams, and all he wanted in return was the occasional giggle (and straight A's on every report card).

Maybe Nancy missed Zhiyu so much she'd unconsciously channeled him.

Reincarnated him.

But like the fortune she stashed in her pocket to be read later under the lights of the promenade, this little revelation had to be put aside. The tide would not wait. She turned up the volume on the detector and settled into a rhythm with her swings. Each step just a few inches. Ten feet from the water's edge she detected the faintest variation in the sound, at the edge of the detector's sensitivity. A signal she would have once dismissed as noise. It was something pretty deep if it was something at all.

She set the detector down beside the hot spot. She stepped on the scoop to drive it into the dense, dark sand. She levered, lifted, deposited. Digging as Eric once did into the La Jolla ground. She dug in deeper. Then deeper still. A pile took shape beside the hole. Nancy waved the antenna over this pile. Thousands of invisible waves intermingled with millions of sand grains—and with something else, too, it seemed. The beep was louder now.

She toed the sand even as she continued to wave the detector over it. The pile slumped apart. The beep was coming from a clump. Nancy bent and took the clump in her hand. Loose sand fell away. Something remained.

A watch. She rubbed away the clinging sand. It was an Omega. Her hand flew up to cover her mouth. She stared down at this artifact. It came to life in her hand. The detector and scoop fell away like discarded crutches. She splashed out into the knee-deep water to rinse the thing off and examine it in the moonlight. She needed to be absolutely sure of something this frightening, this impossible.

But also right there, in her hand.

She was transported to the drive home from the awards banquet. Eric seated dutifully in the passenger seat, the little box open in his lap. Those bastards, he'd said. It's not even a women's watch.

You take it, Nancy had said.

Eric had slipped it on. Modeled it for her.

It looks nice on you, she'd told him.

Alright, he'd said. I'll wear it with disdain.

Nancy was wet and shaking. She angled her hand to capture what light she could from the pier lights. She could almost make out the watch's roughened face. She thought there should be a company logo there. But the glass was so corroded and the light too dim to know. Her mind raced. *Was this even possible? If so, how? A day at this beach a decade ago? . . . Eric backstroking out past the breakers with the watch on, and . . . click, the clasp giving out . . . the intricate little mechanism fatigued by years of tension . . . the band slipping off, sinking . . . ?*

Nancy gave this half-baked hypothesis the benefit of the doubt. Took it a step further, even, asking: *Was there sufficient data, then, to assign responsibility? Could she blame the man for being so careless, so carefree? Or should she blame the watch itself, some flaw in its production? What about the woman who'd earned it by spending all her time away from him? What about the waves themselves?*

Nancy waded back in and fished her cell from her pocket. She always kept it powered off while she was detecting, and so was forced to wait as it came back to life. By the time she dialed, she was getting frantic. It rang and rang. Finally:

Mom?

Charlotte! So glad you answered. I just found something.

Holy shit, Mom. This is so *random.*

Charlotte's voice was slurred. Nancy was deflated by the non-randomness of *that.*

Where are you? Nancy asked.

Oh my god, I'm *scared*, Mom. I was actually thinking of calling *you.* It's so late, though. I didn't want to—

Nancy could hear banging. Charlotte shouted something. She was crying.

Charlotte, Nancy said. Tell me what's wrong.

I'm in the bathroom. At this bar. Carter's out there. I locked him out.

What's going on? Did he hurt you?

No. But I think he, um . . . I don't know . . .

Tell me where you are.

I can't be like this anymore, Mom. Everything's just a fucking *waste* . . .

Nancy slipped the watch into her vest pocket. She felt like she'd just been struck twice in a row by lightning. She wanted to be in that bathroom with Charlotte more than she'd ever wanted anything. The watch could wait.

It's going to be okay, Nancy said. You stay right where you are. I'm coming.

You don't even have a fucking car, Mom.

Then I'll get fucking limo! said Wacky Metal Detector Mother.

Epilogue

I, Z (2012)

AS I SAID BEFORE, THE VIEW AFFORDED ME, Z, peering out from the front seat of my Jeep into Carter's truck's highly tinted, partly scrolled-down passenger-side window, is different than the view afforded Nancy and Charlotte from my back seat. *I* can look deep enough into the truck's cabin to see Charlotte's unhinged ex-boyfriend awash in the alien green light of his instrument panel. He has one hand on the steering wheel, the other on a pistol.

What's he doing? Nancy asks.

Nothing, I say. Just staring at me.

I think I should call him, Charlotte says.

No, I say with too much emphasis. I try again, this time calmer: No.

The light turns green. I stay put. I want to see if he'll drive away. No luck.

I ease my Croc off the brake pedal. The tow hitch groans. Jeep and Airstream creep into the intersection. As Nancy's window draws flush with Carter's, she and Charlotte are afforded a fleeting glimpse into Carter's cabin, too.

Jesus Christ, he has a gun! Nancy says.

Yes, I say.

Carter's truck recedes in my side mirror.

Is he just staying there? Charlotte asks. He's not going?

I keep watch in my side mirror. Actually, I say, he's following us now.

We're in a poorly lit section of downtown. The buildings here are mostly commercial, their metal gates locked shut at this hour. The road parallels the freeway. Two blocks further on, I opt onto an onramp, and accelerate. Nancy and Charlotte plaster themselves against their respective windows. They try in vain to see backward, around the Airstream.

How does he have a gun? Nancy asks. Did you know he had that?

Not tonight, Charlotte says.

Not tonight? Nancy says.

No, Charlotte says.

Did he get on the freeway too? Nancy asks.

Yep, I say.

The truck rides our tail. It veers back and forth over lane lines, its headlights higher than those of the traffic around it.

I drive north, past the airport, past Mission Bay—the same drive Nancy took in the limo when she first arrived here.

I'm calling the police, Nancy says, producing her cell.

Let's wait a sec, I say, aware that I, like Carter, may be over the legal limit.

Nancy pokes her head into the front seat. Oh, she says. So, you have a better idea?

I'm thinking, I say.

I don't have an idea. Yet. Not one in particular. All I know is, my gas gauge is pegged on F, so maybe the question is: just how far north is this fucking kid—with his stunted attention span and his atrocious gas mileage and his criminal blood-alcohol level—just how far is he able and willing to drive tonight? Because I'll drive until dawn. Waiting is one game I've learned I can win.

We come to my La Jolla Parkway exit. I don't take it. This prompts questions from the back seat. I do not answer them.

I'll tell you one thing, Nancy says. Charlotte's staying with me tonight.

Carter knows where *you* live, too, Mom, Charlotte says.

Carter accelerates. His truck gets out ahead of us. His tattooed arm emerges from the driver side and he lofts a tallboy beer can back at us. It sails over the Jeep and clunks against my trailer. Black smoke belches from his dual exhausts as he speeds up again. Then he brakes and works his way back around in the traffic until he's alongside us again.

The hell's he doing? I say, just as he swerves sharply, nearly sideswiping us. Charlotte screams. I veer out over the shoulder line. My tires hum loudly on the rumble strip. I brake. Carter brakes. I speed back up. Carter speeds back up.

Twice more he swerves his big, blunt truck at us.

Asshole! Charlotte yells, pressing her middle fingers to the window.

Suddenly there's the sound of muffled heavy metal music, accompanied by a buzz, coming from the back seat. Charlotte fishes her phone out of her bag. She studies it, then looks at Nancy. The music overdrives the phone's speaker.

It's Carter, Charlotte says.

I'm still in the slow lane. Carter's truck remains right outside my window. I share a quick glance with Nancy in the rearview. Ahead of us, there's a semi-truck in Carter's lane. My lane is clear.

Charlotte answers: Babe, what the fuck are you doing?—I *see* that.—Because you're *drunk!*—No.—*No.*—We're not doing this over the phone . . .

Hang up, Nancy says.

Charlotte holds the phone out. I see her face awash in the light of its screen. She goes to tap it.

No, I say. Wait.

Why? Nancy says.

I sneak a look out my window. I see Carter with his cell to his ear. He stares over at us. His voice enters his phone and travels a vast network before reaching our car a split second later, pitting the sight and sound of him at odds.

Just keep him talking, I say.

Charlotte puts the phone back to her ear. Yes, she says. I'm right fucking here.

I stamp the gas pedal to the floor. Carter's truck easily matches my acceleration.

This is insane, Charlotte says.

I can't tell if she's talking to Carter or to me. She listens to the phone, then dives right back in: It doesn't fucking matter! she yells. Babe, *please* stop doing this.—I know.—Yeah, well, this isn't helping.—Exactly, because you're being such a selfish, fucking . . .

And that's when Carter drives headlong into the back of the semi-truck trailer that has slowed for the traffic ahead. While we glide past the semi on the right. The sound of the collision is violent and unnatural and followed closely by a screeching of tires.

Did he just . . . , Nancy starts to say.

Oh my god oh my god . . . Charlotte is saying. Oh my god . . .

Nancy leans forward and puts her hand on my shoulder.

I flinch.

What do we do? Nancy asks.

I am speechless. I don't know what do except to keep driving. My Jeep and trailer have a momentum that I mindlessly obey. There aren't any exits for a few miles.

The headlights of the semi-truck have long receded. The traffic had begun to clog up behind it as it left my sight. I wonder if I've killed that boy. I wonder if I feel bad about it.

Charlotte is hysterical. She's demanding we turn around, go back. Nancy is of similar mind. And then, ghost-like, the heavy metal starts up again.

Charlotte gasps. Carter? she says into her phone.

She listens.

I thought that maybe . . . , she says. He interrupts her. I know babe, she says. Are you hurt?

Nancy and I stare at each other in the mirror. Charlotte is getting an earful.

What's he saying? Nancy asks.

He's pissed, Charlotte says. He's a fucking mess.

Nancy wrests the phone from Charlotte's grip and taps it, ending the call.

Charlotte is aghast.

I keep driving. Driving is really all I feel capable of doing at the moment.

Nancy slides across the seat and wraps her arms around her daughter. Both of them break down sobbing and shaking and describing for each other the horrific thing we'd all thought might have just happened—a thing none of us had dared voice for fear saying it might make it true. I exit the I-5 and head east on the Ted Williams freeway.

I hear a zipper. I look back to see Nancy produce something from a pocket of her cargo vest. She turns on the dome light and dangles it out for Charlotte to see. It's a watch.

I found this tonight, Nancy says. At the beach.

So? Charlotte says.

Don't you recognize it?

Dad had an Omega.

Yes. This is it.

Charlotte turns to look away, out her window.

It seems impossible, I know, Nancy says. But he must have thrown it in the water . . .

That's not it, Mom, Charlotte says.

I know exactly what it looks like, Nancy says. I'm the one who gave it to him.

Right, Charlotte says. Then he gave it to me.

He did?

He did.

Why would he do that?

He didn't want it anymore.

Well, then, do you still have it?

Charlotte reaches down to rummage her bag. When she sits back up, she drops something in Nancy's lap.

What's this? Nancy asks.

What's it look like? Charlotte says.

I turn around to see what it is but I can't see it, and don't want to interrupt.

I found that in a pond, Charlotte says, in Amarillo. Texas.

I don't understand, Nancy says.

The watch is gone, Mom, Charlotte says. Like, *gone* gone. I threw it in a pond when I was angry and when I went back to look for it, all I found was . . . *that*.

A bottle cap, Nancy says.

Charlotte nods.

And you kept it, Nancy says.

I did, Charlotte says.

Why?

As a reminder, I guess.

Of your father, Nancy says.

No, Charlotte says. That things change.

Nancy seems hurt by this. She stares out into the darkness beyond the freeway's aura. A silence strangles the car. A hundred things go unsaid.

Nancy speaks first. I'm too easy to fool, she says. All my life, I've been like that. Not about everything—just everything to do with *me*.

Who cares if it isn't Dad's watch? Charlotte says. It doesn't matter, right? It wouldn't bring *him* back.

I know, Nancy says. I know. It just seemed like it was *meant*. Like he'd lost it and it was waiting for me to find it.

Nancy seems ready to say more. Charlotte and I watch her.

I miss the way things were, Nancy says, before everything fell apart.

Okay, good, Charlotte says. So you found *that.*

Nancy makes no reply to this. I take the liberty of driving on. As if I am only, and have only ever been, the chauffeur—as if I've been politely tuning out their conversation all along. As if I'm not privy to the details and tragedies of their lives. A fly on the wall. The man at the wheel. I head toward the only place that makes sense to me. I hear no complaints. I drive northwest into the middle of this new night. Just a late-model Jeep lugging a vintage Airstream up a wide-open freeway.

Eventually, Charlotte rightly wonders where the fuck I'm going.

The desert, I say.

I watch in my rearview mirror for a reaction, from either of them. I see the effort Nancy puts into not showing me one. Charlotte just shakes her head. I slide a CD into the player. It starts to play.

Charlotte sits up. The hell's this? she says.

Yanni, Nancy mutters.

They titter together. It's the most beautiful sound. There is so much pent up within these women, trying to get out. So I say: Actually, this is *Enya*. Learn your composers, ladies.

Just to hear the beautiful sound again.

We reach Joshua Tree's southern entrance a little after 3 a.m. I put my window down. The night air is cool and brittle, the road deserted. I swerve to miss a rabbit and am heartened by the sight in my side mirror of its white scut vanishing unharmed into the brush. I have been driving nonstop since midnight. I am not tired.

The sight of lofty ocotillo and puffy cholla are Pavlovian for me. They trigger a feeling of belonging. No, *returning*. Maybe reverting? In days of old, untenable men escaped to the sea. For me, it's always been the desert. This desert.

Nancy and Charlotte are asleep against their windows. Mouths agape, breathing loudly. Like sisters. Long before Nancy knocked on my door begging to borrow this Jeep, I'd booked a trailer site in the Cottonwood Springs campground just ahead, starting today. However, check-in isn't until mid-afternoon. I head there anyway, just to see if the site is open.

My little train glides through the temporary neighborhood of the campground. The sun is not up. Camp chairs sit empty around smoldering campfires. Nylon trailer awnings flap in the breeze. It is the darkest hour of the day.

I hear a seatbelt unscroll. Nancy pokes her head into the front seat and rubs her eyes.

Hey, we say.

I drive around the loop past the bathroom and the communal water spigot to the edge of the campground. We reach my site. It is empty. I stare into the headlight-bathed scene: a picnic table, a fire grate, and a broken boulder. The things I love about this campsite, and about the desert itself, diminish as I view them through the eyes of a host. It's not delicate and austere here, it's barren. Never once have I needed to defend this place to anyone. I've merely had to *occupy* it, by myself. Through the years it has provided me with just enough. It return, it has expected nothing. I close my eyes for the first time in hours—not to rest them, but to avoid looking at what's right in front of me. *Why the hell have I dragged them here?*

I back the trailer onto the asphalt pad. The moment I get out of the Jeep, Nancy and Charlotte follow suit. The open-door binging is the loudest sound in the campground.

Charlotte rolls her head around on her neck. Nancy tiptoes barefoot to the picnic table. How can it be freezing? she asks.

I can feel their eyes on me as I lug my leveling blocks into position. Charlotte heads off to the bathroom. I get back in the Jeep and back it up, watching the trailer list. I set the brake, get back out, retract the trailer's metal doorstep, unlock the door, and step inside. The spring-loaded door shuts itself, and

I enjoy my first moment alone since meeting my date at the restaurant—when? . . . nearly eight hours ago. I have put in a decent shift.

I savor the dimness of the cabin, its musty air. To my left is a dinette table and bench seat. To my right, a kitchenette. Across the alley is a bathroom barely wide enough to sit in. At the back is a bedroom with a queen mattress. Tour over.

I flip on the dome light and fish a level from a silverware tray. I set it on the table. The bubble glides lethargically out of its den and settles near the centerline. I start to putter. By the time I get back outside, Charlotte is lying barefoot atop the table and Nancy is waddling off in Charlotte's shoes.

You forget there's this many stars, Charlotte says.

I follow her gaze, up.

I always think about how long that light's been traveling, I say. Some of those stars went out when the dinosaurs were walking around. But we still think they're twinkling.

The waves, of course, go both ways, I think. *Radio messages and novels and cries for help forever seeking, seeking, seeking.*

You sound like my dad, Charlotte says.

I'm not sure how to take that, so I disappear into chores. I chock the wheels, unhook the trailer. As I work, I recall the night I first spoke to Charlotte, two years ago. Eric had just died, though I didn't know that at the time. I said something sad about stars and darkness—not what I would have said, had I known. But maybe I established an important precedent that night. Maybe that's why Charlotte took to me. I treated her like an equal right from the start. I have never babied her. Never tried to be her dad.

What am I to her, then? An uncle of sorts? A grandpa? A drinking buddy? Am I part of her problem, or part of her solution?

I take hold of the jack and turn its crank until the wheel meets the asphalt, then a bit more. Pebbles crackle under the pressure. Back inside the trailer, I rotate the level ninety degrees on the table. The bubble slightly favors the trailer's front end. I put the level back in the tray, go back outside to the jack, and crank the handle back the other way three rotations.

Nancy and Charlotte are huddled at the picnic table, shivering in the dark. The sight of them makes me feel vaguely perverted—as if I've abducted them.

I feel my entire life coming completely fucking unhinged.

All set, I announce cheerily.

Nancy and Charlotte look to be awaiting instructions.

We can unpack in the morning, I say. I think we should just hit the hay.

They get up from the table and, at my invitation, step up into the trailer. Both of them pause with unnecessary ceremony at the threshold.

It's an Airstream, I say. Not an altar.

Their eyes dart around the cabin. Their hands reach out to feel curtains and cabinets, as if to confirm it's all real. I usher them into what will be their bedroom. They both walk with a crouch despite the ample headroom.

You two can share the queen, I say.

I take down an extra pillow from the overhead cabinet and toss it onto the bedspread. Dust rises from the fabric.

Where will you sleep? Nancy asks.

I point at what is currently a table. Nancy stares at it.

It folds out, I say.

Nancy seems to process this. I'm not certain about the folding out thing, actually. Years ago, a salesman demonstrated how the dinette converted into a mattress, but I've never had the need.

No one moves. Until, suddenly, we all move at once, and create a logjam in a narrow passageway in a small trailer in the middle of nowhere. I get out of the way by stepping into the bathroom.

Nancy sits down on the corner of the bed. This is crazy, she says. Right?

I chuckle, in full agreement.

I'd kill for a toothbrush, Charlotte says.

I produce a crumpled, body-temperature pack of Doublemint from my pocket. I offer it out like a pack of cigarettes. Mother and daughter step forward. They each tug out a piece. I take one, too. I see Nancy looking around for a trash can, so I hold out my palm. She and Charlotte set their wrappers in it.

The trailer's musty air suffuses with exhaled mint.

I manage to make the fold-out work. It doesn't have sheets on it, though, so I nab a spare blanket from the drawer next to the sink. I give Nancy and Charlotte the only two pillows. I fashion one for myself by stuffing a sweater into a T-shirt.

We settle in for what remains of the night. I hear them talking in whispers in the bedroom. Eventually, I think they've both fallen asleep. Then I hear the kind of sniffling that accompanies tears. Later, one of them begins to snore. Then the other.

I envy them. My mind is still reeling at the way the night turned on its axis. The trailer closes in on me. I toss and turn.

I sit up, pull on my jeans, my Crocs, a sweatshirt. I slip outside. There are a few high clouds, but otherwise the sky is clear. Constellations galore. Breezes stir the underbrush. I check my watch: 4:35 a.m. I've been keeping it set nine minutes fast to be on time more often. All I've improved is my ability to subtract nine from any number.

I get an idea, imperative from the moment it arrives.

I rummage my duffels in the back of the Jeep. I strap on a headlamp. The other trailers and tents around us are unlit and tranquil, making my light conspicuous. I switch it off. The moon is bright enough to see by anyway. I start walking up the main road. I go to the trailhead for Mastodon Peak, a three-mile loop I've done many times—though never in the dark. I take it.

I descend on the hardpack path toward Cottonwood Springs Oasis. A few lonely, spring-fed palms there. A set of rock stairs ascend the opposite bank. Back when I could still piss a strong, steady stream and naturally maintain an erection and many other things, I used to take these stairs two at a time. Tonight, I take two steps per stair. Everything—the sand and the yucca and the ocotillo and the boulders—are awash in the purplish moonlight. I stop to rub my aching hip. I cough and spit downwind.

I will quit drinking, I decide. *With Charlotte. A show of solidarity. Maybe not for good. But for a while.*

The trail turns rocky. A few times I have to get on all fours to scramble up and over the big rocks.

Crocs were a poor choice.

I summit. I sit. The broad Salton Sea shimmers to the south. Light brims over the eastern edge of the world. The higher clouds have started to pinken. Contrails of early-morning flights scar the sky above Los Angeles.

This is how lizards feel, I decide, *waiting for the sun to warm their blood.* The light, when it finally, gradually, washes over me, does not bring the warmth I've somehow convinced myself it will. The wind has by then chilled my sweat. My legs have fallen asleep against the rocky ground. I rise, grunting. I can feel it now, all of it: the toll of the drive and the lack of sleep and the foolhardy scramble up this mountain. I think about Eric and wonder: what if *I* had a heart attack? Who would feel a loss? I am an only child, my parents long dead. What friends I might claim live in L.A., not La Jolla, and they are mostly Christmas card connections at this point.

I go so far as to imagine a funeral: a mahogany-lined old boys' clubroom, casket in the corner, and all the women I've ever dated in attendance. None of them would *actually* come to my funeral, of course. My imagination, as you may have guessed, is both a curse and a career. Smartly dressed, these ladies would surely eye each other suspiciously at first. But they would quickly move on, past the topic of me. They would find much better commonalities. I envision them tilting back flutes of champagne. Wailing with laughter at my expense. They would leave the clubroom in locked-arm two- and threesomes, in search of a more happenin' spot.

Charlotte's right: things change.

Can people?

Can old dogs?

The sky turns the diluted blue it will remain all day. The mountain slopes are sun bleached and stubbled with obstinate desert plants. I start back down.

It's warmer off the windy summit. I cast a gangly shadow over the madcap flora and Dr. Seuss geology. I round a bend and startle a small herd of bighorn. They stop to stare, jaws working, horns like nautilus shells. I stare back, panting. A big male turns to clamber over a rise and his herd follows.

I can't wait to tell Charlotte and Nancy. This land is not barren! I will tell them. It can support entire families! My pace quickens.

The campground in sunlight looks a different place than the one I left in moonlight. Scattered generators hum. Wood smoke and the scent of bacon drift on the breeze. I bid good morning to a man walking a pair of corgis. I wave to a woman sipping coffee on the step of her trailer.

The curtains are still drawn on the Airstream. I hesitate at the door. A door upon which I've never in my life knocked. Not once. I tap twice with a fingertip. No response. I enter.

Charlotte and Nancy are asleep.

I saw bighorn, I whisper in their direction.

I step out of my Crocs. I curl up in the dinette/bed.

A silver fox in a silver henhouse.

I wake to the sound and smell of crackling grease. Nancy holds tongs over a skillet. I take my watch off the table and squint at it: it's 10:00. I have an erection. As a younger, more successful man, erections pestered me when I didn't need them. Like literary agents. I no longer take either for granted.

We got hungry, Nancy explains.

I grab the dowel dangling above my head and tow the attached curtain around on its track. A swath of sunlight expands across the cabin. I see Charlotte sitting outside. She is hunched over some project at the picnic table.

Nancy holds up a carton of eggs to peer at its underside. Is there supposed to be a date on these? she asks.

They're good, I mutter.

I look around inside the trailer. Tiny changes are detectable here and there. Items in different nooks, cabinets not properly latched.

We didn't know where you kept anything, Nancy says. So we just started opening stuff. There isn't much of a *scheme*.

I choose not to dignify that with a reply.

We did find pancake mix, she says. So I'm making that. And bacon!

You could have woken me up, I say. I know exactly where everything is.

You were snoring, she says, smiling down at her skillet.

Yeah? I retort. So were you.

I woke up in the middle of the night and you weren't here, she says.

I hiked up that, I say, pointing out the window. I saw the sun come up.

How Z of you, she says.

I saw this herd of—

We were worried, you know . . .

Oh.

You can't just *leave*.

I'm sorry. I can get a little . . . *claustrophobic*.

You brought us here, dude.

(*Dude?*) I didn't mean it like that, I say.

Nancy adjusts the propane burner. So, brave leader, she says. What's next? I feel like I'm on a Girl Scout camping trip.

My erection has subsided enough that I can risk standing up. I fold up my blanket and jam it into the drawer beside the sink—where it *goes*. There's a magnificent goddamn scheme!

Nancy transfers cooked bacon to a plate, dripping grease on the counter. I hold my tongue. She has not cooked for me since the night she smothered carbonized pork chops with cold apple sauce from single-serving kiddie cups. I reach past her and nab a piece of bacon. She elbows me in the chest as I chew. It's slightly burnt: perfect. My doctor has told me to eat oatmeal for breakfast. And I do. In La Jolla.

All bets are off in the desert.

Nancy watches, waiting for my review. I pretend to choke.

I have a little cork board on the wall. It has, as of late, had only three things pinned to it: the scorecard from my best-ever round of Frisbee golf; a Post-it note with useful phone numbers, including the spa in Palm Springs where I stop sometimes for a massage; and a running resupply list, to which I'll add items using the Sharpie kept in the silverware tray beside the level, per The Scheme. As such, a little strip of paper added to the board catches my attention. It's a fortune-cookie fortune. I lean in to read it. It says: *Failure is the mother of all success*.

It was in my pocket, Nancy explains.

You trying to send me a message?

You're not the only one sleeping in this trailer.

I nod, and say, Next time, though, please go through proper channels. We can't have folks just posting propaganda in here . . .

Understood, Nancy says. She salutes with her spatula. I unlatch the door and slip outside. The fresh air, the big sky. The sunlight. It's not very warm though.

Charlotte looks up from the picnic table. She's wearing one of my sweatshirts over the clothes she had on last night. Her face is shaded by a straw cowboy hat I keep on a nail in the trailer. On the ground beside her bare feet is a stack of empty blue plastic sacks held down by a rock. She has scattered the sacks' contents—rusty nails and other pointy odds and ends—over the weathered wooden table.

For the second time since waking up, I feel embarrassed and exposed. One day a few months ago, I'd been leaving my bungalow when I noticed a small blue sack on my porch. It looked like it might contain dog shit—the leavings of a prankster—but the contents *clinked*. It was full of rusty nails.

Nancy's stunted sense of humor reminds me of this kid I knew growing up. He didn't have a TV. He heard so few good jokes that he laughed at the cheap ones. Perhaps the bag was Nancy's way of apologizing for dumping perfectly good wine into my imperfect lap. Standing on my porch that day, I knew Nancy might be watching through her window shade, giggling, so I'd pocketed the bag as if it were nothing. Later I'd absently tossed it in the back of my Jeep. Where it remained, unnoticed, for weeks. I'd rediscovered it while unpacking at Joshua Tree a few weeks later, and for some reason I'd relegated it to an unused drawer in the trailer. I never mentioned any of this to Nancy, of course. Over the coming weeks, though, she made a running joke of the bags. She left more and more of them on my porch. I just kept squirreling them away in the drawer. Throwing them away hadn't seemed right.

Charlotte taps the brim of my hat at me. I start to give an explanation for the bags, but she preempts me. My mom's so weird, she says.

I sit down across from her. Examine the collection. The nails vary in length and type, and in degree of oxidation. I pick up one of the rustier ones. It's brittle and orange, swollen along its length. Small flecks break loose in my fingers. I toss it back into the pile and stare off into the desert.

She likes you, Charlotte says.

I don't know, I say. I think she figured out what kind of man I am.

What kind is that?

Oh, the usual. Like that boyfriend of yours.

You're the *complete* opposite of him.

I'm him in forty years.

You have a heart.

I'm an old lizard.

Charlotte sniffs. Whatever, she says.

I really look at her. She's a mess inside, I can see it. I look at the table. I'm used to talking with Charlotte behind Nancy's back, but I'm not in the mood today.

She is making us pancakes, I say by way of argument. And bacon.

Yeah, but you can't mess up bacon, Charlotte says.

True, I allow.

Charlotte scans the nails. She lifts one out and holds it over the wobbly little structure she's building. This structure is roughly circular, and hollow in the center. She pinches the nail between her pointer finger and thumb, then tenderly adds it to the stack.

Like pick-up sticks played in reverse.

She loves you, I say.

She's got some making up to do, Charlotte says—more authority in her voice than she has a right to, in my opinion. And I wonder if I've always been too easy on Charlotte. Is this how one spoils a daughter?

She retracts her hands into the cuffs of my big sweatshirt. Thank you, she says, for coming to get me last night.

Your mother was not to be stopped.

Charlotte smiles.

Did you find out what happened? I ask.

You mean, after we just drove away? she says, her tone accusatory.

I do.

Truck's totaled, she says. Carter spent the night in jail. They're charging him with drunk driving. And something else, I can't remember.

I nod.

My mom says we're both alcoholics, Charlotte says.

Me and you?

Me and *Carter*.

Right, I say.

I went to that bar to find him, you know.

So I heard.

Because I thought I was pregnant. Did you hear *that*?

I try to catch her eye to see if she's joking.

I thought you guys broke up, I say.

We did.

She looks up at me and smiles a pathetic smile. She's near tears. Last night, she says, I was in a grocery store, buying beer. I walked past the tampons and I realized I was *late*. I've been partying so much I—I kind of lost track of things. Anyway, I bought a pregnancy test and I went to find him . . .

I don't have to say anything for Charlotte to say, I *know*.

I wasn't thinking, she continues. But I just didn't want to deal with it all by myself. It didn't seem fair. So I found him. I took him with me into the bathroom. He probably thought we were going to hook up! Then I told him what was going on. How we were going to find out, together, right then and there.

I'm beginning to see why he was chasing us.

He got crazy, Z. He pushed me into a wall. I screamed. Got him to leave.

Did you end up taking the test?

Charlotte makes a plus sign with her index fingers.

I don't know what that means, I say.

It means *positive*, you idiot, Charlotte says. And so I was just sitting there on the fucking toilet, crying. I haven't felt that hopeless since . . . my Dad. It actually crossed my mind to call my mom. But I didn't. Then my phone rang and it was *her!* How is that possible?

I want to take her hand but she has both of them inside the sleeves of my sweatshirt.

I don't know how to be a mother, she says. I don't even know how to be *myself*.

You're not the first young woman to feel this way, I say. We'll figure it out.

She looks at me and forces a smile she can't sustain and I can't bear to look at.

My idle hand gravitates to a metal rod the size of a golf tee. It has a smooth pin extending from a threaded headpiece. I pick it up. It's less oxidized than the nails—a higher grade of metal, almost bluish—though still encrusted by the sea. By time.

Weird nail, I say—still not realizing what it is, not having been there, not in person, when Charlotte poured it into the waves with the other remains of her father.

I know, Charlotte says. I feel like I've seen it—like I know what it goes to.

I offer it to her. She nods at the pile. I lay the piece down as steadily as I can upon the little structure, which shifts under the weight. I suck air through my teeth. One nail rolls partway off. Charlotte puts the pad of her finger on its sharp tip and levers it back into place.

So this is Joshua Tree, she says.

None other, I say.

She cocks her head and screws up her face, as if suddenly channeling spirits. When next she speaks, it's with a thick, ludicrous drawl: Place is so dern dry the birds build nests outta barb wire!

I have to laugh. Where'd *that* come from? I ask.

My Texas mother, Charlotte says.

I nod—knowing, as I do, *that* story. I know nearly all of their stories.

I think you need to talk to your *actual* mother, I say. Tell her what you just told me.

I have, Charlotte says. She's not too pleased, of course. But, neither am I. I mean, this isn't exactly what I was trying for.

There is a moment during which I decide not to ask her what, exactly, she *has* been trying for.

She resituates herself on the bench. I'm actually glad my mom's not taking this well. Like, we finally fucking agree on something. We're both mad at *me*. We both hoped I'd turn out better.

You haven't had time to turn out, I say. You're still young.

I'm pregnant, Charlotte says. Game over.

It's an attitude I'd expect from someone like . . . well, me. All the years I've known Charlotte, I've enjoyed hearing my kinds of words come out of her mouth. Suddenly I don't.

Wrong, I say. It's another quarter in the machine. New game.

Charlotte looks at me funny. Nancy opens the trailer door. She's got on my Crocs. They're like clown shoes on her. She shuffles over to the picnic table. Sits down on my side. She's got an egg in her hand. I can tell she wants to speak, but won't.

Yes, dear? I say.

The box says to add an egg, Nancy says. So, do I kind of beat it first, like a scrambled egg? Or do I just break it in there and *then* mix it in, or . . .

Charlotte and I share a look. I put my arm around Nancy's bony shoulders. She scoots away—aware I'm humoring her—but I tighten my embrace. She lets herself be tugged back against me. Tilts her head. I can feel its weight come to rest upon my shoulder. I am grateful beyond words for this weight.

The cook's in charge, I tell her.

Charlotte—drawling again—says: Do whatever ya like with that there egg, darlin'.

Nancy looks down at the delicate little structure we've begun. She reaches out.

Nestles the egg in it.

Acknowledgments

WHEN I WAS IN HIGH SCHOOL, I DEVOURED WALTER VAN TILBURG CLARK'S *The City of Trembling Leaves* from the University of Nevada Press, with a foreword by the press's founder, Robert Laxalt. Their words inspired me to commit to writing as a lifelong pursuit. Smash cut to three decades later . . . to see the press's mountain logo share a spine with my name gives me goosebumps. Curtis Vickers was there from first to final drafts; thank you for cracking open your door and giving this book a home. Thank you, too, to the hardworking staff of the biggest little press around, especially JoAnne Banducci, Caddie Dufurrena, and Ryan Masteller. Robin Dublanc did far more than copyedit; she inspired fresh material.

This book took fifteen years; the seed, for Nancy, was planted in my mind by a short story, "The River Nemunas" by Anthony Doerr, that appeared in *Tin House* in 2009. The Zhiyu/Jerry branch/chapter sprouted in 2017 and was published in an earlier form in *The Rumpus*.

Thank you to the Nevada Arts Council and the Sierra Arts Foundation for generous grants and support over the years.

For lending precious time and thought to early drafts, and precious encouragement and friendship over decades, I am indebted to Christopher Coake, Adam Dedmon, and Gabriel Urza.

For her wisdom and perseverance and belief in this book from day one, I cannot thank Marian Young enough.

Tom Lin had invaluable insights about the manuscript that showed me the story more clearly and how to tell it truer—I am in your debt, Tom!

For explaining to me amateur radio and barrel racing, respectively, I say thank you, respectfully, to Nicholas Manzo (W7NIK) and Lita Scott.

Thank you to Jason Ludden and the Cabal Book Club of Gardnerville for their helpful hot takes.

Shoutout to Sundance Books and Music and its thirty-six-year run as a haven for readers and writers, and to Danilo John Thomas at Baobab Press for such thoughtful editorial counsel.

The list of others who imparted inertia and insight along the way is long, but certainly includes Mena Dedmon, Joe Goodnight, Matt Herz, Ben Clyne, David Torch, Kam Leang, Ilsa Brink, Ryan Tung, CJ Dudley, Steven Malekos, many of my colleagues at NevadaNano, Claire Vaye Watkins, Kenny Ching, Michael Sion, Colin Robertson, Luke Franklin, Todd Sala, Cynthia Reeser, Melanie Perish, Joe Crowley, Willy Vlautin, Other People's Porches, Heather and Matt Ashbach, Don and Judy Rogers, Brooke Rogers, Judd and Lindsay Rogers, Tyler and Julia Rogers, Reid and Logan Hamilton, Pam and Steve Hamilton, Scott and Phyllis Bedford, Mary Bedford, Stewart Bedford, and the whole Rogers clan. Special thank you to Tom and Virginia Rogers for pioneering our family's annual pilgrimage to La Jolla.

Blessed are the teachers. For me, when it comes to writing, I am especially indebted to the time and care taken—and the high standards set—by Anne Marie Utter, Tom Meschery, Jake Highton, Donica Mensing, Travis Linn, Mikalee Byerman, and Richard Davies. And by Sandy Rogers, my mother.

Ulysses! You cannot read or write. Yet I kid not when I dub you a coauthor on this puppy, dude! Grace! You kept me company at all hours as this thing took shape. Miss you . . .

Thank you to my parents, Jim and Sandy, whose support of everything I've ever pursued has been unequivocal and unqualified, and remains so to this day. Dad, thank you for lending your heart and marketing mind to my little creations.

This book is dedicated to my daughters, Quinn and Sydney. Ladies: the whole time I was writing this, you were growing up. I was sure for a long time that the story was about metal detecting; then, ham radio; then, particle physics. No. It was definitely about La Jolla. Until the day when I realized it wasn't truly about any of those things. The fathers and daughters in this book are not us. But nor would they be who they are on the page without what I've felt or understood because of what we have off the page. Both of you are masterpieces in progress. I love you both beyond what I believe you'll fully comprehend unless/until you have children of your own.

No one has read more bad first drafts or shaken more pom-poms in support of my writing (and everything else) than Jill. Thank you for letting me stare into empty space sometimes and for being there every time I come back to the spaces we share (spaces *you* create). I love raising daughters with you. And I love *you*.